PREACHER'S
BLOODY
RAMPAGE

LOOK FOR THESE EXCITING WESTERN SERIES
FROM BESTSELLING AUTHORS
WILLIAM W. JOHNSTONE AND J.A. JOHNSTONE

The Mountain Man

Luke Jensen: Bounty Hunter

Brannigan's Land

The Jensen Brand

Smoke Jensen: The Beginning

Preacher and MacCallister

Fort Misery

The Fighting O'Neils

Perley Gates

MacCoole and Boone

Guns of the Vigilantes

Shotgun Johnny

The Chuckwagon Trail

The Jackals

The Slash and Pecos Westerns

The Texas Moonshiners

Stoneface Finnegan Westerns

Ben Savage: Saloon Ranger

The Buck Trammel Westerns

The Death and Texas Westerns

The Hunter Buchanon Westerns

Will Tanner, Deputy U.S. Marshal

Old Cowboys Never Die

Go West, Young Man

Published by Kensington Publishing Corp.

THE FIRST MOUNTAIN MAN

PREACHER'S BLOODY RAMPAGE

WILLIAM W. JOHNSTONE

AND J.A. JOHNSTONE

PINNACLE BOOKS
Kensington Publishing Corp.

www.kensingtonbooks.com

PINNACLE BOOKS are published by

Kensington Publishing Corp.
119 West 40th Street
New York, NY 10018

PUBLISHER'S NOTE: Following the death of William W. Johnstone, the Johnstone family is working with a carefully selected writer to organize and complete Mr. Johnstone's outlines and many unfinished manuscripts to create additional novels in all of his series like The Last Gunfighter, Mountain Man, and Eagles, among others. This novel was inspired by Mr. Johnstone's superb storytelling.

First Printing: January 2024
ISBN-13: 978-0-7860-5067-3
ISBN-13: 978-0-7860-5068-0 (eBook)

10 9 8 7 6 5 4 3 2 1

Printed in the United States of America

CHAPTER 1

"Look out!" Preacher said as he lunged forward, grabbed his companion's arm, and jerked the tall young man back.

The big wagon, loaded heavily with barrels, rumbled past. The team of massive draft horses never slowed as the driver slapped their rumps with the reins.

"Watch where you're goin', you blasted red heathen!" the man yelled at the tall, buckskin-clad youngster standing beside Preacher. The young man had gotten distracted by his crowded surroundings and strayed too far into the street.

"If this is civilization, I'm not sure I like it," he said as he watched the wagon careen on down the cobblestones. "It is too dangerous here."

Preacher laughed and slapped him on the back. "Civilization ain't that much worse than the frontier, Tall Dog. It's just got a different set of dangers to look out for, that's all."

The young man called Tall Dog asked, "What was in those barrels the wagon was carrying?"

"Not much tellin'. Beer, whiskey, sugar, flour, gunpowder . . . could've been just about anything you can fit in a barrel. It don't matter. If those horses had knocked you down, chances are they'd have trampled you to death before the wagon ever ran over you."

Tall Dog gave the mountain man a solemn nod. "Then you've saved my life yet again. I will never be able to repay all the debts I owe you, Preacher."

"Don't be so sure about that. You've pulled my fat outta the fire more'n once, remember?"

Tall Dog nodded. They set off along the street once more, trailed by a big, shaggy cur that appeared to be as much wolf as dog.

The two of them made a pretty impressive pair. Tall, broad-shouldered, and muscular, Preacher was in his forties but looked younger.

Years in the mountains had left him with a deeply tanned face that didn't really show his age. Only scattered strands of silver threaded through his thick dark hair, mustache, and beard.

The broad leather belt around his waist supported a pair of holstered Colt Patersons, the newfangled repeating revolvers that had been given to Preacher a while back by a company of rangers down in Texas. He also carried a sheathed hunting knife and had a tomahawk tucked behind the belt.

Tall Dog towered over Preacher by several inches but was built whipcord lean. The reddish tint to his skin testified to his Crow heritage, but the dark blond hair, shaved on the sides and left long on top to work into a braid that hung down his back, revealed the other side of his lineage.

His father was Olaf Gunnarson, a Norwegian who had immigrated to America and become a fur trapper and mountain man. Once in the mountains, Gunnarson had met, fallen in love with, and married a young Crow woman who had seen quite a bit of the western half of the continent during her various captivities and wanderings.

The Maker of All Things Above had blessed their union with only one child, a boy who had grown tall and strapping and strong. Olaf had called him Bjorn, but he usually went by his Crow name, Tall Dog.

Today he was armed with a couple of flintlock pistols and, in a scabbard that hung down his back from a strap around his shoulder, a Spanish conquistador's sword with a curved hilt around the handle. His mother had picked up the weapon, an *Espada ancha,* during her travels as a young woman down in the Southwest.

During the year since their first meeting, Preacher and Tall Dog had become staunch friends and shared several adventures. They had worked together during the fur trapping season and amassed one of the best loads of pelts Preacher had taken in quite a while.

Now they were in St. Louis. That load of pelts was sold and had been stored in a fur trader's warehouse, and Preacher had money in his pocket.

He figured on spending some of it at Red Mike's.

No trip to St. Louis was complete without a visit to the tavern not far from the riverfront. Preacher had been stopping in there for years, every time he was in town, for a few drinks, some chin-wagging with the burly Irishman who ran the place, and occasionally some companionship from one of the buxom wenches who served drinks.

If Tall Dog was going to live the life of a mountain man, going to Red Mike's was a vital part of his education.

The youngster seemed to be having second thoughts about it. He said, "Perhaps it might be better if I went back to the stable where we left our horses and gear."

"Don't you want to see Red Mike's for yourself, after hearin' me talk about the place?"

"Is it noisy and crowded and smells bad like the rest of this city?"

"Well . . ." Preacher grinned. "Some might say that's a pretty fittin' description."

"You go ahead, Preacher," Tall Dog said. "I will await your return at the stable."

Preacher wasn't going to argue with him, although to be honest, he was a little disappointed. He'd wanted to see what sort of reaction Tall Dog would provoke from the other customers in the tavern.

After all, it wasn't every day a fella laid eyes on a half-Viking, half-Crow warrior carrying around a conquistador's sword.

But the decision was Tall Dog's to make, so Preacher was about to say that he'd see him back at the stable when Tall Dog suddenly stood up a little straighter and frowned. That made him tower over his surroundings even more than before.

"Something wrong?" Preacher asked.

"That woman. I have never seen anyone such as her before."

Preacher looked where Tall Dog was looking, across the street to where a young woman was hurrying along. She wore a gray dress and a dark blue cloak with the hood thrown back to reveal tumbling waves of auburn hair.

From this distance and angle, Preacher couldn't see her eyes, but he was willing to bet that they were green and that she had a scattering of freckles across her face. He knew an Irish colleen when he saw one.

"Do you know her?" Tall Dog asked.

"You reckon I know everybody in St. Louis? I never saw her before, but I agree, she's mighty easy on the eyes."

"Her hair . . . it's so bright. Like the late afternoon, when the sun is low and the air begins to thicken with the approach of dusk."

"You know where she's going?"

Tall Dog's gaze snapped around to Preacher. "Of course not. Do you?"

"Not for sure, but I can tell she's an Irish lass, so she's probably on her way to Red Mike's."

She might not be headed anywhere near the tavern, Preacher thought, but Tall Dog didn't know that.

"Perhaps I should go there after all."

"Maybe you should. And even if that gal ain't there, some other good-lookin' wenches will be."

Tall Dog shook his head. "None to compare with that one." He looked over the heads of the crowd in the busy street and went on with a note of alarm entering his voice, "I don't see her anymore."

"Let's see if we can find her."

Tall Dog didn't say anything else about skipping Red Mike's. He strode along beside Preacher with a determined expression on his face.

The auburn-haired girl had disappeared into the throng of people. Preacher and Tall Dog didn't spot her again as they made their way toward Red Mike's.

Preacher honestly believed that they might find her at the tavern, but if they didn't, that would be all right. Looking for her was just an excuse to get Tall Dog to come along without being stubborn about it.

After leaving Dog outside with a command from Preacher to stay, they paused just inside the tavern's doorway. Tall

Dog looked around, his keen eyes searching intently for the object of his interest.

"I do not see her, Preacher."

"The place is pretty busy. Maybe you just didn't notice her. Come on over to the bar with me. We'll ask Mike if she's been here."

Several customers called out Preacher's name by way of greeting. He grinned and nodded to them.

"It seems as if everyone here knows who you are," Tall Dog commented.

"Well, I been comin' here a long time, and sometimes you just want to be—"

Preacher stopped short as a young woman hurried up to him. The neckline of the dress she wore scooped low enough to reveal generous portions of her creamy, ample breasts.

Blond curls tumbled around her face to her shoulders, which were also left partially bare by the garment. She carried a currently empty round tray in her left hand.

"Preacher!" she said. She reached up, wrapped both arms around his neck, and pulled his face down to hers. Her lips pressed against his in a long, urgent kiss.

Whoops of approval erupted from some of the men in the tavern.

When Preacher finally broke the kiss and lifted his head, he saw that Tall Dog was staring at him with one eyebrow cocked quizzically.

"Um, this here is Molly," Preacher said. "And dang it, girl, I've told you before, I'm old enough to be your pa."

Molly still had her arms around his neck and her body pressed close to his. She grinned and said, "Yeah, but you ain't my pa."

Abruptly, her forehead creased in a frown as she went

on, "You aren't my pa, are you, Preacher? I mean, you've been coming to St. Louis for a long time, and my ma worked in a place like this . . ." The frown went away and the grin came back. "Oh, well, I don't care. I'm just glad to see you again, Preacher."

"Yeah, I, uh, got that idea." Preacher nodded toward his companion. "Molly, this here is Tall Dog, a good friend o' mine."

Molly finally let go of Preacher and boldly surveyed Tall Dog from head to foot. Judging by her expression, she liked what she saw.

"I don't reckon I've ever seen an Indian like you before," she said.

"That's because he's half Norwegian."

Tall Dog said, "Have you seen a young woman with hair like the late afternoon sun? She was wearing a gray dress and a blue cloak and was headed in this direction."

The frown reappeared on Molly's face. "Don't you know better than to ask a girl about some other girl?"

"He's lived in the mountains all his life, with his ma's people," Preacher said.

Molly let out a disgusted snort. "That's no excuse. Would he ask some Indian girl if she'd seen some other Indian girl?"

"I doubt that it would cause offense if I did . . ." Tall Dog said with a tentative note in his voice.

"Oh, I'll bet it would. You'd probably just be too thick-headed to see it, you big—"

From behind the bar, the burly, mustachioed Red Mike called, "If you're through welcomin' Preacher and his friend, Molly, I've got drinks here that need to be delivered."

"I have to get back to work," the blonde said, "so I

suppose I'll just have to forgive you, Tall Dog. That was what Preacher called you, isn't it?"

"Yes, I—"

She came up on her toes, kissed him on the mouth, and then twirled around to head for the bar and pick up those drinks.

Tall Dog gazed after her with a somewhat stunned expression on his face. After a moment, he said, "Does she always act like that?"

"Fussin' at you one second and kissin' you the next?" Preacher laughed. "You really don't know much about gals, do you?"

"I still say it is different back home."

"I ain't gonna waste time arguin' with you. Come on, let's talk to Mike."

On the way to the bar, Preacher paused a few times to greet old friends, although thankfully none of the whiskery, buckskin-clad frontiersmen planted kisses on him as Molly had.

Red Mike's customers were split about evenly between fur trappers who were just visiting St. Louis but spent most of their time in the mountains or out on the plains and rivermen who lived in town and worked on the docks or the vessels that plied up and down the Mississippi.

Preacher got along all right with the rivermen, for the most part, but he didn't feel the same kinship with them that he did with other mountain men.

The fur business was in a serious decline. Preacher knew that within a few years it would be difficult for a man to make a living by trapping.

He wasn't sure what he'd do then, but his wants had always been simple and he'd never had any desire to be rich.

The river, on the other hand, would always be there and would always need men to work on and along it.

Not Preacher, though. He couldn't stand being tied down even that much.

"Howdy, boys," Red Mike said as Preacher and Tall Dog reached the bar. "Who's your friend, Preacher?"

"This is Tall Dog. We've been trailin' together for a spell. His ma's a Crow, and his pa's a fella named Olaf Gunnarson who came over here from Norway."

Mike nodded and said, "I thought you had a bit of a Scandihoovian look about you, son." The tavernkeeper smiled. "I reckon your ancestors and mine fought each other tooth and nail about a thousand years ago, but you're sure as blazes welcome here in my tavern today."

Mike extended a big paw across the bar, and the two men shook. Tall Dog said, "I've heard stories from my father about the days when the Vikings went to war against the Irish. Those were epic battles."

"Aye, so they say. Those days are long past. What can I get you, fellows?"

"Beer for the both of us," Preacher said, "but I'll have a shot o' whiskey with mine."

Mike hesitated and looked at Tall Dog. "No offense, lad, but I know that some members of your blessed mother's tribe have a difficult time with spiritous drinks."

"My father has also told me stories about the mead halls and the prodigious amounts of mead my ancestors could consume. I believe I will be all right to have one mug of beer."

"Comin' right up, then," Mike said as he reached under the bar for a pair of pewter beer steins. He filled them from a keg, set them on the bar in front of Preacher and Tall Dog, and then snagged a bottle of whiskey and an empty glass from a shelf.

Preacher and Tall Dog took hold of the steins and lifted

them, but before they could drink, a harsh male voice spoke behind them.

"What the hell is this, Mike?" the man demanded. "Since when do you allow filthy, heathen redskins to drink in your tavern?"

Chapter 2

Preacher stopped with his beer stein halfway to his lips. He looked over his shoulder and saw a big, broad-shouldered man standing behind him and Tall Dog.

Preacher could tell by the rough work clothes that the man labored on the docks. He glared at Tall Dog with intense dislike on his beard-stubbled face. Thick black hair fell down over his low brow.

"Back off there, Dechert," Mike said. "I'll be havin' no trouble in here, you know that."

"If you don't want trouble, you shouldn't let savages in here."

"Take it easy, friend," Preacher said. His words were civil enough, but his voice held a hard edge.

The riverman called Dechert turned the glare on him. "I know who you are. You don't scare me, Preacher."

"Not tryin' to scare anybody, just don't want to ruin a peaceful visit to my favorite tavern."

"It's my favorite tavern, too, or at least it was until it started stinkin' of Injun."

Tall Dog had been looking over his shoulder at the stranger, too, but now he pointedly turned back to the bar in a dismissive gesture.

"I would like to ask you a question," he said to Mike. "We are looking for a young woman—"

Dechert said, "Keep your dirty redskin hands off the gals around here, you damn—"

As he spoke, he grabbed Tall Dog's shoulder. Dechert was pretty big, but he had to reach up to do that.

Preacher didn't wait any longer in the hope that trouble could be averted. It was too late for that now.

He crashed the beer stein in his hand against the left side of Dechert's head.

The stunning blow was enough to drive the riverman to his knees. Preacher dropped the beer stein and pivoted to throw a left-hand punch into Dechert's face.

The clout drove the man over backward and left him sprawled senseless on the tavern's sawdust-littered floor. A couple of men sitting at a nearby table had had to jump up and back to keep him from crashing into them.

"Blast it, Preacher!" Red Mike burst out. "Why'd you—"

"Didn't figure you'd want one of your customers gutted right here in the tavern," Preacher interrupted to say. "That's what would've happened mighty quick-like if he'd kept on tryin' to manhandle Tall Dog."

With a solemn nod, Tall Dog said, "I would have been forced to defend myself."

"Well, it ain't over yet. Look out!"

Preacher heeded Mike's warning and jerked his head around in time to see a flung chair sailing through the air at him. He didn't have time to duck, so he threw an arm up and deflected the chair so that it clattered against the bar.

However, that wasn't the end of it. Four men who had been sitting at a table had surged to their feet. One of them had thrown the chair. Since their clothing marked

them as rivermen, too, Preacher assumed they were
Dechert's friends.

One of them confirmed that by shouting, "We can't let
him get away with what he did to Otto! Get the cowardly
schwein!"

They charged at Preacher and Tall Dog. A few men who
happened to be in the way scrambled to get clear.

Red Mike yelled curses and told the men to stop, but
they ignored him. Preacher and Tall Dog turned to meet
the charge.

Tall Dog reached up and closed his hand around the
grips of the sheathed sword on his back, but Preacher
snapped, "Leave that blade where it is. We don't want to
kill these idiots."

Tall Dog glanced at him, shrugged, and let go of the
sword.

The way the attackers were clumped together, Preacher
and Tall Dog couldn't separate them and tackle two apiece.
They all came together in a knot of slugging, flailing fists.

Preacher didn't bother much with trying to fend off any
blows. He just absorbed the punishment and dished out
some in return.

The battle continued in that furious fashion for a
moment, until one of the rivermen worked his way around
behind Tall Dog and jumped on his back. He wrapped
his arms around Tall Dog's neck and his legs around the
warrior's waist and yelled, "I got him! I got him!"

Tall Dog reached back with both hands, grabbed the
man's ears, and twisted them as he bent forward at the waist.
The man howled in pain and his arms and legs loosened.

Quick as a flash, Tall Dog shifted his grip and caught
hold of the man under the arms. With a powerful heave, he

sent the man flying over his head to crash into another of the attackers.

A few feet away, Preacher caught one of his opponents with a straight, hard right to the face and felt the satisfying crunch as the man's nose flattened under the impact. Hot blood spurted across the mountain man's knuckles. The man reeled back, clutching his nose and groaning as crimson streamed from it.

That exchange gave the other riverman just enough time to set himself and hammer a punch into Preacher's midsection. Preacher's belly was ridged with muscle and hard as a washboard, but the man who hit him was large and powerfully built. The blow was enough to drive Preacher back against the bar.

With little room to maneuver, Preacher wasn't able to avoid the man's lunge. The punch also knocked most of the breath out of him, so he didn't react quite as quickly as he normally would have.

As a result, the riverman was able to clamp both hands around Preacher's neck and bend him back even more. He aimed a knee at Preacher's groin in a vicious thrust.

Preacher expected that and twisted the lower half of his body just in time to avoid the worst of it. The riverman's knee caught him on the thigh. That made Preacher's leg go numb for a moment, but the choking hands held him up so he didn't collapse.

Bright red rockets began to go off behind Preacher's eyes. He knew the lack of air would make him lose consciousness in another minute or so, and that would end the fight.

Even though his muscles didn't want to obey his commands, he brought his arms up and hacked down with the edges of both hands, driving them against the spots where his opponent's shoulders met his neck.

That paralyzing double blow made the man let go of Preacher's neck. He stumbled as he tried to stay on his feet. Preacher lifted a right uppercut from his knees.

It landed under the man's chin. His feet came off the floor, his legs flew up, and he slammed down on his back. Blood leaked from his mouth. Preacher spotted something lying in the sawdust next to the man that might be the bitten-off tip of his tongue.

Keep your tongue behind your teeth during a fight. That could be a painful lesson to learn, Preacher thought as he leaned on the bar and tried to catch his breath.

All four of their attackers were down, either unconscious or bloody and moaning. Dechert, who had started the fight by harassing Tall Dog, still lay senseless in a puddle of spilled beer. But at least it was over.

Then Preacher realized that wasn't the case at all. Half a dozen more rivermen were on their feet and advancing deliberately toward the bar. Three of them held large knives, while the other three gripped makeshift clubs that were actually chair legs wrenched free.

Preacher glanced at a nearby table where several frontiersmen sat. He knew one of them and asked, "You boys plan on takin' cards in this game, Cullers?"

The man grinned back at him. "Why would we do that?" he wanted to know. "We're havin' too much fun watchin' you hand these river rats their needin's!"

"These men are armed, Preacher," Tall Dog said. He reached up, closed his hand around the sword again, and cocked an eyebrow.

"Go ahead," Preacher said.

Steel whispered against leather as Tall Dog drew the *Espada ancha*.

The sight of the sword's broad blade made the gang of

rivermen hesitate for a second. The weapon gave Tall Dog greater reach . . . but there were six of them.

Besides, they had made it obvious to everyone in the tavern that they were entering the fray. They couldn't back down now, not without injuring their pride.

With sudden, harsh yells, they charged the tall warrior.

Preacher stepped back, figuring he might as well watch the show, too.

The man with the longest club leaped over a fallen combatant and reached Tall Dog first. He gripped the bludgeon in both hands and swung it with speed and power.

Tall Dog swatted it aside with a flick of the blade that seemed effortless. He could have back-handed the sword across the man's throat and opened it up with the razor-keen edge, but instead, he slapped the flat of the blade against the man's head.

That made the man stumble, fall, and pitch forward to ram his head against the bar. He dropped senseless to the floor.

Tall Dog shifted to the side so he wouldn't trip over the man he'd just put out of the fight. Again, he didn't seem to hurry, but he was standing there in one place and then he wasn't, in less than the blink of an eye.

That caused the man who tried to rip him open with a downward knife stroke to miss badly. Tall Dog lifted the sword and slammed the heavy brass pommel at the end of the grip into the man's head.

He fell next to the man with the club, who was also out cold.

Tall Dog whirled out of the way of the next man, whose club struck the bar with enough force that he lost his grip on it. With his free hand, Tall Dog grabbed the back of the man's neck and shoved his head down.

The man's face bounced off the bar, and his knees buckled. He crumpled next to the other two.

That accounted for half of the fresh wave of attackers.

The trio still on their feet had learned from watching how the fight worked out for their companions. Instead of coming within reach of the sword, one of the men drew back his arm and threw the knife he held at Tall Dog.

The *Espada ancha* flickered in the lamplight as Tall Dog whirled it in an arc. Metal clanged against metal as the sword struck the flung knife and knocked it away.

While Tall Dog was doing that, the remaining man holding a club sprang close enough to him that he was able to ram the chair leg into the warrior's side.

Tall Dog grunted in pain but didn't give ground. He swung his left forcarm in a sweeping blow that caught the man on the side of the head and drove him against the bar.

The next instant, Tall Dog was behind him, his left arm looped around the man's neck and the sword at his throat. Utter silence gripped the tavern because everyone in there knew that it would take only a slight motion of Tall Dog's wrist to cut the man's throat from ear to ear.

Only one of the rivermen who'd wanted trouble was left. He held a knife, but he threw it on the floor with a quick motion.

"It's over!" he said. "Don't kill him, mister."

"I never kill anyone unless I have no choice," Tall Dog said. He added into the ear of the man he held on the brink of death, "Is the fight over?"

The man started to swallow but stopped as he realized that would put more pressure on the blade pressed to his neck. He licked his lips instead and said, "Y-yeah. No more t-trouble."

"Very well." Tall Dog took the sword away from the

man's throat but kept the grip on his neck. "Gather up your friends and leave."

"We . . . we sure will!"

From where Preacher leaned casually against the bar, the mountain man said, "Don't get no ideas about lurkin' around outside and jumpin' us later, neither. Won't be no askin' polite-like next time. Just killin'."

Tall Dog finally released the man he held and gave him a little shove. He stepped back and with another of those economical movements sheathed the sword on his back.

Preacher straightened and stepped over beside him. They watched as the two rivermen began hauling their companions to their feet. Several other men who worked on the docks came forward to help.

Some of the men who'd been knocked out regained enough consciousness to stumble from the tavern under their own power. Others had to be carried out. But within minutes they were all gone.

"Sorry about the ruckus, Mike," Preacher said as he and Tall Dog turned again to the bar.

"You fellas didn't start it," Red Mike replied with a shrug, "and for a change, there's not any blood on the floor to clean up. A few chairs got broken, but I reckon I can repair them. As brawls that you're mixed up in go, it wasn't too bad, Preacher."

That brought a laugh from the mountain man. "Maybe we'll try harder next time. And I pretty much steered clear of this one."

"I noticed." Mike looked at Tall Dog. "I believe you were about to ask me something when the trouble broke out, son."

"Yes, I was, sir. We came here looking for a woman."

Mike lifted a bushy eyebrow. "Well, I suppose something can be arranged, as long as the gal is agreeable—"

"Not like that, Mike," Preacher said. "Tall Dog's talkin' about a particular woman we saw on the street headed in this direction. Mighty pretty gal with dark red hair. We didn't get a real good look at her, but she appeared to be Irish, to me."

Mike surprised them by responding, "Wears a blue cloak with a hood on it?"

"That is her," Tall Dog said with a note of excitement in his voice. He looked around. "She is here?"

"Not right now. She was here earlier today, though." Mike stroked his chin and frowned, evidently in thought. "You know, this is a mite strange."

"What is?" Preacher asked.

"The fact that you fellas came in here lookin' for her just now, because when she stopped in before, *she* was lookin' for *you,* Preacher."

CHAPTER 3

"Lookin' for me?" Preacher said with a puzzled frown. "That don't make any sense. I never laid eyes on the gal until today and don't have nary an idea who she might be."

"Maybe not, but she knows you, at least by name. She said she was looking for a mountain man called Preacher and that she was told he came in here whenever he was in St. Louis."

Tall Dog said, "Preacher, are you sure you did not recognize her when we saw her on the street?"

"I've got a good memory for faces, especially pretty ones that belong to young women. I'm plumb certain I don't know her. She didn't say why she was lookin' for me, Mike?"

The tavernkeeper shook his head. "Nope. I asked her if there was any message I could give you, if I happened to see you, and she said, no, she needed to talk to you personal-like." Mike shrugged. "That's all I know."

Preacher tugged on his right earlobe and then scratched at his bearded jaw, two signs he was deep in thought. Then he shook his head and said, "It's a mystery, sure enough."

"That ain't the only mystery, Preacher."

"What is it now?"

"That redheaded gal isn't the only one who's been

looking for you. Today was the first time I'd seen her, but somebody else has come in here and asked about you several times."

"And who might that be? Another good-lookin' gal, I hope?"

"Hate to disappoint you, but this was a fella. Good-sized, rugged-looking gent with fair hair and a beard, both starting to go gray. Middle-aged but still pretty active, like he'd spent most of his life outdoors. Like you, in that way. He wore buckskins, too, and if I had to guess, I'd say he was probably a mountain man."

Preacher considered that for a moment and then said, "I know quite a few men that description might fit, but the problem is that you'd know 'em, too, Mike. 'Most everybody who's still in the fur trade comes to Red Mike's sooner or later."

"True enough. Not only did he ask about you in here, I've heard that he's been checking at some of the other taverns in town, seeing if he can get on your trail. Whoever he is, Preacher, he's sure eager to talk to you."

"Or to ambush you," Tall Dog pointed out. "This man could be an enemy with a grudge against you." The creases in the warrior's forehead deepened. "But how does that explain the woman with hair like the sun?"

"Maybe it don't have to," Preacher said. "Maybe it's two totally different things."

"That would seem to be quite a coincidence."

The mountain man shrugged. "Such things are known to happen now and then. Mike, do you have any idea where I could find that fella?"

"Not for sure, but Molly might know something. She takes a big interest in anything that has to do with you." Mike chuckled. "She's sweet on you, you know."

"I know," Preacher said, trying not to sigh. "But she's a whole heap too young for me."

"Try telling her that."

"I have. It don't seem to do much good."

Mike set another full beer stein on the bar to replace the one Preacher had bent over the troublemaking riverman's head. Preacher picked it up now and said to Tall Dog, "Let's go talk to Molly and find out what she can tell us."

During the time Preacher and Tall Dog had been talking to Red Mike, things had settled down in the tavern. Overturned chairs had been picked up, and men who had moved to avoid the brawl had returned to their tables.

Molly was standing beside one of those tables, talking to the men sitting there. Her laugh said that she was flirting with them, but when Preacher stepped up behind her and spoke her name, she immediately turned her attention to him.

That didn't sit well with a couple of men at the table, but after witnessing the ruckus, they didn't try to start another one. They settled for scowling briefly at Preacher and then went back to drinking.

Molly had a big smile on her pretty face as she asked, "What can I do for you, Preacher? You know I'll do anything you want. Absolutely anything."

"Uh, how about we just sit down and talk for a minute?" Preacher suggested. "Maybe at that empty table over yonder in the corner."

Molly looked vaguely disappointed, but she nodded and said, "Sure. Is your friend coming along, too?"

"Yeah, Tall Dog'll sit with us."

Preacher knew the warrior could take care of himself, of course, but he figured it might be a good idea to keep Tall Dog close by, just in case anyone else in the tavern was thinking about starting a ruckus.

Although that seemed mighty unlikely when they had all seen the havoc Tall Dog had unleashed on those rivermen . . .

"What do you want to talk about?" Molly asked when the three of them were seated at the table.

"Mike was tellin' us about a fella who's been in here askin' questions about me."

That was all Preacher had to say. Molly nodded eagerly and said, "That's right! After the second or third time he came in, I started worrying that he might mean you harm. The next time he was here, it was almost closing time, so I took off early and followed him when he left."

Tall Dog said, "That might not have been wise. The man could be dangerous."

Molly laughed and said, "Sweetie, I stopped worrying about men being dangerous a long time ago. That's just a waste of time and energy for a girl like me." She gave him a confident look and added, "Besides, I can take care of myself."

Brazenly, she pulled her dress up to reveal her bare right leg. Strapped to her sleek thigh was a sheathed dagger.

"There's one on the other leg, too," she said, "and I've got a derringer hidden on me, to boot, although I don't think we're quite well enough acquainted yet to show you where that one is."

Tall Dog's face turned even redder at that comment.

Molly looked at Preacher again and went on, "I trailed the fella to Hanlon's boarding house. You know it?"

Preacher nodded. "I do. Not exactly a fancy place."

"Not hardly," Molly agreed. "But I reckon there's worse in this town."

"I don't suppose you talked to him?"

She shook her head. "No. I asked Fergus Hanlon about him, but that old coot claimed not to know anything and ran me off. I think he took me for a doxie trying to drum up some business. If I'd offered him a cut, he might've been more cooperative. That's not what I was after, though."

"How long has it been since the man came around looking for me?"

Molly frowned in thought for a moment then said, "Three days? Maybe four?"

"Remember when we asked you earlier about a red-headed gal?"

Molly made a face. "What about her?"

"You didn't tell us that she was in here askin' about me, too."

"Well, why would I? It's not my job to help other gals find what they're looking for. I've got enough to do to keep up with my own business."

"So you did see her?"

"Maybe," Molly replied with a shrug.

"Do you know where she went?"

"Out of here, that's all I care about." Molly sniffed. "I've got enough competition from the other girls who work for Mike. I don't need more of 'em wandering in off the street."

Preacher could tell that he wasn't going to get any more information out of the blonde. He took a coin from his pocket and slid it across the table toward her.

"We're much obliged to you, Molly."

She picked up the coin, bit it, and said, "This'll buy you more than some talk, if you want it to, Preacher."

"I reckon we'll call it square, at least for now."

"Well, then, I suppose I can hold out some hope, anyway."

Preacher and Tall Dog left her sitting at the table and headed for the door.

"Is that young woman always so . . . so brazen?" Tall Dog asked as they left the tavern.

Preacher chuckled. "Sort of comes with the job, I reckon."

"She sells herself to men?"

"Well, I don't know about that from personal experience, mind you, but I suspect she does. That ain't part of what goes on at Red Mike's, but he don't object when the gals who work for him make arrangements of their own with the customers."

Tall Dog shook his head. "Such things are seldom practiced among my people."

"Your people tend to have different ideas than white folks about most things."

"This is true. Where are we going now?"

"Hanlon's boarding house," Preacher replied. "I want to see if we can find that fella who's been lookin' for me."

Dusk had settled over St. Louis while they were inside Red Mike's. They followed the cobblestone streets through the gathering shadows.

There wasn't as much traffic on those streets now, so Preacher didn't have to worry about keeping Tall Dog out of the way of any wagons that might run over him.

Hanlon's boarding house was several blocks farther away from the Mississippi than Red Mike's, but Preacher knew rivermen often stayed there because it was cheap. The same was true of the mountain men who came to St. Louis to sell their furs.

Because of the frequent hostility between those two factions, it wasn't uncommon for dead men to be found in the alleys around the boarding house, their throats cut or their skulls stove in. The authorities paid little or no attention to such killings, the thinking being that anybody brave enough—or foolish enough—to venture into the neighborhood had better be able to defend himself.

Preacher wasn't worried about that where he and Tall

Dog were concerned. Between Tall Dog's sword and the pair of Colt Patersons on his hips, he figured they were a match for anything unless a whole army jumped them.

And they'd give a mighty good account of themselves against an army.

Enough light lingered in the sky for the dwellings and the people to be visible. The big cur trailing the two men expressed his opinion of their surroundings by growling deep in his throat.

Tall Dog looked around at the poorly constructed buildings and the shambling, raggedly dressed people and commented, "And the white men say that my people live in squalor."

"Some of these folks are doin' the best they can," Preacher said. "The rest just don't give a damn. I feel sorry for the kids who live in places like this because they can't help it, but that's about all the sympathy I got."

Their destination was a two-story, unpainted clapboard building. The boards of which it was constructed were so warped the whole place looked like a strong wind would blow it over. Preacher told Dog to stand watch outside while he and Tall Dog went in.

Unlike some boarding houses, this one had nothing homey about it. The street door opened onto a room furnished with a long table and some benches where meals were served, generally stew with only a few chunks of meat of questionable origin.

The stairs to the right had a small counter beside them where a short, ferret-like man with gray hair stood. A candle burned on the counter in front of him.

"Sorry, boys, we're full up," he announced. Then his lip curled as he looked at Tall Dog and went on, "I don't rent to redskins, anyway."

"We ain't lookin' to rent a room, Fergus," Preacher said.

The old man peered at them with rheumy eyes that obviously didn't see very well. "Do I know you? Is that . . . Oh, hell, Preacher! I didn't recognize you at first. I didn't mean no offense—"

Preacher waved off the apology. "Never mind that. We're lookin' for a fella who may be stayin' here." He repeated the description that Red Mike had given them. "Anybody like that here?"

"Sure, his room's on the second floor, Preacher. I don't believe I've seen him in a day or two, but you go right on up, Preacher. Second door on the right. You goin' up there, Preacher?"

"Reckon we will, if that's all right."

"Sure. Go on up, Preacher."

The mountain man nodded and then turned toward the stairs. They were too narrow for him and Tall Dog to ascend side by side, so Preacher went first with the warrior close behind him.

"Did you notice the way he kept saying your name, and rather loudly, at that?" Tall Dog asked quietly.

"I noticed," Preacher replied with a grim note in his voice. A glance over his shoulder revealed that Fergus Hanlon wasn't behind the counter anymore. The old man had scurried off somewhere, vanishing like the rat he was before trouble could break out.

Preacher's fingers brushed the smooth wooden grips of the Patersons. The light from the candle didn't reach very far up the stairs. The hallway at the top of them was a black hole.

He had never run from trouble and didn't intend to start now, but neither had he waltzed blindly into it without a care. Pausing before he reached the landing, he slipped the tomahawk from behind his belt and with a gentle toss threw it into the darkened upper hallway.

The tomahawk landed with a clatter. A female voice cried, "Look out, it's an ambush!"

An instant later, muzzle flashes ripped through the darkness and guns boomed.

The warning surprised Preacher, but the ambush didn't. He had figured out pretty quickly that somebody had paid Hanlon to tip them off if Preacher showed up looking for the mysterious stranger.

But who was the girl who'd tried to help Preacher and Tall Dog escape death?

Was it too far-fetched to think that—

Preacher didn't waste time pondering that possibility right now. Instead, he drew the revolvers as he crouched on the stairs. Pistol balls hummed through the air not far above his head and thudded into the wall.

From the sound of it, several bushwhackers had waited on the second floor, their guns trained on the landing, primed to open fire as soon as the visitors reached the top of the stairs after Hanlon tipped them off.

Chances were, at least some of them wouldn't have a spare weapon and would have to reload.

Preacher eared back the Patersons' hammers, dropping the triggers into place, and then charged up the last few steps into the second-floor hallway.

At the far end of the corridor, a tongue of muzzle flame lashed out. Preacher returned the shot in a fraction of a heartbeat, the left-hand Paterson roaring and bucking against his palm. A man cried out in pain.

A heavy footstep sounded from his right. He sensed as much as saw the large figure lunging at him from the first door on that side.

The right-hand Paterson boomed. The muzzle flash lit up the face of the man Preacher had just shot in the chest.

He fell back and dropped the empty pistol he had tried to use as a club.

Another man burst out of the same room, right behind the first one. This attacker had an axe lifted high above his head and yelled incoherently as he brought it sweeping down, aiming to split Preacher's skull.

Before Preacher could shoot the varmint, the blade of Tall Dog's sword intervened, catching the axe handle. With a twist of the sword, Tall Dog trapped the handle and jerked the sharp-edged tool out of the would-be killer's hands.

A quick step and a thrust with Tall Dog's powerful muscles behind it drove the sword all the way through the attacker's body. The man gasped in mingled surprise and pain as he died.

It was too dark for Preacher to know if his first shot had found its target, but a flurry of rapid footsteps from the end of the hall told him that some of the bushwhackers were still in the fight. He yelled, "Hold it!" but the rush of feet continued and more shots thundered.

Preacher wasn't hit and hoped that Tall Dog wasn't, either. He got to work with the Colts, switching back and forth from right to left as he thumbed off several shots with each revolver.

In these close quarters, the reports pealed out in a deafening wave. When Preacher stopped shooting, his ears still rang. Other than that, ominous silence filled the corridor.

He lifted his voice to ask Tall Dog, "You all right back there?"

"Fine," the warrior replied. "They were not very good shots."

"Ain't likely they'll have a chance to get better."

The silence that followed the exchange of gunfire spoke volumes. Nobody was even groaning. Preacher figured the hail of lead he'd sent along the hallway had scythed down the ambushers and ended their threat permanently.

That would be a shame in a way, if it turned out to be true. He wouldn't have minded asking those varmints why they wanted to kill him.

But there hadn't been time to do much of anything else.

He was about to tell Tall Dog to go back downstairs and fetch the candle from the counter, when the hinges of the second door on the right creaked. Preacher swung the Patersons in that direction as Tall Dog stepped up beside him, the sword gripped in his hands and poised to strike again.

Light spilled through the slowly widening gap as the door swung open. A figure stepped forward holding a lamp.

Preacher's eyes, which had adjusted to the darkness, squinted against the glare. He could see well enough to make out the shape of the person holding the lamp, and after hearing the voice that had called the warning to them, he wasn't surprised to realize the shape was female.

Nor was it much of a shock to see the tumbling mass of auburn hair, along with the green eyes and lightly freckled features he had guessed at.

In fact, the way this evening was going, he would have been surprised if the girl who tried to help them had turned out to be anyone else.

CHAPTER 4

"Don't shoot," the girl said unnecessarily.

"I hardly ever gun down women," Preacher said, "and it don't appear you're armed."

Although, like Molly back at Red Mike's, this girl might have a knife or a pocket pistol hidden somewhere under her dress. More than likely not, since the garment was tight enough to display the nice curves of her body to her advantage.

Preacher took note of that, strictly from a practical standpoint, of course.

"Are you Preacher?" she asked.

"I am."

She looked at the towering warrior. "And you must be Tall Dog."

He couldn't have looked more taken aback if she'd slapped him. "You know my name?"

"I do . . . Bjorn."

This had gone beyond mystifying, Preacher thought. Now that he had gotten a better look at the girl in the lamplight, he was more certain than ever he had never seen her before that glimpse in the street an hour or so earlier.

He pouched his left hand iron and reached out. "Mind loanin' me that lamp for a minute?"

"Of course."

She gave it to him. He used the light from it to check the three bodies sprawled farther along in the corridor. The men were dead, riddled by lead from the Patersons.

The first man he'd shot was a goner, too, Preacher saw when he turned back toward the landing, as was the man Tall Dog had run through with the sword. It was hard for anybody to survive several feet of cold steel being rammed through his innards.

"Why has no one come to see what all the shooting was about?" Tall Dog wondered.

"In a place like this, folks get in the habit of mindin' their own business," Preacher told him. "Anybody stayin' here will keep their doors closed and hunker down to wait for the commotion to be over. The same is true of Fergus downstairs. He'll have figured out by now that we're still alive, so he'll make himself scarce in case I decide to hunt him down and make him pay for helpin' these killers."

"He deserves whatever happens to him, the vermin," the girl said with surprising vehemence. "I'm convinced these men killed Rolf, and he probably was in on it."

"Rolf?" Tall Dog repeated.

The girl looked quickly at him. "You know that name?"

"I do. I heard it from my father."

Things were still going around too fast and puzzling for Preacher to keep up with them. He said, "Let's go somewhere else we can talk. Some place that don't stink of powder smoke and fresh-spilled blood." He looked at the girl. "You have anything in that room you need to get?"

"Just my cloak. I'm staying somewhere else." She hesitated. "A place called Ruby's."

"Oh," Preacher said.

Her green eyes flashed angrily in the lamplight. "I'm

not a trollop! It's true I work there, but . . . but only serving drinks."

"We can talk there, anyway," Preacher said.

The girl stepped back into the room to fetch her cloak. Then, while she held the lamp, Preacher reloaded both pistols.

He didn't expect to run into any more trouble, but you could never be sure about things like that. Danger had a way of coming at a fella when he least expected it.

Once the Colts had full wheels again, Preacher led the way back down the stairs, with the girl behind him and Tall Dog watchfully bringing up the rear.

"Are we going to just leave those men up there?" the girl asked.

"Those dead varmints who were tryin' their best to kill me and Tall Dog? Yeah, I reckon we'll leave 'em where they lay. We'll let ol' Fergus worry about 'em."

Hanlon would drag the carcasses out of the building and dump them in the alley, Preacher knew. What happened to them after that wasn't his problem.

He didn't holster the Colts until they reached the street. Dog was still sitting there, apparently untroubled, so Preacher knew no immediate threat was nearby.

Even then, his hands hovered near the gun butts, ready to draw.

But nobody tried to bother them. Evidently, the ambushers hadn't had any friends lurking outside.

The girl cast a wary eye toward the big cur and said, "Is that a wolf, right here in town?"

"Dog? Naw. Well, he might have some wolf blood in him. I ain't sure about that. But he's tame . . . enough."

"His name is Dog?" The girl looked at the warrior. "And your friend is Tall Dog?"

Preacher shrugged. "Ain't my doin' what folks are

called. Anyway, I've known a heap of fellas named John or James or such-like."

"And it is easy to tell Dog and I apart," Tall Dog added with a touch of the dry humor that cropped up in him from time to time.

The girl made a little sound of annoyance at that and said, "Why don't we get out of here?"

"That's the plan," Preacher said.

Ruby's was a tavern in the same neighborhood as Red Mike's, close enough to the river to get most of its traffic from the men who worked on the docks.

However, it had an attached building in the back containing rooms where the girls who worked there took customers. Mike didn't care if his serving wenches had a sideline in slap-and-tickle, but such things were an integral part of the business at Ruby's.

Except, maybe, for the auburn-haired girl, who insisted that she didn't sell herself.

Preacher didn't care whether she did or not. He just wanted an explanation for all the strange and violent things that had happened this evening.

The girl led them into the tavern and pointed to an empty table, saying they could sit there and talk.

Before they reached it, a heavyset, middle-aged woman with an enormous bosom threatening to spill out of her dress blocked their path. Preacher knew she was Ruby, the proprietor of this place, who was said to have a hard enough right-hand punch to knock out a riverman, as well as appetites that could wear him down to a nub if she was in a different mood.

Right now she was annoyed, as she said, "Damn it,

Betsy, you can't work here and just come and go as you please."

"I'm sorry, Ruby. I . . . I had something important come up—"

"You always do," Ruby snorted. "And you're too good to make it up the way you ought to when you leave me in the lurch—"

"Take it easy, Ruby," Preacher drawled. "The young lady's with me and my friend now, so why don't you send a bucket of beer and a bottle of whiskey over to that table?"

Ruby's eyes narrowed as she looked at Tall Dog. "I don't normally allow Injuns in here."

"How about fellas from Norway?"

"Norskis? Sure, they're all right, I suppose."

"Well, Tall Dog here is half Norski, and you can't let that half in without lettin' the Crow half in, too."

Ruby squinted even harder. "Is he civilized?"

"I'll vouch for him," Preacher said. He saw anger smoldering in Tall Dog's eyes and figured the boy would have something to say if this kept on. He took hold of Tall Dog's arm and steered him toward the table the girl had pointed out. Ruby let them go with a sour look but no objection.

Out of habit, Preacher sat down so that his back was to the wall. Tall Dog was across from him, with the girl between them to Preacher's left. He said, "Your name's Betsy?"

"That's right. Betsy Kingsley."

"So now we know your name," Tall Dog said. "But that does not explain how you know ours."

"Rolf told me about you. Rolf Pedersen. When he asked me to help him, he told me who he was looking for."

Tall Dog tensed and leaned forward. "Where is Rolf Pedersen now?"

Betsy swallowed hard and said, "I . . . I'm afraid he's dead."

"Yeah, you mentioned something about that back there," Preacher said. "You said those gents who ambushed us killed him."

"I don't know that for a fact, but it's the only thing that makes sense. He told me there were enemies after him and they might hurt him, or even try to kill him." Betsy's voice caught a little. "They . . . they succeeded. When I went to Hanlon's this morning to talk to Rolf, I found him. He . . . he looked like he'd been beaten to death."

"Where's his body?" Preacher asked in a flat voice.

Betsy shook her head. "I don't know. I was so shocked, I ran out of there. When I went back later, Rolf was . . . was gone."

Preacher nodded slowly and said, "Hanlon would've gotten rid of the corpse. The killers probably paid him to, just like they paid him to tip them off if I showed up." A thought occurred to him, and he frowned. "How'd they know my name and that I was somebody to watch out for?"

"Rolf had been looking for you for a while and asking about you in the taverns. I'm sure if those men were keeping an eye on him, they could have found someone to tell them who he was searching for."

"Yeah, I reckon," Preacher said. "This is kind of a muddle, but it makes sense if you squint your eyes and hold your mouth right. Be a lot easier to know what's going on if we'd been able to grab one of those fellas alive and ask him a few questions." The mountain man shook his head. "Just didn't work out that way."

"Perhaps the answers are in that letter you spoke of," Tall Dog said to the girl. "Do you know where it is?"

"I do," she said. "And things should be a lot clearer if I just let you read it. At least I hope so, since I can't make heads nor tails of it myself and only know what Rolf told me."

She reached into a pocket on the inside of the cloak and withdrew a folded piece of paper. At one time, it had been sealed with a blob of wax, but that seal had been broken.

One of the other girls who worked at Ruby's arrived at the table just then with a bucket of beer, two tin cups, and a bottle of whiskey. She smiled at Preacher, regarded Tall Dog with a wary but appreciative glance, and glared at Betsy.

"Two fellas and you don't even know what to do with them," she said to the auburn-haired girl, then let out a disgusted snort and walked off.

Anger sparked in Betsy's green eyes, but she controlled the reaction.

"The other young ladies who work here don't like you?" Tall Dog asked.

"They're not ladies . . . and no, they don't like me. They think I think I'm better than them."

Preacher didn't have any interest in getting into that. He uncorked the bottle, took a swig of the whiskey, and then dipped the tin cups in the bucket of beer.

"You were gonna let us read that letter," he reminded Betsy. He held out his hand.

She said, "It's actually meant for Bjorn. But Rolf said he'd be accompanying you, and since you're so well known in St. Louis, you're the one he asked for."

She extended the folded paper to Tall Dog.

He took the missive, opened it, and began reading. After a few seconds, a smile curved his lips.

"You could not read it anyway, Preacher. It is written in Norwegian."

"You read that lingo?"

"I do. My father taught me, along with English. My grasp of his native tongue is perhaps not quite as fluent as it might be, because we had little chance to practice it except between ourselves. But I understand enough to make out that this letter is from my grandfather, Axel Gunnarson."

"Back in Norway?"

Tall Dog shook his head. "No. According to this, my grandfather is the leader of a group of settlers who have made their home in the British provinces of North America, far north of here."

"What they sometimes call Canada?"

"Yes, I believe so."

"Have you ever met your grandfather?"

"No, but I knew that he and my father exchanged letters from time to time. Not many, and not often, because you know how difficult it is to communicate on the frontier."

"That's sure enough the truth," Preacher agreed.

"He sent Rolf Pedersen to St. Louis with this letter, knowing from my father that I have been traveling with you. Grandfather thought it likely that we would come here sooner or later to sell our furs."

"That was a good guess on his part. I reckon this Pedersen fella is the one who went to Red Mike's lookin' for me?"

"Yes, hoping to find me through my association with you."

"Just like I said," Betsy put in. "Rolf and I became friends after we met here at Ruby's."

"Took a shine to you, did he?" Preacher asked.

Betsy's face glowed red in the lanternlight.

"No, it was nothing like that," she said. "He helped me one night when some men were bothering me, and then he . . . I believe he thought of me more like a daughter and wanted to protect me. I offered to try to help him find you, but he seemed to think that might be dangerous and so he refused." She nodded toward the paper Tall Dog held. "He did give me the letter for safekeeping, though, in case his enemies found him before he found the two of you."

Tall Dog said, "So when he was killed, you took up the effort to locate us."

"I thought I owed him that much," Betsy said.

The picture had become clearer, but there were still some missing pieces. Preacher took a healthy swallow from the cup of beer and leaned forward.

"Who in blazes were those fellas who were after him? Why did they kill him?"

"They were trying to keep him from finding us," Tall Dog said. "They did not want Rolf Pedersen to deliver this letter from my grandfather."

"Why not?"

"Because it is a plea for help," Tall Dog said. "It asks that I go north and save my grandfather and his people from the man who wants to destroy them."

Chapter 5

"My grandfather's Viking heritage is very important to him," Tall Dog explained after he had studied the letter more and digested its contents. "When he decided to come to this continent, he gathered a group of men who felt similarly, and they and their families traveled to the British provinces and headed west, away from civilization."

"Sort of like folks down here who don't want to be hemmed in head for the Rockies," Preacher said.

Tall Dog smiled. "From what I am told, the Rocky Mountains extend far up into British territory. Nothing really changes at the border, as far as the land is concerned."

"That's true, I reckon. But I've heard that the Vikings were sea-goin' folks. Why would they take off for the land-locked middle of a continent as big as this one?"

"They were told stories about giant lakes as big as seas and thought perhaps they could settle on one of them."

"The Great Lakes," Preacher said. "They're big, all right, but there are quite a few settlements around them already. Ain't exactly what I'd call the frontier."

"My grandfather and his followers discovered the same thing. So they pushed on farther west until they came to another lake, not as large as the ones you call great, but big enough for their purposes and with a large stream flowing into and out of it on the north and south. So there they decided to settle and built the village of Skarkavik."

Preacher scratched his jaw. "Good fishin' and huntin' in the area, I reckon?"

"Very good, according to my grandfather. They live off the abundance of the land."

"But don't Vikings have to go out and, what do you call it, pillage from time to time?"

Tall Dog shrugged. "My father's and my grandfather's people believe in adventure and glory and honor that comes through battle. In that they are no different than, say, the Crow and the Blackfeet."

"Good point," Preacher acknowledged.

"But living in peace and raising good, healthy families is important to them, as well," Tall Dog continued. "At a certain point, even Ragnar Lothbrok, the greatest Viking of them all, wished to put violence and raiding behind him and live the simple, peaceful life of a farmer. It was not his fault that circumstances never allowed him to do so."

"So you're sayin' your grandpa Axel and the folks with him just want to hunt and fish and be left alone."

"That is correct."

"But somebody don't want to let them do that."

"His name," Tall Dog said, "is Decker Galloway."

Galloway, the warrior went on to explain, was a logger and sawmill operator who had made a considerable amount of money by cutting timber in the eastern provinces.

"Evidently, Galloway believes that the forests of the western region hold even more riches than those of the east. Galloway wants to establish a sawmill in that untouched wilderness and cut down countless spruce, fir, and pine in order to make himself even richer."

"And he has his sights set on the land around that lake where . . . What was the name of the place again?"

"Skarkavik."

"Where your grandpa founded Skarkavik. That about the size of it?"

Tall Dog nodded. "The forest is particularly thick along the east side of the lake. Galloway is accustomed to getting what he wants, and he will stop at nothing to accomplish that goal."

"Includin' sendin' killers after Pedersen to try to keep that letter from ever gettin' to us."

Tall Dog's broad shoulders rose and fell. "It is the only explanation that makes sense."

Preacher looked at Betsy. "You knew some of this."

"Rolf told me basically what the letter says. He told me I needed to know what was going on, so I could protect myself if anything happened to him."

"Sounds like he really took a shine to you."

"I told you before, there was nothing improper between us," she snapped. "You can believe that or not, I don't care."

But she did care, Preacher could see, and that made him lean toward believing she was telling the truth. And whether she was or not, it didn't really change the question that now lay before them.

He looked across the table at Tall Dog and asked, "What are you gonna do?"

"I am going to Skarkavik," the warrior answered without hesitation. "I cannot refuse a plea for help from my family, and that side is as much blood of my blood as my mother's people."

"Your grandpa must've sent Pedersen with that letter a good while back for him to have come all this way down here to St. Louis. Whatever was gonna happen likely already has."

"It does not matter. I must go and help if I still can."

Tall Dog folded the letter and placed it solemnly on the table in front of him, almost as if it were some sort of holy relic.

"Do you even know how to get there?" Preacher asked.

"This tells me how to find Skarkavik." Tall Dog tapped the letter.

"And it'll take weeks to get there, I'm thinkin'. That's that much more time for this Decker Galloway to run your grandpa and his friends off their land."

"Everything you say is true, Preacher, but it does not change the duty I have. I cannot refuse a call for help from my family without compromising my honor and my name."

"I just wanted to make sure you knew what you were gettin' into . . . and the fact that we might be too late."

"We?" Tall Dog repeated. "You are going to Skarkavik, as well?"

"What in blazes do you think?" Preacher picked up his tin cup. "To Skarkavik."

"To Skarkavik," Tall Dog echoed as he picked up his cup. "And to vanquishing our enemies."

The cups clinked together. The two men drank.

"And what about me?" Betsy Kingsley asked.

Preacher frowned at her. "What about you? We're much obliged to you, but you've done what that fella Pedersen asked you to do. You put that letter into Tall Dog's hands."

"I warned you about that ambush, too. I was afraid the men who killed Rolf might still be around, waiting for you to show up looking for him, so I kept a watch in his room at Hanlon's, when I wasn't out trying to locate you myself."

"And we appreciate that," Preacher said, not mentioning that he had already tumbled to the threat of ambushers lurking on that darkened second floor.

"So, doesn't that give me a right to come with you?"

"To the great woods in the north?" Tall Dog asked, unable to contain his surprise. "We cannot take you all that way."

"Why not?"

"Because you are a woman." Tall Dog sounded as if that were the most obvious thing in the world.

"I don't have any family," Betsy said. "My pa was a riverman until the Mississippi took him a couple of years ago. My ma and I got by until she passed about six weeks back. Since then it's just been me."

A note of desperation crept into her voice as she went on, "I got this job serving drinks, but it's going to turn into more than that. Ruby won't have it any other way, and she'll keep the pressure on me until I give in. You know that."

"I'm sorry," Preacher said gruffly, "but that ain't our look-out. There are likely a whole heap of girls in your situation—"

"And you can't save all of them, I know. But you can help one. Me."

"By taking you into even greater danger?" Tall Dog said.

"Who says it's greater danger? Did you ever hear the expression 'a fate worse than death'?"

"The only fate worse than death is living without honor."

"That's right," Betsy said softly. "That's what I'm talking about."

Preacher shook his head and said, "You go back and talk to Red Mike again. Tell him I said to give you a job. He'll treat you better than Ruby."

"You really think he'd hire me?"

"I'm sure of it, if he knows I'm askin' it of him as a favor."

"I don't want to be a burden to anybody," Betsy said. "That's not the way I was raised."

"You won't be a burden. You'll work plenty hard at Mike's, and you won't have to do nothin' you don't want to do."

She sat there looking back and forth between Preacher and Tall Dog for a long moment, then let out a sigh.

"I suppose there's nothing else I can do."

"I believe this will be for the best," Tall Dog said.

Preacher dropped a coin on the table. "Come on. Let's head back to Mike's right now. No point in hangin' around here."

As they started toward the door, Ruby got in their way again and planted her fists on her more than ample hips.

"Where are you goin'?" she demanded of Betsy. "I've let you lollygag around long enough—"

"The young lady is leaving your employment," Tall Dog said.

"Oh, so that's the way it is," Ruby responded with a leer. "You fellas made a private arrangement to keep her all to yourselves, did you?" She pointed a stubby finger at Betsy. "You'll see for yourself how long that lasts, dearie. They'll get tired of you and put you out on the street. You're better off stayin' here where I can look after you—"

"If I had more time, I might get offended at that, Ruby," Preacher said. "You ought to know that ain't the sort of fella I am."

The heavyset proprietor scowled. "Well, what am I supposed to think? This gal goes traipsin' in and out like she figures she's better'n all of us. She'll get her come-uppance one o' these days—"

"But not from you," Tall Dog said. He took hold of Betsy's arm. "Come along."

"See?" Ruby said as she edged aside to let them pass. "You'll let a redskin put his dirty paws on you, but you're too high and mighty for all the honest men in here!"

"That's enough," Preacher said in a low voice.

Ruby moved aside even more, paling a little at the quiet menace in the mountain man's voice.

Once they were outside, with Dog trotting along in front of them, Tall Dog let go of Betsy's arm and said, "I apologize for being forward."

"Nothing to apologize for," she assured him. "You were just trying to help. I might not have gotten out of there if it weren't for you two."

"Civilization is still not doing much to win me over, Preacher," Tall Dog said." I think Skarkavik will be better."

"I'm a mite curious to see what a Viking village looks like, my own self," Preacher said.

It didn't take them long to reach the block where Red Mike's was located. By this time, the taverns were the only businesses still open. The streets were largely empty.

Most men with families were home asleep by now. Those who wanted to drink and carouse were busy doing that inside the taverns. A figure would stumble out now and then and head for whatever squalid domicile he called home.

Preacher intended to see Betsy settled at Red Mike's— the tavernkeeper had some spare rooms he rented out, and Preacher was willing to pay for one of them—and then he and Tall Dog would head back to the stable where they had left their horses and pack animals and gear. Preacher had arranged with the stableman for them to sleep in the loft.

They were still twenty paces from Red Mike's door when several figures emerged from a narrow passage between buildings across the street. Alarm bells went off in Preacher's head as half a dozen men moved quickly to block the street.

The rasp of boot leather on cobblestones from behind told Preacher that direction was blocked, too.

Betsy gasped quietly and said, "Are they thieves?"

Before Preacher or Tall Dog could answer, one of the figures in front of them stepped forward and spoke in a guttural accent.

"So, mountain man, things are different now for you and your filthy redskin friend."

The accent, as well as the words, identified him as the riverman who had started the earlier trouble by grabbing Tall Dog's arm.

Preacher moved forward slightly, putting himself in front of Betsy in case the men were armed and started shooting.

"I told you there wouldn't be no warnin' next time, only killin'," Preacher said. "Did you forget? I can understand somethin' slippin' a man's mind, so if you want to skedaddle right now—"

"You're outnumbered five to one," the riverman interrupted. "I don't count that whore with you."

"I'm no whore!" Betsy said. "You take that back, you ugly—"

Tall Dog stopped her by saying, "The lady has no part in this. Allow her to leave in peace."

"No, she can stay right there and watch while we beat you boys to death, Injun. Then she'll want to go with us, since by then she'll know we're real men, not buckskin-wearing frauds."

"Real men," Preacher repeated. He laughed. "That's

rich, mister. Gang up on folks and then claim to be real men. I'll admit, though, five to one is pretty heavy odds. What do you think, Tall Dog?"

"Yes, they are bad odds," Tall Dog said. "But what should we do? Give them time to see if they can find five or ten more cowardly dogs such as themselves to make things more even?"

The import of those words took a few seconds to sink in on the rivermen. Then angry yells erupted from several of them, and with the hurried slap of boot leather, they charged, front and rear. Enough moonlight filtered down into the street for Preacher to see that they were all brandishing long clubs.

He had told them not once but twice what would happen if they started more trouble.

His hands swept down to the butts of the Colt Patersons.

CHAPTER 6

Before Preacher could draw the guns, hoofbeats thundered and two riders swept around a nearby corner to charge directly into the midst of the attackers in front of Preacher, Tall Dog, and Betsy.

The rivermen instantly forgot about settling their grudge and scrambled to get out of the way. One of them didn't make it, going down with a terrified screech under the hooves of one of the horses.

Hearing rapid footsteps and harsh breaths behind them, Preacher and Tall Dog swung around to face the four men coming from that direction. Tall Dog gave Betsy a shove that sent her stumbling toward the side of the street, where she ought to be safer.

Preacher decided against gunplay. That wasn't personal enough. He was mad, and he wanted to settle this with his bare hands.

The closest man swung the long pole gripped in both hands, aiming the blow at Preacher's head. Preacher ducked at the last second, cutting it so close that the pole knocked the wide-brimmed brown felt hat from his head.

Then, like an uncoiling spring, Preacher shot up and grabbed the pole while its wielder was off-balance. His hands wrapped around the pole in firm grips and drove it backward.

The other end thumped hard into the man's chest, just below his throat. The impact knocked him back a couple of steps. Preacher jerked the pole away from him, spun it for a second, and slammed it across his face.

The man went down hard.

A few feet away, Tall Dog was ready with the sword in his hand. The heavy blade flashed back and forth with seemingly effortless ease, moving too fast for the eye to follow as the warrior parried the blows from the long poles swung by two attackers.

Those two were close enough that it was inevitable they would get in each other's way. When they did, one man stumbled and went to a knee. The other tripped over him and dropped the pole. It clattered away.

Tall Dog stepped in and struck downward with the brass ball at the end of the sword's pommel. It thudded against the skull of the kneeling man, who pitched forward and didn't move again.

The other man was trying to get up, but as he started to rise, the heel of the warrior's foot landed in his chest. The man flew backward, arms flung wide, and landed on the cobblestones on his back with such force that he slid for several feet before stopping, even on that rough surface.

Sensing danger to his left, Preacher shifted in that direction, slid his hands apart on the pole he held, and thrust it into the air above his head. That blocked the pole in the hands of another man who had tried to bring it down in a crashing blow. Preacher felt vibration shiver up his arms when the two bludgeons met with such force.

The pole held by the other man rebounded upward. Preacher lunged forward, still holding his pole horizontally, and rammed it across the man's throat.

The man gasped and gagged and struggled to drag air through his crushed windpipe as he fell. Preacher kicked him in the head and knocked him out.

The varmint might choke to death while he was unconscious, but Preacher didn't care.

They'd been warned.

That took care of the four men on this side of the fight, Preacher saw when he glanced around and spotted Tall Dog standing there, tall and straight, with the sword still in his hand.

"You all right?" Preacher called to him.

"Yes. What about you?"

"Varmints never touched me."

Preacher moved to join Tall Dog, and they stood side by side as they turned to see what had happened in the rest of the fight after their two mysterious benefactors on horseback joined in.

Devastation was what had happened. One tall, massively built form stood in the middle of the street with limp, broken figures sprawled around him in all directions, as if he had waded into the rivermen and tossed them around like children's toys.

As Preacher recognized the huge man, he thought that might have been exactly what happened.

"Evenin', Nighthawk," Preacher said. "How are you doin'?"

"Umm."

"Yes, it was indeed a stimulating bit of exercise . . . while it lasted," said a small man still mounted on horseback.

He slid out of the saddle and dropped to the street with graceful ease that belied the somewhat twisted nature of his short legs. He stood only a little more than three feet tall but had a powerful, broad-shouldered, muscular torso.

"Preacher! How delightful to see you again," he said as he walked toward the mountain man.

"Likewise, Audie," Preacher greeted him. The two men clasped hands with the firm familiarity of old friends. "Have you and Nighthawk been lookin' for me, or is meetin' up like this just pure coincidence?"

"Coincidence, I assure you," Audie replied. "Or perhaps I should say, as is so often the case with you . . . fate."

Preacher had no better friends in the world than Audie, the diminutive former college professor turned mountain man, and Nighthawk, the giant Crow warrior who matched Tall Dog in height but was even more powerfully built. The two of them roamed the frontier together and had thrown in with Preacher on many adventures in the past.

"We spotted what appeared to be a very unequal battle shaping up," Audie went on, "and as you know, such things always rub us the wrong way."

"Umm," Nighthawk added.

"Indeed. Then we heard your voice, Preacher, and knew that perhaps the odds were not as unequal as we first believed." Audie laughed. "But we didn't want to pass up the opportunity to enjoy a bit of exercise. I hope you'll forgive us for intruding into what appeared to be a personal matter."

"Naw, that's fine," Preacher assured him. "These fleas needed squashin', and I don't particularly care who done it."

"Umm," Nighthawk said.

"Yes, what happened to the young lady who was with you?" Audie said as he looked around.

Tall Dog seemed to be wondering the same thing. He called, "Miss Kingsley?"

"I'm here," Betsy said as she stepped out of a darkened alcove in front of the door to a nearby business. "I tried to stay out of the way while I waited to see what was going to happen."

"Wasn't much doubt about that," Preacher said. "Even less once Audie and Nighthawk showed up."

"Yes, I see your, uh, friends . . ."

Audie took off his hat and bowed low to her, which considering his lack of stature to begin with put him pretty close to the cobblestones.

"Good evening, young miss," he said. "My name is Audie, and my friend here is Nighthawk. It's an honor and a pleasure to make your acquaintance."

Preacher saw that Betsy was staring at them. He chuckled and said, "Yeah, you won't find many out here like this pair. But they're good fellas and have been pards of mine for a long time. Boys, we were on our way to Red Mike's and would be plumb pleased if you'd join us."

"Of course," Audie answered without hesitation. "We'll take our horses on to Patterson's Livery and be there shortly. We just arrived in town, you know."

As Audie and Nighthawk walked off leading their mounts and the pack animal tied to Nighthawk's horse, Betsy said, "I suppose we're going to leave these bodies where they fell, too?"

"When the ones who ain't dead come to, they can deal with the ones who are," Preacher said.

"That's an efficient method, I suppose," Betsy said somewhat dubiously.

Red Mike saw them come into the tavern, and so did Molly. The blond serving wench planted herself in front of them and said, "I see you found her."

"We did," Preacher agreed. "And we're gonna sit down at that big table in the corner. Audie and Nighthawk'll be joinin' us in a little spell."

Molly glared at Betsy for a second longer and then

moved out of the way. Red Mike came out from behind the bar and met them at the table.

"I see you found her," he said with a nod toward Betsy.

"Yep. Mike, this is Betsy Kingsley. She could use a job and a place to stay, if you've got one to spare."

Mike nodded and said, "I reckon we can do that, Preacher, since you're the one who's asking. Miss Betsy, when do you want to start?"

"I . . . I don't know . . ."

"How about tomorrow night?" Preacher suggested. "We've still got some things to talk over tonight."

"That'll be fine," Mike agreed. "But you can have the room starting tonight, miss."

"Thank you," Betsy said. She looked at Preacher and Tall Dog. "I don't know what I would have done without your help."

"You were trying to help us," Tall Dog said. "You even risked your life to do so. Helping you find a place is the least we can do."

"I'll have Molly fetch you some drinks," Mike said.

"Make it coffee," Preacher said. "And have Molly bring the pot, since Audie and Nighthawk are gonna be joinin' us."

"They are?" Mike grinned. "Been a while since I've seen that mismatched pair of varmints. It'll be good to say howdy to them."

He moved back to the bar. Betsy said, "He's right, your friends really are . . . well, odd. No offense meant."

"None taken," Preacher assured her. "Audie would be the first to tell you there ain't anybody else out here on the frontier like them. Audie used to be a professor at some fancy college back east. Taught philosophy and natural history and things like that. Not to mention, the little fella's memorized just about all there is in the Bible and Shakespeare and a bunch of other poetical scribblers. When you get him to spoutin' that stuff, he can go for hours without runnin' down."

"But he dresses like a mountain man."

"That's because that's what he is," Preacher said. "One day, he took it in his head to leave the college and head west. I reckon he just up and decided it was time for him to live a simpler life. Once he got to the mountains, he met Nighthawk, and the two of them just hit it off right away. They been best friends ever since. Audie says it's because he's the only one who can put up with all of Nighthawk's jabberin'."

Preacher looked over at Tall Dog and went on, "You know, it wouldn't surprise me if Audie knows a whole heap about Vikings. Seems like the sort of thing he'd be interested in. If he and Nighthawk don't have any other pressin' business, they might want to come along with us to Skarkavik."

"Even though it may be a dangerous journey and more dangerous when we get there?"

"Shoot, that'll just make 'em more eager to throw in with us. There's nothin' those two like better than a good scrap. They was with me a while back when I run into a bunch of Aztecs in a hidden city up in the mountains . . . No, never mind about that, it was a plumb loco story to begin with. Let's just say that what we're fixin' to do is just the sort of thing to get them interested."

"We will discuss it when they get here," Tall Dog said, then added, "From what I saw outside, they are good fighters."

"You won't find any better," Preacher declared.

Audie and Nighthawk arrived back at the tavern a short time later, and when they came in, they received the same sort of exuberant welcome Preacher always did. They spotted Preacher, Tall Dog, and Betsy at the table and crossed the room to join them.

"All the garbage we left in the street has been cleared away," Audie reported after he'd climbed nimbly onto one of the chairs. "What was that about, Preacher? Have you gotten yourself mired in some sort of difficulties again?"

Preacher waved a hand. "That ruckus was just a bunch of soreheaded river rats who didn't like the idea of Tall Dog comin' in here. Tall Dog had a little tussle with 'em earlier and handed 'em their needin's. Tarnal fools were too stupid to take their beatin' and let well enough alone."

"Men who were not overly fond of our red-hued brethren, eh?"

"Yeah, that's about the size of it."

"Umm," Nighthawk said.

"You're right, old friend, prejudice is a terrible affliction," Audie said. "A man should be judged by his actions and little else." He smiled across the table at Tall Dog. "I recognize the Crow beadwork on your clothing, my friend, but I hope you'll take no offense if I say that otherwise you don't resemble any other Crow warrior I've ever seen."

"That's 'cause he's one of a kind," Preacher said. "Audie, Nighthawk, meet Tall Dog, otherwise known as Bjorn Gunnarson."

Audie cocked an eyebrow. "Kin to Olaf Gunnarson?"

"My father," Tall Dog acknowledged. "Do you know him?"

"I know of him. Our paths have never crossed as far as I recall. But he's well-spoken of in the mountains." Audie nodded slowly. "Come to think of it, I believe I had heard that he took a Crow wife. That would be your mother, I take it."

"Yes. I was raised among her people."

"But he's still half Viking," Preacher put in. "Which

leads us to a problem we're havin' right now that you two fellas might want to help us with."

"Umm," Nighthawk said.

"Yes, will there be excitement and adventure?" Audie asked.

"Don't reckon we'll know for sure until we get there."

"Where are you going?"

"North," Preacher said. "Way up north."

CHAPTER 7

Before Preacher could continue with the explanation, Molly arrived at the table with a pot of coffee and a tray with five cups on it.

"Mike says you're going to be working here, so I have to get along with you," she said to Betsy.

"I don't want to cause any trouble," the auburn-haired girl said.

"Then don't go trying to sink your hooks into Preacher. I'm going to convince him sooner or later that the two of us ought to get together."

"I've told you, Molly, you're a whole heap too young for me—" Preacher began.

"We'll see," she said confidently. "Women are born older than men."

"Anyway," Preacher said, "I ain't gonna be in town, because Tall Dog and me are about to set off on a trip. So you and Betsy won't have any excuse not to get along just fine, and I'd take it as a personal favor if you did, honey."

Molly sniffed and said, "Well, in that case . . . Welcome to Red Mike's, I guess. Betsy, that's your name?"

"Yes, Betsy Kingsley."

"I'm Molly. I'll be around."

The blonde left to go back to the bar.

"Thanks," the auburn-haired girl said. "I'm getting pretty tired, so I'm just about ready to turn in." She looked at Preacher. "You said you're leaving in the morning on a boat called the *Argosy*?"

"That's right. It'll be pretty early."

"Then I should say goodbye now, I suppose, in case I don't see you in the morning. Good luck to all of you. If you can, settle the score for Rolf Pedersen. He treated me decently."

"We will see him avenged," Tall Dog vowed.

She reached across the table, clasped his right hand with both of hers for a moment, and said, "Thank you."

Tall Dog looked a little embarrassed. He slipped his and free and cleared his throat.

"Honor demands it," he said.

"Not all men are honorable."

"You're right about that, honey," Molly said. "Come on me. Don't you have a bag or anything?"

"ust what I'm wearing," Betsy said.

She told Preacher, Audie, and Nighthawk goodbye and wished them well on the journey, then vanished down a allway at the rear of the tavern with the blonde.

"I am surprised she did not put up more of an argument ut wanting to come with us," Tall Dog said.

"So am I," Preacher agreed.

fact, he was a mite suspicious that Betsy might be g some sort of trick.

, there was no sign of her at the boat the next n Preacher and the others arrived to load their plies.

g sidewheelers that chugged up and down

"I'm sorry if I've caused trouble between the two of you," Betsy said.

Preacher shook his head. "Don't worry about it. No matter what Molly says, there ain't no 'two of us.' Once that gal gets an idea in her head, it's hard to get it out."

When they all had cups of coffee, Audie said, "Now, Preacher, we want to hear about this northern journey you propose to take."

For the next several minutes, Preacher laid out the situation, with help from Tall Dog who explained about his grandfather and the Viking settlement on the shore of the great northern lake.

"Wait a moment," Audie said. "You mean to tell me these are actual Vikings such as the ones who lived in the Scandinavian countries a thousand years ago? The ones I've studied in the eddas and sagas?"

"They ain't a thousand years old," Preacher said, "but they live the same way those old boys did. Ain't that right, Tall Dog?"

"Yes, that's my understanding. They probably have firearms, but other than that, they hunt and fish and live just as our ancestors did."

"Remarkable! After reading about them, I must see this for myself. Do you have any objection to Nighthawk and me accompanying you?"

"Matter of fact, we were hopin' you would," Preacher said. "There's a good chance we can use a couple more good fightin' men."

"It's settled, then. When do you plan to leave?"

"As soon as we can. It's already taken a while for word of his grandfather's troubles to reach Tall Dog, and it'll take almost as long for us to get up there where we're goin'. There are riverboats that go all the way up the Mississipp' to Fort Snelling and St. Peter's. We can take one of them that far, but from there on we'll have to travel on horseback."

"Where, exactly, is our destination?"

Tall Dog had placed the letter from his grandfather in a fringed pouch that hung from a strap over his shoulder and around his neck. He took it out, opened it, spread it on the table in front of them, and began to trace the foreign words with a fingertip as he translated them.

The directions Axel Gunnarson had provided were detailed and sounded fairly easy to follow. When Tall Dog had laid out their route, Preacher asked, "Have you and Nighthawk ever been up that way, Audie?"

The former professor shook his head. "No, we've never ventured that far north."

"Neither have I," Preacher said. "You know me, though. I've always got a hankerin' to see some country I've never laid eyes on before."

"I think that's common to all men of our nature. I'm sure you realize, Bjorn, that we may not arrive in time to provide much help to your grandfather and his friends."

"Preacher said the same thing. All I know is that I must try to do what I can."

"We're in complete agreement there." Audie smiled. "I was right, Preacher. It was fate that brought us all together, and there's no point in struggling against fate, is there?"

"Not one damned bit," Preacher agreed.

Red Mike kept up with all the comings and goings of the steamboats on the river. Later that evening, when Preacher explained to him where they were headed, the burly Irishman said, "You're in luck, then. The stern-wheeler *Argosy* is headed up to St. Peter's and Fort Snelling in the morning."

"Reckon there'll be room on deck for our horses and gear?" Preacher asked.

"If you're willing to pay, Cap'n Chidsey will find room."

Tall Dog was standing next to Preacher at the bar. He said, "I cannot allow you to continue paying for everything, Preacher. This is my family's problem, not yours."

"We're partners, ain't we? Besides, we got that money from sellin' those furs that we worked on trappin' together, and it'll burn a hole in my pocket if I leave it sittin' ther[e] for too long. I'll see Captain Chidsey first thing in t[he] mornin' and see about payin' for our passage."

"You'll have to take along your own provisions," Mike warned. "The *Argosy* is primarily a cargo boat [tak]ing goods upriver and furs back down. It doesn't [carry] many passengers."

"Henry Sibley still runnin' things at St. Peter's?"

"That's right. The place had a hard go of it for a y[ear] after the American Fur Company sold out to Pierre Ch[outeau] a few years ago and then went belly up. The fur trad[e is] not what it once was, which you know as well a[s any]body. But Sibley's still hanging on. I hear he's tryin[' to get] farmers to move in up there."

"That far north?" Preacher said with a dub[ious look.] "Can't be much of a growin' season."

"You know what farmers are like, [If] there's some empty ground, they'll [ ] hope."

Having come from a farm[ing family so far] back that he could barel[y remember it, Preacher knew] what Red Mike meant[ ] make it up there, he th[ought.]

A short time later, back[ ] and said to Betsy, "I can s[ ] any time you want."

the Father of Waters between St. Louis and New Orleans, the steamboats that navigated the upper reaches of the Mississippi were smaller, had shallower drafts, and carried their paddlewheel at the stern. The *Argosy* was about two thirds the size of the riverboat Preacher had ridden to New Orleans a couple of years earlier.

Preacher had been at the dock an hour before sunrise, when the engineer was just starting to get steam up in the boiler. He had met with Captain Donald Chidsey in the lamplit pilot house, and the sight of the gold coins Preacher had placed on the chart table had convinced the captain that there was room aboard for some unexpected, last-minute passengers.

The deck would be crowded with four saddle mounts and three pack horses, but the crew had moved the cargo around to make room, Preacher saw in the dawn light as he and his companions led the animals aboard. Dog trotted up the boarding ramp after them and went to the boat's bow, where he sat down and looked out at the river like a carved figurehead.

Captain Chidsey came down from the pilot house to welcome them. "We'll be casting off in just a few minutes," he said.

"How many other passengers do you have?" Preacher asked.

"Just four. Three soldiers bound for Fort Snelling as replacement troops, and a clerk who's going to work for Sibley."

"A red-headed gal didn't show up this morning and try to cajole her way on board, did she?"

"I don't know what you're talking about," Chidsey replied. "It doesn't seem likely any woman would want to travel to such an out-of-the-way place. As far as I know, the only woman up there who isn't an Indian is Sibley's wife."

Preacher accepted Chidsey's answer because there was nothing else he could do. He was still surprised, though, that Betsy hadn't tried to finagle her way into coming with them.

Maybe she and Molly were getting along better now. Preacher hoped so.

Molly stifled a yawn as she stepped out the back of the tavern and stumbled through the gloom toward the privy. Even though the weather was nice, a little chill drifted through the air from the river.

She didn't have to be awake this early, but nature didn't always take that into account. On the way to the tavern's back door, she had paused to knock on Betsy's door and see if the auburn-haired girl was awake, too.

She knew that if Betsy was still asleep, the knock might wake her, and that was a little petty, Molly supposed. But even though she had promised Mike she would get along, she still resented Betsy a little.

Betsy hadn't responded, though. Evidently, she was a really sound sleeper.

Molly yawned again. A few streamers of mist curled through the open area behind the tavern. She opened the privy door . . .

A rush of footsteps behind her was the only warning she had. Then someone hit her from behind, wrapped an arm around her waist, and bulled her on into the little, foul-smelling building.

The door slammed behind her.

Molly's heart hammered in fear as a hand closed over her mouth and nose, cutting off her air. The man who had grabbed her jerked her back against him, pressing their bodies tightly together because there wasn't room in here to do anything else.

Molly was used to men touching her, of course. Some even got a little too rough with her from time to time. That was why she usually had the two knives and her derringer within reach.

This was different somehow. This was terrifying.

And her weapons were inside her room in the tavern. Bent on the errand she was, the possibility that she might need them hadn't entered her head.

The hand over her face kept the smell inside the privy from being overwhelming, but it prevented her from breathing, too. Her heart slugged harder as her body began to struggle for air. She writhed as much as she could, but she couldn't get loose.

"Listen," a harsh voice rasped in her ear, "if you promise not to yell, I'll let you breathe. All right?"

Molly didn't hesitate. She nodded her agreement.

Then when the hand lifted, she opened her mouth to scream.

The man clamped his hand over her nose and mouth again before she could get out more than a squeak.

"I figured you were lying to me," he said. "Now do as I tell you and you won't get hurt. Understand? But if you nod again, this time you'd damned well better mean it."

Molly had expended what little air was left in her lungs. She nodded. She didn't have any other choice.

When the man took his hand away this time, she whispered, "Wh-what do you want?"

She figured she knew the answer to that. She was wearing only a thin nightdress, so her writhing became more calculated, no longer an attempt to get away. She didn't like being handled so roughly, but she could put up with it for a little while, she supposed.

She expected the arm around her waist to move upward and caress her, but instead he maintained his grip, pinning her to him.

"Tell me about Preacher," he said.

The question took her completely by surprise. "I . . . I don't know what you mean."

"You were around while he and the others were talking last night. You must have heard at least some of what they said. Where are they going?"

"I don't know. I swear! I . . . I wasn't paying that much attention. I was mad at that girl—"

"Pedersen's little redheaded friend?"

"I don't know any Pedersen," Molly replied honestly. "No, wait. Maybe I heard the name . . . but I don't know who he is."

"Was," her captor hissed. "He's dead."

She moaned. "I don't know anything about any of this, I tell you. I . . . I just work in the tavern serving drinks." She tried to gather some courage. "You'd better let me go. When Mike finds out about this, you'll be sorry."

"Tell me where they went, and I'll let you go."

"All I know is they said something about a riverboat . . . the *Argosy,* I think they called it . . . and Fort Snelling. I don't know where that is. I think I've heard of it, but I'm not even sure about that!"

For a moment, the man holding her was silent. Then he said, "I know where that is. And it makes sense they'd go there. Damn it! Things shouldn't have gone so wrong."

"I don't know anything about it," Molly said. "And I won't say anything about this, mister, I swear. Just turn me loose and you can go on your way. Nobody will bother you."

"Nobody's going to bother me," the man said.

Just to make sure he didn't hurt her, Molly said, "If you want me to do anything else before you go . . . I mean, this isn't a very nice place, but——"

Her captor interrupted her with an impatient grunt. "I don't have time for this," he said.

She hoped that meant he was finished with her.

Then she felt pain across her throat that somehow was burning hot and icy cold at the same time, and something hot flooded down across the bosom of her nightdress, and as he let go of her and her knees buckled, she realized that he was finished with her, all right.

The whole world, which had never treated her well to start with, was finished with her.

But despite that, she clung to it until the overwhelming nothingness carried her away.

CHAPTER 8

This was Tall Dog's first time on a riverboat. For the first few days, he stood on the deck watching with great interest as the shoreline seemed to unroll endlessly on both sides of the broad stream.

The countryside provided plenty of varied scenery: some wooded landscape, some open fields, occasional limestone bluffs that rose sheer and rugged from the water. Once the *Argosy* passed the confluence of the Mississippi and Missouri Rivers, the stream became smaller but was still impressive.

When Tall Dog commented on that to Preacher, the mountain man said, "You ought to see it farther downstream on the way to New Orleans. There are places where the Mississipp' is a good mile wide. Looks more like a lake than a river. A regular lake, that is, not like those great big ones up north or, I expect, like the one where your grandfather and his people settled."

"In his letter, he did say that lake is vast," Tall Dog said. "He wrote that it takes more than a day to row across it, and several days to go from one end to the other."

Preacher nodded. "Sounds like a good-sized puddle o' water, all right."

"Huge fish live in its depths, according to Grandfather

Axel, and moose and bear and elk roam the land around it. The hunting is very good."

Tall Dog looked to the west, toward the unseen mountains where he had lived his life with the Crow.

"I never thought about it until now," he went on, "but it seems to me that my mother's people and my father's people live in much the same way, completely free and content with the bounty the land gives them. It is not surprising that the two of them have always been happy together."

"No, I reckon not," Preacher agreed. "Those Vikings, though, from what I hear they were more fiddlefooted. Restless folks who always wanted to go somewhere new. The Crow roam around some, of course, dependin' on where the huntin's good and the time of year, but they stay in the same general area. Audie tells me that the Vikings come over here to North America a long time ago, hundreds of years before that Columbus fella. Said they explored all over Europe and Asia, too, and maybe even down into Africa and over to China. Fought wars everywhere they went, too."

Tall Dog nodded. "There are many such stories contained in the eddas and sagas Audie mentioned, the histories of the Vikings. He has promised to tell me all about them. I want to know more about my father's people."

"Well, you're half-Viking, so I reckon that's understandable." Preacher clapped a hand on the warrior's shoulder. "Maybe you'll decide to stay up there in Skarkavik, once we get this little problem taken care of."

"No, my home will always be with the Crow. But a man can have two homes, can he not?"

"I expect you'll find out," Preacher said, thinking about all the decades that had passed since he had had a real home, other than the frontier.

But that was the life he had chosen for himself. Tall Dog had the right to make the same choice.

The *Argosy* stopped every day so members of the crew could go ashore and chop firewood for the boiler.

However, Captain Chidsey kept the boat chugging on past most of the small villages that dotted the riverbank. He explained to Preacher that he didn't want the crew visiting the taverns in those settlements. A hungover man might not notice a snag in the river ahead or forget to keep an eye on the boiler's pressure gauge. Such lapses could prove disastrous.

The captain's decision was fine with Preacher and Tall Dog. It was going to take long enough to reach their destination as it was. They didn't want any unnecessary delays.

The riverboat might have to stop at some of the villages, though, because someone there had cargo to go upstream, Chidsey explained to Preacher. In those cases, a flag would be raised on a pole next to the landing that extended out into the river, and the *Argosy* would put in at the dock.

The boat had been steaming upstream for five days when Chidsey spotted such a signal flag at the landing for a small settlement called Deaver's Mill. The captain used the speaking tube that connected the pilot house to the engine room below decks and ordered the engine to slow. He turned the wheel so that the *Argosy* swung toward the west bank.

Since the riverboat had only two cabins for passengers and both of those were occupied, Preacher, Tall Dog, Audie, and Nighthawk had been camping out on the cargo deck, not far from the makeshift corral where their horses were kept. The weather had been nice so far, and all four men were used to sleeping outdoors anyway. The roof of a cramped cabin over their heads would have just seemed confining.

When Preacher saw that the boat was headed ashore, he cupped his hands around his mouth and called up to the pilot house, "What's this, Cap'n? Why are we stoppin'?"

Chidsey leaned out the open window of the boat's topmost structure and pointed.

"Signal flag at the landing up ahead! We shouldn't be stopped for long."

"I hope not," Preacher said to Tall Dog, "although I reckon in the big scheme o' things, five or ten minutes here and there don't mean much."

"Every delay is that much longer before we reach Skarkavik," Tall Dog replied with unassailable logic.

However, Chidsey was the captain and ran the riverboat the way he saw fit. As the steady beat of the paddlewheel at the stern slowed, the *Argosy* eased toward the dock that extended about fifty feet into the river.

A couple of wagons loaded with crates were pulled up close to the dock. When Preacher saw them, he figured whatever the cargo was would be loaded onto the boat.

That would make the deck even more crowded, but hauling cargo was Chidsey's business. Preacher couldn't very well tell the captain to turn down freight he'd get paid for transporting.

With practiced skill, Chidsey brought the riverboat alongside the dock. One of the crew easily made the leap from the deck to the dock's planking and dropped the loop of the thick rope he carried over a round piling sticking up for that purpose.

The *Argosy*'s paddlewheel came to a stop with water sluicing off of its wide paddles.

The man sitting on the driver's seat of the closest wagon was named Gabe Simon. He was a burly, craggy-faced man with a thatch of black hair, a drooping mustache, and cold gray eyes under a wide-brimmed black hat.

"Be ready back there," he said from the corner of his mouth without turning his head.

"We're ready," a harsh voice answered from the hiding place within the stacks of crates where three men crouched and waited for Simon's signal. "You better be ready to pay us what you agreed to once those men are dead."

"You'll get your money, don't worry about that," Simon replied.

Payment wasn't a problem, since he still had most of the gold coins Decker Galloway had given him before he came down here to the States to stop that stupid squarehead Pedersen from causing trouble. Simon had promised those coins to the men he had recruited in St. Louis to help him accomplish that task.

They had failed—spectacularly—but at least they'd had the good graces to get themselves killed in the process, so he hadn't had to fork over the loot after all. He'd paid them a little, to keep them on the string once Pedersen was dead, but when he discovered that the letter Pedersen carried had vanished, he had refused to pay the rest until the job was truly done.

That meant finding the letter and then making sure nobody picked up the trail from it.

Pedersen had been asking around the taverns for a man called Preacher. Somehow, that message had reached its intended recipient, which meant Simon had to set a trap for Preacher and slam that door shut, once and for all.

It should have worked, too. It would have worked, if he'd had better men to carry out the plan.

That was the problem. You had to take what help you could get, like these thick-headed galoots hidden in the wagons, waiting for the riverboat to dock.

There were eight in all, though, counting himself, Simon mused. Eight against four. Two to one odds.

But five to one odds hadn't been enough back in St. Louis, Simon reminded himself. Not nearly enough.

That's why, as soon as he got the chance, he was going to draw the pistol tucked behind his belt and shoot that blasted mountain man called Preacher before anybody knew what was going on.

With Preacher dead, the rest would be easy . . .

Preacher, Tall Dog, Audie, and Nighthawk stood on the cargo deck and watched as the crew member secured the *Argosy* to the dock. Preacher hoped it wouldn't take long to load those crates and wondered if he and Tall Dog and Nighthawk ought to volunteer to help, just to speed things up.

Captain Chidsey had come down from the pilot house and descended to the cargo deck himself to deal with whoever was shipping the crates. As Chidsey reached the deck, Preacher started toward him.

At that moment, a voice rang out clearly and shouted a warning.

"Preacher, look out! It's an ambush!"

The mountain man's mind barely had time to register the fact that the voice belonged to a woman before his instincts took over. He darted into the cover of some crates already on the deck as his hands dipped to the holstered Colt Patersons on his hips.

The man on the driver's seat of the closest wagon bolted to his feet and jerked a pistol from behind his belt. He cursed as he leveled the weapon and pulled the trigger.

The would-be killer had reacted quickly, but Preacher was quicker. The pistol ball missed by several feet as it hummed past him and thudded into the wall of the cargo deck structure.

Preacher returned the fire. Both Colts boomed and bucked in his hands as flame gouted from their muzzles.

His shots weren't quite quick enough, either, as the man leaped frantically off the wagon, evidently unharmed.

More shots blasted from the back of the vehicle. Preacher realized that several men were concealed there, and in the back of the other wagon as well. They opened fire, too, sending a wave of lead toward the *Argosy*.

A long, swift jump carried Tall Dog to Captain Chidsey's side. The captain was standing there with a confused look on his ruddy face when Tall Dog tackled him and knocked him to the deck.

An instant later, several rifle balls whistled through the space Chidsey had just occupied. The men in the wagons were shooting indiscriminately, clearly not caring who else they hit as long as their shots found Preacher and his companions.

Because Preacher knew instantly that he and the others were the true targets of this ambush.

The gunmen were well-armed with extra rifles and pistols and didn't have to reload right away. But with the Patersons, neither did Preacher. He held his fire for a second, waited until one of the men in the first wagon foolishly stuck his head up, and then blasted a round right through it. Blood sprayed as the man toppled backward out of the wagon.

Tall Dog was still stretched out prone on the deck, next to the captain, without any real cover. He had dropped his rifle when he tackled Chidsey.

But that didn't mean he was unarmed. He pulled his tomahawk loose and waited until another of the ambushers rose in hopes of a better shot, then threw the 'hawk in a blindingly fast sidearm motion.

The tomahawk spun through the air with deadly accuracy. It skimmed over the barrel of the rifle the man was aiming and struck him in the forehead, right above the eye he'd been squinting at the rifle's sights. The sharp steel head embedded itself in the man's skull and cleaved into his brain. He dropped the rifle and slumped forward.

Audie and Nighthawk had reached cover like Preacher and sent shots blazing back at the men in the wagons. The man on the driver's box of the second vehicle clapped a hand to his chest but couldn't stop the bright blood that welled between his fingers. He toppled to the ground.

Less than a minute into the fight, Preacher and his friends already had whittled down the odds considerably, enough so that the remaining ambushers were thinking twice about this. One man stood up, evidently intending to leap over the sideboards and flee, but Preacher drilled him before he could do so. The man twisted and pitched out of the wagon in an ungraceful sprawl.

That left one man alive in each wagon, and they'd had enough. Their guns sailed out of the vehicles as they tossed them away, and their hands reached for the sky.

"Hold your fire! Hold your fire, damn it! We quit!"

"Stop shootin', boys," Preacher told Audie and Nighthawk. He kept his own fingers taut on the triggers of the Colts, but the twin revolvers fell silent for the moment.

The mountain man's keen eyes studied the scene on the riverbank next to the landing. Five bodies lay motionless on the ground, either dead or next thing to it.

Preacher realized that the man who'd been on the driver's box of the first wagon was nowhere to be seen. His jaw tightened in anger and frustration. The fella had taken off running and gotten away once it became obvious the ambush had failed.

Rising from his cover behind the crates, Preacher kept his guns trained on the remaining bushwhackers.

"Climb down outta there, slow and easy," he told them. "Don't try any tricks."

"Don't worry, we won't," one of them said. "We weren't paid enough to throw our lives away like the rest of these boys did!"

Without taking his eyes off the men he was covering, Preacher said, "Tall Dog, is the cap'n all right?"

The warrior was on his feet again, helping Chidsey up. The captain slapped at his stocky body as if checking for bullet holes and said, "I think I'm fine, thanks to this young fellow."

Preacher told Audie and Nighthawk, "Keep an eye on those varmints while I go ashore."

"We have them in our sights, Preacher," Audie assured him as he pointed his specially-made rifle at the men standing nervously beside the wagons.

Preacher didn't holster the Colts as he hopped lithely from the riverboat to the dock. He strode along it toward the wagons, keeping the revolvers leveled at his waist as he did so.

"You're not gonna gun us down in cold blood, are you?" one of the ambushers asked nervously.

"You mean the way you were plannin' to kill us?" Preacher snapped as he came up to them. "If you want to keep on bein' wastes of perfectly good air, you'd best tell me who you were workin' for."

"Fella said his name was Gabe, that's all we know," the other man replied. "Honest, mister. He found us in the tavern and offered a twenty-dollar gold piece for each of us if we'd help him get rid of some troublemakers."

"He said he just, uh, wanted to scare you off," the first man put in.

"Don't insult me by lyin' like that," Preacher said. "He wanted us dead."

The men glanced at each other and shrugged.

"Did he pay you that money?"

"No," one of the men replied bitterly. "He said we'd get the coins when the job was done. And now he's gone and taken off for the tall and uncut, damn it!"

Preacher narrowed his eyes and asked, "Does the name Decker Galloway mean anything to you?"

Both men blinked stupidly and looked genuinely baffled.

"Never heard of him," one of them said. "Who is he?"

"Never mind," Preacher said. His gut told him the men were telling the truth. They were just none too bright bruisers that Gabe, whoever he was, had found to do his dirty work, promising them enough money to keep them in cheap liquor and whores for a good long time.

"Mister, uh . . . what are you gonna do with us?"

"Is there any law hereabouts?" Preacher asked. He suspected he already knew the answer to that question.

"None to speak of."

"Well . . . I can shoot both of you in the head right now. You've got it comin', and that way I could be sure I'd never have to worry about you in the future."

Both men paled and looked sick.

"You d-don't have to do that!" one of them stammered.

"Just let us g-go. We'll leave these parts so quick we'll be a mile away before you even know we're gone."

"I'd have to see that to believe it."

The men glanced at each other again, then jerked around and started to run. They threw fearful looks over their shoulders, as if they thought with every step that Preacher would shoot them in the back, but the mountain man held his fire.

He didn't holster the Colts until they were out of sight, though.

By this time, a couple of the riverboat's crew had put the boarding ramp in place, following Captain Chidsey's orders. As Preacher walked across it to the deck, Tall Dog waited for him and asked, "Are you sure you should have let them go?"

"I've got a hunch we'll be long gone from here before those two stop runnin'. Did that letter from your grandpa happen to mention a fella name of Gabe?"

"Gabe," Tall Dog repeated. He shook his head. "No, nothing like that. Who is he?"

"The one who hired those ambushers. More than likely, the one who ran off as soon as the shootin' started. Even if the name ain't familiar, I'd bet a hat he works for Decker Galloway and Galloway sent him down here to make sure nobody answers your grandpa's call for help."

Tall Dog nodded. "That sounds reasonable. If it is true, we may see him again."

"I got a good look at him, even though it was a fast one. I'll know him again. And I wouldn't mind seein' him again . . . as long as it's over the barrel of a gun."

Captain Chidsey approached them. "I take it there actually isn't any cargo bound for Fort Snelling?"

"Nope, it was just a trap," Preacher said. "Those fellas figured on stoppin' us from goin' north."

"None of my business," Chidsey said. "At least as long as no one is shooting at me and my boat, that is. Do you think it's likely such a thing will happen again?"

"Can't really say. You gonna put us off the boat, Cap'n?"

Chidsey sighed and shook his head. "No, I can't very well do that. We'll be more careful as we proceed upriver, though."

"Fair enough. Now, I got another bone to pick with you."

"You do?" Chidsey said with a frown. "What's wrong now?"

Preacher pointed and said, "I want to know what *she's* doin' here, when you swore to me back in St. Louis that you didn't know who I was talkin' about."

In response to that, Chidsey, Tall Dog, Audie, and Nighthawk all turned their heads and looked up at the texas deck, where Betsy Kingsley stood at the railing looking back down at them.

CHAPTER 9

Five minutes later, Preacher and Tall Dog were in the pilot house along with Chidsey and Betsy. Even with big, open windows on all four sides, the uppermost chamber on the riverboat seemed a little crowded with all four of them in there.

"The young lady asked me for my help," Chidsey said defensively. "I don't know about you two, but I was raised to be a gentleman and accommodate a lady's wishes whenever possible."

"Also, she paid you to lie to us and hide her out on board, I'm guessin'," Preacher said.

"Don't blame the captain," Betsy said. "I insisted. I swore to him that it was a matter of life and death that I come along on this journey."

"Death, more'n likely. Yours. You don't know what a heap of danger we're headin' into."

"To be fair, neither do you," Betsy pointed out. "You have no idea what you're going to find up there in the British provinces. This whole trip could be for nothing. You may get there too late to help."

Tall Dog said, "I refuse to believe that. Somehow inside me, I would know if our quest was hopeless. My grandfather and his people are there and still need my help."

Betsy nodded. "I hope that's true. I really do. And I'd like to help, too. Rolf Pedersen was one of them, and he was kind to me. Even though I didn't know him long, he seemed almost like an uncle to me."

"That ain't no reason for you to go traipsin' off into the wilderness where you could get killed," Preacher said.

Betsy laughed, but the sound held no genuine humor. "Correct me if I'm wrong," she said, "but it was the two of you who almost got killed a few minutes ago, along with your friends. There's a good chance you would have if I hadn't spotted those ambushers hiding in the wagon and warned you." She smiled. "I seem to be making a habit of warning you about traps. It seems to me that someone like that would be handy to have around."

Tall Dog glanced at Preacher as if about to say that she had a point there, but the mountain man forestalled that comment with a slight shake of his head.

"Where have you been stayin'?" he asked Betsy. "We haven't seen any sign of you since leavin' St. Louis."

Chidsey said, "The young lady has been staying in my office. I moved a cot in there." The captain's forehead creased in a stern frown. "And before either of you cast any aspersions on her character or on mine, I can assure you that absolutely nothing improper has transpired. I am a happily married man, despite being away on the river a great deal of the time."

Preacher figured that being away on the river most of the time had a lot to do with the captain having a happy marriage, but he didn't see any point in commenting on that.

Instead he asked, "Are we liable to run into any river-boats headin' downstream?"

"I know what you're thinking," Betsy said. "You want to put me on another boat and send me back to St. Louis!"

Preacher scowled. "The thought crossed my mind."

"Well, I won't let you do it."

"Or we could just put you ashore and leave you," he suggested.

"You wouldn't dare!"

"And I wouldn't allow it, either," Chidsey said. "That would be a dangerous, not to mention ungentlemanly, thing to do. So unless you plan to stage a mutiny, sir, which I highly doubt would be successful since my crew is exceedingly loyal to me, you can forget about the idea of abandoning the young lady."

"Aw, hell, I wasn't really serious about doin' that," Preacher muttered. "What about the other riverboats?"

Chidsey shook his head. "Very unlikely. Not many vessels ply the upper reaches of the Mississippi. I believe Miss Kingsley will be with us until we reach Fort Snelling."

"If that is the way it must be, then we will not argue," Tall Dog said.

Preacher frowned. He still felt like arguing a little more, although he conceded to himself that it wouldn't do any good.

When he looked at Tall Dog, though, he realized the warrior was gazing at Betsy with admiration in his eyes. Evidently, she still impressed him just as much as she had when he'd first spotted her auburn hair back in St. Louis.

Preacher supposed they could let Betsy continue on to Fort Snelling with them, especially since they didn't seem to have any real choice in the matter. That would allow Tall Dog to spend more time with her and get to know her better.

Once they got there, though, Preacher would have to put his foot down. If she refused to go back downriver on the *Argosy,* Betsy could stay at the fort, or at St. Peter's, the settlement across the river from the outpost. But she wasn't going with them.

Yes, sir, Preacher vowed to himself. He'd have the last word on this.

"I believe we should take her with us," Tall Dog declared with a serious expression on his face.

"Have you plumb lost your mind?" Preacher asked him. "We'll be weeks on the trail just gettin' to your grandpa's village. And if Galloway's man rounds up some help and tries to stop us again, there ain't no tellin' how much fightin' we'll have to do along the way."

"This is true," Tall Dog admitted, "but Miss Kingsley has sworn she will not go back to St. Louis on the *Argosy*, and I believe she will be safer with us than she would be staying here."

With Dog sitting beside Preacher's feet, the two men were standing on the dock where the *Argosy* was tied up. From there, a sloping dirt trail ran up the side of the bluff on which Fort Snelling was located.

It was an impressive structure, built in the form of long, connected, brick blockhouses arranged in a rectangle around a central courtyard. At the southwest corner, overlooking the spot where the St. Peter's River ran into the Mississippi from the northwest, a round tower gave lookouts a prime vantage point for watching all around.

Across the river lay the settlement of St. Peter's, easily reached by rowboats since the Mississippi had narrowed a great deal where it ran between the surrounding wooded bluffs and was no more than fifty feet wide at this point. The buildings in the settlement were constructed of stone or logs, for the most part. Some of the residences were sturdy structures of brick, such as the one where Henry Sibley lived.

Sibley had been in charge of the American Fur Company branch here and was still running things even though Pierre Chouteau, a member of the family that had founded St. Louis, owned the company these days.

Preacher looked across the river and thought that Tall Dog might be right about Betsy being safer with them. Even though Sibley was a firm, efficient manager of the fur trade in these parts, the settlement was still a raw, untamed place. Sibley's wife was probably the only respectable white woman over there.

Lieutenant Colonel Seth Eastman was the commanding officer of the fort. Preacher knew him only by reputation, which was a good one. The officer was supposed to be a fine painter and a top-notch mapmaker. He had spent several years at West Point, teaching cartography.

Preacher figured Eastman would allow Betsy to stay at the fort and would try to look out for her, but again, she would be surrounded by a lot of rough, uncivilized men.

He turned his gaze back to Betsy, who was standing on the river bank a short distance downstream, talking to Audie and Nighthawk. About a hundred yards away, several of the peaceful local Indians had put up tipis and were fishing in the river. Their canoes were pulled up on the bank.

Betsy was taking in the scene with interest. Judging by the way Audie gestured emphatically as he spoke, he was telling her all about it, slipping back into his old habits as a lecturer and teacher.

During the time they had traveled upriver to this point, Betsy had become good friends with Audie and Nighthawk. Preacher felt sure that both of his old friends would sacrifice their lives to protect her.

Tall Dog shared that devotion to Betsy, although he was still a bit tongue-tied and awkward around the auburn-haired girl. But Preacher knew he would never allow any harm to come to her if he could prevent it.

The same was true of the mountain man, of course, although he wasn't sweet on Betsy like Tall Dog was.

The problem was that nobody could ever foresee all the dangers that might crop up on the frontier. Deadly threats could come out of nowhere, with no warning whatsoever.

But that was true in civilization, too, Preacher reminded himself, as they had seen demonstrated vividly in the trouble they had encountered in St. Louis.

"Dadgum it," he said now with feeling. "There just ain't no good answer to this problem. Once she got away with hidin' on that riverboat and leavin' St. Louis, we were gonna wind up saddled with lookin' out for her."

"She has been helpful in the past."

"Yeah, sort of," Preacher grumbled. "But that ain't no guarantee she won't get us all killed in the future."

Betsy had turned from the river and was strolling toward them now, trailed by Audie and Nighthawk. She smiled as she came up to them and said, "This is magnificent country, and those Indians are fascinating. Audie has been telling me all about them and the way they live."

The smile went away as she gazed intently at Preacher and Tall Dog and went on, "You two have been talking about me, haven't you? I can tell by looking at you."

"We been talkin' about what in the world we're gonna do with you," Preacher said.

Anger appeared in her green eyes. "Don't I have any say in the matter? Or are you going to just hogtie me and put me back on the riverboat?"

"Don't tempt me," Preacher said ominously. "You know, this ain't the first time some mule-headed gal has followed along after me and figured I wouldn't be able to send her back. And every blasted time, it's led to trouble."

"And what happened to those women? Did you let them go with you?"

"Didn't have any choice in the matter," Preacher said with a frown.

"And did they lose their lives?"

"Well, no," Preacher said. "They all come through it all right."

"And did having them around work out well?"

"I reckon in the long run, you could look at it that way—"

Betsy folded her arms across her chest, nodded, and interrupted him to declare, "Then I think the question is settled, isn't it?" She looked at Tall Dog. "Don't you have anything to say about this?"

"I have told Preacher I think it would be best for you to come with us," Tall Dog said.

"Thank you!" Betsy looked at Preacher. "Finally somebody with some sense. You should listen to him."

"For what it's worth," Audie said, "Nighthawk and I have no objection to Miss Kingsley accompanying us, even though the journey is likely to be a dangerous one."

"Umm," Nighthawk said.

"Indeed, she seems to be quite a courageous young woman and well aware of the risks inherent in the journey. As she has pointed out, she warned you about that trap those fellows set for you at Hanlon's place in St. Louis, even though that could have put her in great danger."

"Yeah, yeah," Preacher said. "I ain't claimin' she lacks for nerve." As he looked around at the four of them, frustration welled up inside him. He blew out a breath and went on, "I can tell when I'm outnumbered. All right, gal, you can come along . . . on one condition."

"Name it," Betsy said.

"You follow orders. Any time I tell you to do somethin', or Tall Dog or Audie or Nighthawk tell you, you do it right away without arguin' or askin' a heap of questions. Because your life's liable to depend on it. You understand that?"

"Of course. I know you're all much more experienced in the ways of the frontier than I am. I'd have to be a fool not to listen to what you tell me."

And he'd have to be a fool to drag some gal along into the heart of the wilderness, where a war between a bunch of would-be Vikings and a ruthless timber baron waited, Preacher told himself.

But fool or not . . . here they were.

CHAPTER 10

Preacher didn't know exactly how far it was to the vast inland lake where the village of Skarkavik was located, but based on the directions Tall Dog's grandfather had included in his letter, the mountain man figured it would take approximately three weeks to reach their destination.

They would be able to hunt for fresh meat along the way. Much of the country into which they were heading teemed with game. But they would need to take some supplies with them, as well, so they stocked up at the trading post at St. Peter's run by Henry Sibley.

The group had three pack horses to go with their saddle mounts. Audie, who was smart and ciphered well enough that he could have been a quartermaster in the army, took charge of gathering the supplies and seeing that they were packed and loaded properly.

Flour, salt, salt pork, molasses, powder and shot, cartridges for Preacher's revolving pistols, some whiskey for medicinal purposes . . . Audie procured all those things and more at the trading post. When Preacher looked over the work the former professor had done, he nodded in satisfaction and appreciation.

"We ought to be able to get where we're goin'," he said.

"Whether or not we make it back . . . well, I reckon we'll have to wait and see about that."

With cargo for the return trip stacked on the *Argosy*'s deck, Captain Donald Chidsey shoved off for St. Louis after saying his farewells.

"I suspect I'll see you and your friends back here in a few months," he told Preacher as they shook hands. "When I do, I'll be happy to carry you back to civilization."

"Might take you up on that," Preacher said. "Although I might not be ready to go back to civilization just yet. I got a pretty low tolerance for most of the foolishness back there."

Betsy stood on the dock and waved goodbye as the riverboat chugged downstream. Tall Dog was beside her, although he was too dignified to wave.

Audie, watching from the bank with Preacher and Nighthawk, nodded toward the two young people and said quietly, "They make a fine-looking couple, don't they?"

"Don't go gettin' ahead of yourself," Preacher warned. "Two young folks like that, thrown together in a mess like this, are just naturally gonna be a mite interested in each other. But that don't mean anything'll ever come of it."

"Perhaps, but I have a feeling . . ."

"What about what's waitin' for us up yonder in the north country? You got a feelin' about that?"

"Umm," Nighthawk said.

Audie threw back his head and laughed. "Oh, that's all too true, my friend!" he said. "Desperate battles always seem to await whenever Preacher is involved. Why, you and I can spend months of tranquility in the wilderness, and then within days of running into Preacher again . . . nay, within hours or even minutes! . . . all hell breaks loose! You attract trouble the way a lodestone attracts iron filings, Preacher."

"It ain't none o' my doin'," Preacher said darkly. "Just the luck o' the draw!"

Audie reached up and patted him on the arm. "You go right ahead believing that, my friend. You just go right on ahead."

The sound of footsteps behind them made Preacher turn his head to look over his shoulder. One of the young soldiers from the fort stood there.

"Somethin' we can do for you, son?"

The trooper saluted and said, "Colonel Eastman sends his respects, sir. He'd like to speak with you, if you'd be so kind as to accompany me."

Preacher looked at Audie. "What do you reckon the colonel wants with me?"

"There's one sure way to find out."

Preacher nodded and told the soldier, "Lead the way, son."

Lieutenant Colonel Seth Eastman was a solidly built man with dark hair, a closely cropped beard touched here and there with gray, and keen, intelligent eyes.

He shook hands with Preacher and said, "I hear from Henry Sibley that you plan on leading a party north of the border."

"That's the plan," Preacher said.

"You don't anticipate doing anything that our British neighbors might regard as an armed invasion, do you?"

Instead of answering the question directly, Preacher said, "You've seen that young fella who's travelin' with me, haven't you?"

"The one who dresses like an Indian but otherwise appears to be possibly of Scandinavian heritage?"

Preacher chuckled. "That's him. Name of Tall Dog, as far as his ma and her people the Crow are concerned. But his pa called him Bjorn Gunnarson. That half of him is Norwegian. His grandpa on that side lives up yonder north of the border on a big lake, and Tall Dog's goin' to pay him a visit. Me and the other two fellas are just goin' along to keep him company."

"And the young woman?"

"She's just along for the trip, too," Preacher said. "None of us are lookin' for trouble."

Eastman nodded and said, "The fact that you're taking a female along makes me believe you're telling the truth. But there will still be danger from the elements and the wildlife along the way, and possibly from Indians."

"You ain't tellin' me anything I don't already know, Colonel, and I've tried to explain that to the young lady, as well. But she's a mite on the stubborn side."

The officer cocked an eyebrow and laughed. "Like every other woman in the world, eh? I suspected that it wouldn't do any good to try to talk you out of your plans. You see, I've heard a great deal about you. I know that you generally do what you set out to do. So I thought I'd offer you some help instead."

"Sir?" Preacher said. "You ain't figurin' on sendin' soldiers along with us, are you?"

"No, I'm afraid I can't do that, but I can provide this." Eastman took a long, rolled-up tube of paper from his desk and held it out to the mountain man. "You may have heard that I try my hand at mapmaking from time to time."

"Folks say you're mighty good at it."

"This is a map I've prepared of the area between the fort and the border. We haven't patrolled beyond that, at least not intentionally, so I can't sketch from personal knowledge what's past that point. However, I've heard stories and rumors, so I added a few features that may or may not be in exactly the right place. I hope it'll come in handy anyway."

Preacher unrolled the map and studied it for a moment before nodding.

"I'd say it'll come in mighty handy, Colonel. We're much obliged to you."

"There's a way you can repay me for any assistance that it might give you."

"What's that?"

Eastman smiled. "Come back alive so that you can tell me all about what you find up there. I'd love to be one of the first to prepare a decent map of the region!"

After another day of last-minute preparations and making sure all the horses' shoes were in good shape, the group was ready to depart.

Preacher had already figured that following the St. Peter's River to the northwest would be the best route. After studying Lieutenant Colonel Eastman's map and comparing it to the directions in Axel Gunnarson's letter, Preacher and Tall Dog agreed that that plan was the best and they would stick with it.

They had bought a saddle mount and rig for Betsy at the livery stable in St. Peter's, as well as the smallest men's canvas trousers and flannel shirts they could find at the trading post.

"You'll have to ride astride," Preacher had told her while they were shopping for the clothes. "There probably ain't one o' them fancy side saddles to be found within a thousand miles."

"That's all right," she'd assured him. "I'll do whatever I need to, as long as I get to go with you."

"Here," Tall Dog had said as he held out a wide-brimmed, brown felt hat. "You should have this to protect you from the sun."

With a laugh, Betsy had tucked her auburn hair up into the hat's rounded crown and asked him, "How does that look?"

"Very good," Tall Dog told her. "With that hat, once you are dressed in those other clothes, you will look like a man."

"Well, I don't know if I like the sound of that," she teased, which made his face turn red.

"I . . . I didn't mean that anyone would ever mistake you for a man," Tall Dog stammered. "There would still be the, uh, shape . . . uh . . . I mean . . ."

"Don't worry about it," Preacher told him as Betsy laughed again. "She knows what you mean."

Preacher had also arranged to take along four extra saddle horses. He would ride Horse, his rangy gray stallion, for the most part, of course, and Tall Dog's regular mount would be his big paint Skidbladnir, named for a ship in one of those old Norse stories his father had told him. Audie and Nighthawk had horses that had been trail partners with them for quite a while, too. But it never hurt to have spare mounts, because you could never tell when you might need them.

Preacher and Tall Dog led the way, riding along the eastern bank of the river. Betsy was next behind them, and Preacher had to admit that in the hat and trousers and flannel shirt, riding astride like that, she did indeed look like a man.

Audie and Nighthawk brought up the rear. Audie led

the pack animals while Nighthawk had the spare saddle mounts on a lead rope.

Dog, as usual, was out in front, loping along about fifty yards ahead of Preacher. The mountain man had complete faith in the big cur to alert them if any danger happened to be lurking up ahead.

When they had been riding for a while, Preacher looked over his shoulder at Betsy and asked, "Are you doin' all right back there?"

She rocked along easily in the saddle as she said, "Of course. This is no problem at all. It's easy."

"Ever ridden much in your life?"

"No, hardly at all."

"Well, I'm glad you ain't findin' it too much of a challenge, then."

Preacher glanced at Tall Dog and saw the mixture of amusement and concern on the young warrior's face. Betsy might find the journey easy going now, but that would change as she spent hours in the saddle. Both men knew that.

"I just hope she does not find it too uncomfortable," Tall Dog said under his breath so that only Preacher could hear, "once it all catches up to her."

A short time earlier, on top of a wooded rise half a mile away on the other side of the river, Gabe Simon had lowered the spyglass he'd been using to keep an eye on the fort and announced to his two companions, "Well, they're on their way. They just rode out."

"Now what do we do?" the man called McNair asked.

"They've got us outnumbered," added the third man, whose name was Brendle.

They were the two who had survived the failed ambush downriver at Deaver's Mill. Preacher had allowed them to leave instead of killing them, although the cold look in the mountain man's eyes had told them just how close they had come to death. Preacher could have carried through on his threat to shoot them both in the head and never blinked an eye doing it.

He had also warned them never to let him see the two of them again, or else he would kill them without hesitation or warning. Simon knew that McNair and Brendle were both regretting at times their decision to throw in with him again.

But he had promised them a good payoff and provided horses, supplies, and ammunition—all paid for with Decker Galloway's money, of course—and swore that this time, they would kill that blasted mountain man and his friends.

As they mounted up to follow the western bank of the St. Peter's River, Brendle asked, "Is that girl with 'em? The redheaded one who hollered when she spotted us hidin' in the wagons at Deaver's Mill?"

"I never got a real good look at her before all the shootin' started," McNair added, "but from what I could tell, she was mighty easy on the eyes."

"Don't worry about that," Simon snapped. "Our job is to stop them from getting where they're going, that's all."

"Yeah, but if the girl's along, she could liven things up a mite once we've taken care of the others," Brendle said.

Simon shrugged. He didn't give a hang about the girl, one way or the other. But the promise of having some sport with her might help the other two to keep their attention on the job.

"There was a fifth rider," Simon told them. "Dressed

like a man, but small like a girl. I think there's a good chance it was her, but Preacher put her in those clothes to cover up the fact that he's dragging a female along into the wilderness."

"I wish we knew for sure," McNair grumbled.

"There's one way to find out: Kill the other four." An ugly grin spread across Simon's face. "Then you can do whatever you want with the fifth one, no matter who it is."

That seemed to mollify them for a few minutes, but then Brendle said, "I still don't know how we're gonna get rid of them, when there's five of them and only three of us."

"That's why we have to be smart," Simon replied.

And it was a good thing he was along to handle that part of it, he added to himself, because these two men with him were both dumb as rocks.

Preacher didn't set too fast a pace the first day. He knew that he and Tall Dog, as well as Audie and Nighthawk, could push on as hard as they needed to, for as long as was necessary, but that wasn't true of Betsy.

She was holding them back already, he grumbled to himself. But she would toughen up and grow accustomed to the long days in the saddle.

At least he hoped she would.

That evening, when they dismounted to make camp beside the river, Betsy's legs wobbled when she dismounted and tried to stand up. She caught hold of the stirrup to steady herself.

Tall Dog saw that and was beside her instantly, asking, "Are you all right? Do you need help?"

Betsy, to give her credit, forced her back to stiffen and stood up straight.

"I'm fine," she declared. "A little sore, that's all."

Then she let go of the stirrup, tried to take a step, and made a face as her legs started to buckle under her.

Tall Dog was there instantly to grasp her arm and keep her from falling.

"You should sit down," he said. "There is a log right over there. Let me help you—"

She tried to pull away from him but wasn't strong enough to do so. "I need to take care of my horse."

"I can do that for you."

Preacher said, "Let the girl take care of her own mount."

Tall Dog looked around at him with a frown. "She is tired."

"So are the rest of us," Preacher said, although he knew that with the iron constitutions all four of them possessed, the day's ride had been a pretty easy one. "She wanted to come along, so she's got to carry her share of the load."

"That's what I intend to do," Betsy said. "What I'm going to do if this . . . this big ox will let go of me!"

Tall Dog looked hurt at that. "I was only trying to help," he said.

She summoned up a weary smile for him. "I know that, and I appreciate it, I really do. I'm sorry I called you a big ox. But Preacher is right. By insisting that I wanted to come along, I gave up any special privileges. I'm just one of the group now, and I need to work and fight just like the rest of you."

Preacher wasn't sure about the fighting part, but he felt some grudging admiration for Betsy's desire to do her share. He relented slightly and said, "Let Tall Dog give you a hand unsaddlin' and takin' care of your horse. You haven't done it before, so you'll have to learn how to go about it. But Tall Dog, you just tell her what to do and let her do as much of the work as she can."

"Very well. After a few minutes' rest?"

"I'm all right," Betsy insisted. "The poor horse carried me all day. It's my turn to do something for him now."

With Tall Dog explaining to her what needed to be done and occasionally demonstrating, Betsy picketed her horse, got the saddle off, and rubbed the animal down.

Preacher watched the process without appearing to pay much attention, but he saw how Betsy bit her lip from time to time as she moved around, pained by sore muscles and places that had been rubbed almost raw by riding. However, none of that stopped her from doing what she set out to do.

Audie sidled over to where Preacher was tending to Horse and said quietly, "The young lady seems quite determined."

Preacher blew out a short breath and said, "Stubborn as a mule is more like it."

"She has our young friend wrapped around her little finger, as the saying goes."

"And don't think she don't know it, too. Tall Dog's got no idea, though. I figured he had more sense than to lose his head over a pretty gal."

"You can't predict what a young man in the throes of first love will do," Audie said.

"I know. First time he ever laid eyes on her down in St. Louis, it was like somebody walloped him in the head with a wagon tongue. Next time we run into trouble, he's liable to be so busy lookin' out for her that he'll go and get his own self killed . . . or one of us."

"And when do you think we'll run into that trouble?"

"I don't know," Preacher said, "but I reckon it's just a matter of time!"

CHAPTER 11

With each day that passed, Betsy had a slightly easier time of it, as Preacher had hoped would happen. She grew more proficient at taking care of her horse, and she didn't seem to be in as much pain at the end of the day when she dismounted, although she still walked and sat gingerly at times.

Despite the wide-brimmed hat Tall Dog had given her, she got enough sun that her face acquired a healthy tan, which made her freckles less noticeable. The days were warm and she rolled the sleeves of the flannel shirt up to her elbows so that her forearms browned, as well. Her green eyes began to acquire faint lines around them from the wind and sun.

All those things gave her character, Preacher thought, and seemed to make her even more attractive to Tall Dog, who had taken to falling back a little so he could ride beside her. Preacher heard them talking and made out enough of the words to know that he was telling her about his life among the Crow, as well as recounting some of the Norse legends his father had told him when he was a boy.

Preacher had already heard about Thor, Loki, Odin, and all the other Norse gods from mythology and thought they sounded like a right salty bunch, always ready to fight or chase after pretty girls. That Valhalla sounded like just the sort of place where he wouldn't mind ending up, if such a thing existed for scruffy old frontiersmen.

Betsy seemed very interested in the tales, although it might be that she was just letting Tall Dog think so. Women were good at using their wiles like that, the mountain man mused.

But so far, Betsy hadn't been a lot of trouble and Tall Dog didn't seem too distracted by her presence, so Preacher supposed that bringing her along hadn't been too much of a mistake.

Then the Indians showed up.

They were still following the St. Peter's River, always camping within sight of the stream if not right beside it. On this particular occasion, they had made camp under some trees about fifty feet from the water.

Preacher was up before sunrise the next morning, and after rolling out of his blankets he knelt beside the campfire's embers to stir them up and get the flames going again so he could put coffee on to boil.

He glanced around in the gray, pre-dawn gloom and saw shapes stretched out on the ground where Tall Dog, Audie, and Nighthawk slept.

The blankets where Betsy had slept appeared to be empty. Preacher frowned slightly when he noticed that, but he supposed she might have gotten up early to tend to personal business. As a young woman traveling with four men, she probably valued any moments of privacy she could get.

Dog came over and sat down beside him, leaning companionably against him as Preacher worked on the fire. But only a moment later, the big cur stiffened and a growl rumbled deep in his throat.

That by itself would have been enough to warn Preacher

that something was wrong, but a second later, a shrill scream ripped out, shattering the pre-dawn stillness.

In an instant, Preacher was standing up and twisting toward the river where the scream had come from. His hands flashed down to the holstered Colts. He had buckled on the gunbelt as soon as he left his bedroll.

His keen eyes pierced the shadows and found Betsy standing on the riverbank, staring toward the far side of the stream. Shakily, she backed a few steps away from the water as she lifted a hand to her mouth and bit her knuckles in fright.

Preacher saw what had spooked her. Four Indians mounted on ponies sat on the side of the St. Peter's. They weren't moving and didn't appear particularly threatening. They just sat there gazing toward the camp on the other bank.

Betsy's scream had roused Tall Dog, Audie, and Nighthawk, of course. All of them were veteran frontiersmen and could come awake instantly and completely at the first sign of trouble. They threw their blankets aside and grabbed their weapons as they came to their feet.

"Take it easy," Preacher told them in a clear, commanding voice as he strode toward the stream. He hadn't drawn the Colts, but his hands hovered near their butts in case he needed the revolvers.

As he reached Betsy's side, he told her, "Go on back and stay with Tall Dog."

"I . . . I'm sorry I screamed. I was just so surprised. I . . . I had been in the bushes and when I came out—"

"No need to explain," Preacher said, adding again, "Go on back with Tall Dog."

This time she did as he told her. Later, when this was over, he would have to remind her that she had agreed to follow orders without hesitation or question, he thought.

The sky was growing lighter by the second as dawn approached. With an unhurried casualness, Preacher moved closer to the river and looked across at the silent Indians. He nodded to them.

"Mornin'," he said in English. Some of them might savvy the white man's lingo. Or they might not, but it wouldn't hurt to try.

Nor would some hospitality be out of place. He went on, "Would you like to cross the river and join us? We'll have hot coffee and food in a little spell."

The four warriors remained impassive. As the light grew strong enough for him to make out more details, he recognized the decorations and markings on their buckskins as Sioux. Members of the Dakota band, more than likely, since he knew them to live in this region.

One of the Indians spoke quietly to the others. Preacher couldn't quite understand the words, but he heard them well enough for his guess to be confirmed. The Indian spoke in a Sioux dialect.

Preacher was sufficiently fluent in their tongue that he thought he could make himself understood. He said, "My friends and I pass through your lands in peace. We mean no harm to the Dakota people."

They looked a little surprised to hear themselves addressed in their own language. The one who had spoken to the others nudged his pony a little ahead. He was middle-aged, older than the rest and probably a chief, or at least the leader of this foursome.

"Where are you going?" he asked.

Preacher gestured. "Far to the north, to a land of tall trees where there is a great water. Far beyond the Dakota hunting grounds."

"Why do you go there?"

"One of my friends has family there. They need our help."

As Preacher spoke, he half-turned and gestured with his left hand toward Tall Dog. He was happy to see that Betsy had done as she was told. She stood just behind Tall Dog now, no doubt because he had put her there to protect her.

The Indian looked intently at Tall Dog for a moment and couldn't hide the look of puzzlement that passed across his face.

"That man is a Crow," he said. "And yet he is not."

"His mother is Crow," Preacher agreed, "but his father comes from a faraway tribe." The mountain man smiled. "A tribe called Vikings."

"Vi . . . kings," the Dakota repeated, struggling slightly with the word. "I have never heard of this tribe."

"They come from a far land, as I said. And there are not many in this part of the world."

The Dakota grunted. "This part of the world is all the world."

"All the world that matters," Preacher said. "That is why people from those other places want to come here."

"They come here and intrude on Dakota hunting grounds," the man snapped.

"If we hunt, we will take only what we need, and we will not stay. You have my word on this."

"White men have lied to my people before." The Dakota moved his hand in a sweeping gesture. "White men said that none of them would come across the Haha Wakpa, the river that connects all waters and all lives. They said these hunting grounds would remain for the Dakota. But now they are on this side. They build their big stone lodge on the sacred ground of Bdoté, where the rivers come together and all life began. Why should we believe what a white man tells us now?"

Preacher knew the man was talking about Fort Snelling. The confluence of the Mississippi and St. Peter's Rivers was called Bdoté by the Dakota, and as the warrior had said, it was sacred ground to them. So far, that incursion hadn't caused any raids or bloodshed that Preacher knew of, but there was no telling how long the uneasy peace would last.

"We are friends of the Dakota," he said, moving his hand in a circle to indicate all five members of their party. "We do not serve the Great White Father in the east."

All four warriors still wore dubious looks. One of them said something in a low, intense voice to the leader, maybe trying to stir up trouble.

Preacher had another card to play, and he figured it might be time.

"You have not asked my name," he said. "I am called Preacher. I am also called Ghost Killer, the sworn enemy of the Blackfeet."

Again, the tightly controlled expressions on the face of the four warriors showed surprise. Preacher knew that stories about him had spread from one end of the frontier to the other, and he also knew that hardly any of the other tribes got along well with the Blackfeet.

He wasn't sure how the Dakota felt about them, but there was at least a chance that they would consider an enemy of the Blackfeet to be their friend.

"We have heard of a white man known as Preacher," the leader responded after a moment. "It is said this man has killed many Indians."

"Only ones who were trying to kill me or my friends." Preacher shrugged. "And mostly Blackfeet. I have also helped many Indians and gone to war on their behalf. I have killed my own people when they were trying to harm Indians unfairly."

All of that was true, and he hoped these Dakota had heard about it.

The leader turned to his companions. For a couple of minutes, they conversed in tones too low for Preacher to make out what they were saying. When they turned back to him, their faces were still impassive, but Preacher sensed that something had changed.

"You travel with a woman and a child," the leader said. He sounded more curious than hostile now.

Preacher knew the woman he meant was Betsy. She wasn't wearing her hat, and her hair hung loose around her shoulders.

Not only that, but the top button of the flannel shirt was unfastened, too, and that made her femaleness more obvious.

The mention of a child puzzled Preacher, but only for a second. Then he chuckled and said in English without turning around, "Audie, come on up here."

Audie walked forward, bringing his cut-down rifle with him. He stopped next to Preacher.

"Am I being put on display?" he asked.

"These fellas took you for a youngster," Preacher explained. "I wanted 'em to see that they're wrong."

With his graying beard and weathered face, it was evident that Audie was no child. The Dakota warriors could see that now, but they were still very curious about him. People of Audie's stature turned up amongst the tribes now and then, but just like in the rest of the world, they were rare. It was possible these warriors had never seen anyone like him.

"My friend has the strength and wisdom of a full-grown warrior in a smaller body," Preacher told them. "That means his medicine is very, very powerful. He was a mighty shaman but gave it up to become a simple, peaceful man."

Audie said, "I can understand most of what you're saying, you know."

"Yeah, and you understand why I'm sayin' it, too. We don't want to fight with these folks. Might be just four of 'em stopped by here this mornin' to say howdy and check us out, but I'll bet a hat there's a heap more of 'em not too far off."

"I won't take that wager. I suspect you're right."

After a moment, the leader said in the Dakota tongue, "We meant no offense by referring to the shaman as a child."

Audie said, "A wise man passes off unintended offense as a light breeze that harms nothing."

The Dakota murmured among themselves at him answering in their language.

Preacher said, "The offer still stands. You're welcome in our camp."

"We must return to our people," the leader said stiffly. "They are waiting to hear whether you are friends or enemies." The man nodded. "We will tell them you are friends and have leave to pass through our hunting grounds unharmed, as long as you continue on your journey."

"We will not linger," Preacher said. "I give you my word. We need to reach our destination as soon as possible."

"May friendly spirits guide you."

With that, the four warriors whirled their ponies and galloped away, vanishing quickly over a nearby rise.

"Oh, my heavens," Betsy said in a shaky voice. "I thought they were going to kill us all."

"They were more curious than anything else," Tall Dog told her. "Although if we had done anything to anger them, they would have fought. This is their land."

"And they'll protect it, too," Preacher said. "But as long

as we behave ourselves, they ought to leave us alone. A few more days and we'll be past the area where this band ranges."

"Will there be more of them between here and where we're going?" Betsy asked.

"More than likely."

"But we'll be on our best behavior," Audie said, "so that none of the tribes have any reason to attack us."

Nighthawk nodded and said, "Umm."

"Indeed, old friend. Undoubtedly we'll have more than enough trouble from white men to worry about, once we get where we're going."

From the shelter of a cluster of boulders atop a ridge, Gabe Simon, McNair, and Brendle watched the four Indians riding west about a quarter of a mile away. The sun was just below the horizon now, and there was plenty of light for them to see the Indians.

Brendle blew out a breath and said, "I figured we was goners. Good thing you got sharp eyes, Simon, and spotted those savages before they saw us."

"That don't happen often," McNair said. "Usually the redskins know you're there before you know they're there, if that makes sense."

"Well, I'm disappointed," Simon replied. "I was hoping they'd attack Preacher's bunch and whittle the odds down for us. Maybe even wipe them out, if we'd been lucky enough."

"But they would've killed that girl, too," Brendle protested.

Simon shook his head. "The girl's not our objective, as I've told you before. All we care about is stopping them, whether Indians kill them or they get caught in an avalanche or a bear gets them. It's all the same to us."

"Yeah, sure," McNair muttered, but he didn't sound very sincere about it.

Simon hoped these two idiots wouldn't ruin everything because of their obsession with getting their hands on the girl.

As he stared at the Indians who were disappearing into the distance, an idea occurred to Simon. It would be dangerous, no doubt about that, but if it worked, it might solve all his problems and allow him to go back to Decker Galloway and report success.

That was very much what he wanted to do.

Nobody wanted to disappoint or anger Decker Galloway. That was truly dangerous.

"Mount up," he snapped at his two henchmen.

"Where are we goin'?" Brendle asked.

"We're going to follow those Indians and see where they go."

Both men stared at him. It took them a moment to work up enough courage to say something.

Then McNair asked, "Have you gone loco, boss?"

"No, but I may have figured out a way for us to get what we want. Get on your horses. We're riding."

McNair and Brendle looked at each other. Maybe they were considering riding away and leaving him here. Maybe they thought they might be able to kill him and take whatever money he had on him.

Knowing that, Simon kept his hand close to the butt of the pistol stuck behind his belt. If they made a move to double-cross him, they'd regret it. He would kill them both.

But then they shrugged, obviously hoping that if they

played along, a better payday would be coming sooner or later, as Simon had promised.

"I hope you know what you're doin'," McNair said as he swung up into the saddle.

"I always do," Simon said with more confidence than he actually felt.

The three of them rode in the same direction that the Indians had vanished into.

CHAPTER 12

Betsy still seemed a little shaken by the early-morning encounter as they had their breakfast and then broke camp.

Preacher didn't know what she had expected. It wasn't realistic to think they wouldn't run into any Indians on their way north to Skarkavik. But judging by Betsy's reaction, the possibility might not have even entered her mind.

She had no way of knowing that you couldn't travel hundreds of miles across the frontier without bumping into some of the folks who had lived there first.

As they rode north, Preacher said to Tall Dog, "I'm thinkin' it might be a good idea to post a guard at night from here on."

So far they hadn't posted sentries because the country through which they were passing was considered fairly peaceful. Also, Preacher counted on Dog and Horse to let him know if anything suspicious was going on. His trail partners had keener senses than any human.

"That would be a good idea," Tall Dog agreed. "We are far beyond the reach of any authority here, and it's likely that anyone we encounter will not be a friend."

"Ought to make Miss Betsy feel a mite safer knowin' we're standin' watch, too."

Tall Dog nodded. "Yes. She was terrified earlier."

"It was her choice to come along," Preacher reminded him.

"Of course. But I see no reason not to make the journey easier on her if we can."

Sure he didn't, thought Preacher, because he was sweet on the gal.

He figured Tall Dog would just deny it and maybe even argue about it if he said that, though, so he let it go.

The country on both sides of the river was thickly wooded, although not with the towering spruce, fir, and pine to be found in the north woods where they were headed. For the most part, these were aspen, maple, oak, and elm.

These good-sized, sturdy trees would someday provide logs and lumber for settlers' cabins, but for now, such habitations were few and far between. Fort Snelling was the last outpost of civilization in this direction. The only whites beyond it were fur trappers who lived nomadic existences and had no use for cabins.

Henry Sibley was trying to get farmers to move up here into this region. Preacher had no doubt that sooner or later he would succeed. Trees would be cleared and plows would break the soil, and this wild territory would be tamed like so much other land had been. Preacher had witnessed that scenario play out time and time again in other areas.

He was just glad he'd been able to see the frontier the way it used to be, before modern times caught up to it and changed everything.

Ruined everything, some would say . . . and Preacher wasn't sure he disagreed with that stance.

* * *

Numerous smaller streams flowed into the St. Peter's from both directions as the river continued its meandering way northwestward. Two miles to the west, in thick woods at the crest of a ridge, Gabe Simon knelt and looked down at the Indian village located on the bank of one of those tributaries. He and his companions had followed the four Indians back to this spot.

"I don't like it here," Brendle said behind him. "One of those Injun curs is liable to catch our scent and raise a ruckus, and then the savages will come up here lookin' for us."

"The wind is coming from the wrong direction for that," Simon said. "Quit worrying about things that aren't likely to happen."

"Those redskins got sharp eyes, too," McNair said. Like Brendle, he stood behind Simon in the thick shadows under the trees. They were being careful not to expose themselves too much. "If they spot us, we're done for."

"How many times already today have you whined that we were done for?" Simon asked, not bothering to keep the irritation out of his voice.

Soon, if the plan he'd hatched worked, he wouldn't need these two anymore. Maybe he would pay them off and send them on their way.

Maybe he would just pay them off in lead and save the money.

It all depended on what those Indians did.

The edge of the village was about two hundred yards away, Simon estimated. The rifles he and the other men carried would reach that far, easily, with reasonable accuracy.

Pinpoint accuracy wasn't really necessary, though. A group of twenty or thirty Indians—men, women, and children—had gathered to watch some sort of competition. Simon had no idea what the Indians who were running around were trying to accomplish, and he didn't care. The encouraging whoops and cheers from the spectators made it clear they were enjoying the show.

Simon stayed in his kneeling position and raised his rifle.

"Get ready," he told McNair and Brendle.

Reluctantly, they stepped up so they flanked him and lifted their weapons, as well. Simon cocked his rifle and they followed suit.

Then Simon bellowed as loudly as he could, "Preacher, no!" followed by a hissed command to fire.

The shouted words rolled down the slope toward the village. Some of the Indians started to look around, puzzled by what they had heard, when three shots roared from the ridge. Simon lowered his rifle and peered through the haze of powdersmoke.

One of the women cried out as her head jerked and she flung her arms out to the side. As she crumpled, Simon realized that luck had guided one of the rounds. The woman was shot in the head and must have died instantly.

He didn't see if any of the other Indians fell, but it didn't matter. The plan was in motion. Now he and his companions had to finish carrying it out.

"Get to the horses," he barked at McNair and Brendle.

He didn't have to tell them twice. They whirled around and dashed through the trees toward the spot where they had left the horses tied. The animals were close by, so it took only moments to reach them. McNair and Brendle jerked their mounts' reins loose and practically leaped into their saddles.

Simon was only a heartbeat behind them. He might have been annoyed by the constant complaining from his two helpers, but to be honest, he was afraid of the Indians, too. Only a fool wouldn't be.

The three men rode down the far side of the ridge to an open stretch of ground and headed east as fast as they could push the horses. More trees loomed on the far side of the broad valley. As they reached that growth, Simon slowed enough to look back over his shoulder.

A dozen figures on swift ponies came into view. There were probably even more riders behind them, Simon thought. Plenty of warriors, furious at the treacherous attack on their village, to wipe out the men they would blame for it.

Now all Simon and his companions had to do was lead those blood-crazed savages right to Preacher and the rest of the troublesome mountain man's bunch.

By the time they stopped in the middle of the morning to rest the horses for a spell, Betsy seemed to have gotten over the worst of her earlier fright. She smiled and laughed as she stood and chatted with Tall Dog not far from the shallow, gently flowing river.

Preacher, Audie, and Nighthawk stood far enough away to give the two young people at least the illusion of privacy. Quietly, Preacher commented to his old friends, "I'm glad she's settled down some."

"Look at that," Audie said as Betsy laughed again and reached out to rest her fingers lightly against Tall Dog's forearm for a moment. "The young fellow has no idea what she's doing, but she's certainly aware of it."

"Umm," Nighthawk said.

"You're right, he has no chance. He's fallen fully under her spell."

"You sayin' she's a witch?" Preacher asked.

"No more so than any woman," Audie replied. "All of them have powers that might be deemed sorcerous, if we're talking about how men react to them—"

The former professor stopped short and raised his head, turning slightly to gaze toward the west. Beside him, Preacher and Nighthawk were doing the same thing, because they had heard the same thing Audie had.

"Horses," Preacher said.

"Umm."

"Yes, quite a few of them, and coming quickly in this direction." Audie looked at Preacher. "Perhaps we should get mounted—"

"Too late for that, I reckon," the mountain man said. "They're close enough we can't outrun 'em, if it's us they're after. Best pull back into the trees, in case there's trouble."

He turned and called to Tall Dog and Betsy, "Grab the horses and come on! Head for the trees!"

Betsy said, "What—"

"Do as Preacher says!" Tall Dog told her. His jovial attitude had vanished in less than the blink of an eye. He grabbed Skidbladnir's reins and those of the pack horses, as well. "Move! Get into the trees!"

Betsy looked shocked that he would speak to her like that. Preacher was glad to see that Tall Dog wasn't completely mesmerized by her and could still react quickly when time was short.

Surprised or not, Betsy did as she was told and broke into a run toward the trees. Part of that was probably because Tall Dog was right behind her, crowding her and leading his paint horse and the pack animals. She had to keep moving to avoid being trampled.

Nighthawk had the extra saddle mounts as well as his own horse. Preacher led his stallion and Audie's horse.

He glanced around for Dog but didn't see the big cur. That wasn't surprising; Dog often went bounding off to investigate various smells that caught his interest. He was canny enough to take care of himself and avoid trouble unless his human friends needed his help.

The riders came in sight on the far side of the river just as Betsy and Tall Dog reached the trees. Preacher, Audie, and Nighthawk were still in plain sight. The strident whoops that went up told Preacher they had been spotted.

They kept moving, though, until they were under the aspens that grew thickly in this area. A sudden silence struck Preacher as ominous. He swung around and looked across the river to see that several dozen mounted Dakota warriors sat there on their ponies.

The Indians were close enough for Preacher to see the cold, angry expressions on their faces.

"What is this all about?" Audie asked. "I was under the impression that we parted on friendly terms earlier this morning."

"That's what I thought, too," Preacher said. "Those old boys look mighty *un*friendly at the moment, though." He took a breath. "I reckon I'd better go palaver with 'em."

"Some of them have trade rifles, Preacher. The others have bows. If you step out in the open, you'll be within range of both weapons."

"Ain't no other way to find out what it's all about." Preacher looked around and spotted Tall Dog and Betsy behind some trees about twenty feet away. "Tall Dog, I'm goin' out there to talk to those Dakota. If anything happens to me, Audie's in charge."

Tall Dog might not like that. He and Preacher had been partners for a while, and he might think that he should be next in the line of command. Audie was older and more experienced, though. And Tall Dog wasn't likely to argue with Preacher's decision whether he liked it or not.

Without waiting to see one way or the other, Preacher stepped out of the shelter of the trees and walked toward the river. His stride was firm and determined.

Angry shouts went up from some of the Dakota, but none of them made a move to attack him. As Preacher advanced toward the stream, he searched among their faces for the man he had spoken with a few hours earlier. He wished he had gotten that fella's name, so he could call to him.

He stopped when he was still a dozen feet from the river and raised his voice to say, "We are glad to meet again with the Dakota."

One of the younger warriors pushed his pony forward and screamed, "Liar! Killer!" He thrust the lance he carried into the air, howled a war cry, and kicked his pony into a run.

The horse splashed across the shallow river, its hooves throwing water up in a silvery spray. Preacher kept his feet planted solidly on the ground as the warrior charged him, the lance lowered now to run him through.

None of the other warriors moved. They just sat and watched, evidently content to let the conflict play out.

Preacher still didn't know what was going on or why the Dakota were out for blood, but at the moment those questions didn't matter.

What was important was that the young fella coming toward him intended to kill him by ramming that lance clean through him.

Preacher waited until the last second to leap aside. As the lance went past him, the thrust missing by scant inches, his hands flashed out and grabbed hold of it. He dug his boot heels into the ground to brace himself as the pony thundered by.

Preacher's iron grip on the lance meant that the warrior had to either let go or be pulled off the pony. He was too stubborn to let go and tried to wrench the lance away from Preacher.

Instead, with a startled cry, he slipped off the pony and crashed to the ground. The impact jarred the lance out of his grip.

While the young Dakota was stunned, Preacher could have whipped the lance around and driven the point through him, pinning him to the ground.

Instead, he threw it to the side, not wanting to kill anybody he didn't have to.

The warrior rolled to put some distance between himself and Preacher, then came up on his feet gasping for the breath that the fall had knocked out of him. His features contorted in a furious snarl as he fumbled with the tomahawk at his waist.

Preacher noticed that the young man's face wasn't painted for war or anything else. In fact, none of the Dakota had taken the time to paint themselves before galloping away from their village.

There had to be a reason for that, Preacher told himself, and he hoped he lived long enough to find out what it was.

Holding out his open left hand toward the warrior, he said in the Dakota tongue, "Stop. We have no reason to fight."

The young man was too angry to be surprised that Preacher spoke his lingo. He responded, "You killed Brown Robin! You shot down more of my people!"

Preacher shook his head. "I don't have any notion of who this Brown Robin is—"

"She is dead! She was to be my wife!"

"Then I'm mighty sorry something happened to her, son. But my friends and I didn't have anything to do with it—"

"You are the only white men around here! It had to be you who shot your guns into our village."

One of the older men pushed his horse forward. Preacher recognized him.

"We heard one of the others shout at you," he declared. "He called you Preacher. Then the shots, and Brown Robin fell dead. Two warriors were wounded."

Again, the mountain man shook his head. "You may have heard somebody use my name, but I wasn't there and neither were any of my friends. We've been right here on this side of the river, travelin' northwest all mornin'."

The young warrior was in no mood to hear it. With an incoherent yell, he yanked the tomahawk from the rawhide loop holding it at his waist and charged Preacher again.

The mountain man could have hauled out one of his Colts and ventilated his attacker, of course, but doing that would get him and his companions massacred. He had no doubt of that. He wanted to keep from hurting any of the Dakota until he had a chance to talk to them and convince them he and the others were innocent of any wrongdoing.

This young fella wasn't making that easy, though. He lunged at Preacher and brought the tomahawk down in a sweeping blow aimed at splitting Preacher's skull.

Again Preacher waited until the last second to make his move. He darted aside. The tomahawk missed him, causing the young warrior to stumble. With his left hand, Preacher grabbed the man's arm and jerked on it, throwing him even more off-balance.

Preacher's right fist shot up and out in a swift punch that landed with terrific force on the Dakota's jaw.

The blow slewed the young man's head to the side. His

eyes rolled up in their sockets and his knees buckled. As he fell, Preacher slung him to the ground so that he rolled again, coming to a stop on his belly. He lay there senseless.

Yipping and crying out, another of the warriors charged across the river on horseback.

"Blast it," Preacher blurted out, "am I gonna have to fight every one o' you varmints?"

CHAPTER 13

It looked like that might be the case, because this warrior was determined to attack Preacher, too. He drew an arrow from the quiver on his back, fitted it to his bowstring, and fired it at Preacher while the pony was still running.

Preacher had to throw himself aside as the shaft whipped past him. He landed on his shoulder, rolled, and was coming back to his feet when the young Dakota warrior left the pony's back in a diving tackle aimed at the mountain man.

The morning sunlight glinted on the blade of the knife the warrior held. Preacher barely had time to get a hand up, grab the man's wrist, and turn the weapon aside.

The next instant, the warrior crashed into him, and both of them went down hard with Preacher on the bottom. The Dakota's weight coming down on top of him drove the air out of his lungs and left him half-stunned.

He didn't lose his grip on the man's wrist. He knew that if he did, the cold steel of that knife would be buried in his body an instant later. To get himself a little breathing room, Preacher bucked up off the ground and twisted.

The move worked. He threw the young man off to the side. The warrior landed with a grunt.

Preacher went the other direction and made it to his feet this time. As the warrior tried to surge upright, Preacher kicked the knife out of his hand. Then he caught hold of the man's arm, heaved and twisted, and threw his opponent over his hip.

This time when the Dakota slammed into the ground, he didn't try to jump right back up. Instead, he rolled onto his side and lay there breathing hard.

Preacher stepped back, ready to keep fighting if he needed to. The second man who'd attacked him didn't seem to be in any hurry to resume hostilities, though.

The same wasn't true of the two men who drove their ponies through the stream toward him and brandished lances.

"Two at once this time, eh?" Preacher said. He was getting pretty fed up with this. He motioned with his hands. "I don't care! Come on, all of you, if that's what you want!"

Tall Dog burst from the woods and ran toward him. "No, Preacher!" he called. "These two are mine!"

Preacher could have handled the Dakota warriors, but if the whole bunch was going to come at them sooner or later, he supposed it wouldn't hurt to share some of the load. He stepped back and made a "help yourself" gesture to Tall Dog.

The two onrushing warriors sent their ponies toward Tall Dog. He reached for his sword, then let go of the weapon before fully grasping its hilt. He understood the same thing Preacher did, that killing any of the Dakota would bring down doom on their heads.

One of the warriors had drawn slightly ahead of the other. Tall Dog leaped out of the way of that initial charge. The second man tried to swing his lance to bear so that he could run Tall Dog through.

Tall Dog caught hold of the shaft and forced it down so that the point dug into the ground. The pony's momentum made it impossible for the warrior to stop. The lance bent, tore itself out of his hands, and snapped up to strike him across the face. The blow was enough to topple him backward off the racing pony.

Tall Dog grabbed the fallen lance and spun it. The first man had reined in his pony and tried another lunge, but Tall Dog parried it with the lance he held. He sprang closer, reached up and got hold of the warrior's buckskin shirt, and jerked him off the pony. The man lost his hold on the lance. It rolled away.

Tall Dog tossed his lance aside, too. Both of his opponents were unhorsed, but they still had him outnumbered and seemed confident they could defeat him. They pulled tomahawks and rushed him from different directions.

Tall Dog bent to the left from his waist. He lifted his right leg and the foot snapped out in a kick that landed in the belly of the man on that side. The man doubled over and flew backward, dropping his tomahawk.

At the same time, Tall Dog grabbed the arm of the second man in both hands, stopping the blow that was intended to smash his skull. He pivoted on the foot that was still planted and used his right leg to sweep the warrior's legs out from under him. The man had no chance to catch himself. He came down hard on his back and lay there senseless.

The second man to attack Preacher had recovered his wits and breath and leaped at Tall Dog from behind. Instinct warned the half-Crow, half-Norwegian fighter and whirled him around. In a sweeping backhand, he hammered the side of his right fist against the man's head and knocked him down.

Everything had happened so swiftly it was little more than a blur. But the end result was that four Dakota warriors lay senseless but basically unharmed on the ground, while Preacher and Tall Dog still stood almost untouched.

Preacher strode up to the edge of the water and glared across the river at the other warriors. Focusing on the one he had spoken to that morning, he said, "Are you gonna send the whole bunch across or not? We don't want to fight you, but we will if we have to. Can't you tell by the way we dealt with your young men that we don't want to harm anyone?"

The man looked at him for a long moment, then said, "You have faced death with courage. You could have dealt it in return. Yet you did not."

"Because we're friends to the Dakota, which I've been tryin' to tell you all along."

"Or perhaps because you knew that if you spilled more Dakota blood, you and all your friends would die."

"Well, now," Preacher said, "if what you're accusin' us of was true, we'd already be in that situation, wouldn't we? But if I'm tellin' you the truth and we didn't attack your village, then we'd want to be sure and not hurt any of your men before I could make you believe it, ain't that right? You've got to be able to see that."

Again the man regarded Preacher with silence and deliberation. Finally, he lifted a hand and motioned the rest of the warriors back.

"I come across to talk," he said as he kneed his pony into motion.

"And you're welcome, just like before," Preacher told him. "Reckon we'd all feel a mite more comfortable about it, though, if the rest of your fellas stayed on that side of the river."

That was symbolic more than anything else; rifle rounds and arrows could carry easily across the stream. But the Dakota leader nodded and motioned for the rest of the warriors to stay where they were.

Slowly and with great dignity, he rode across the river. The four men who had attacked Preacher and Tall Dog were coming to their senses, and as he moved past two of them who were sitting up, he spoke sharply to them, commanding them to catch their ponies and help the others back across. Sullenly, they set about doing so.

"Go back with Miss Kingsley," Preacher said quietly to Tall Dog. "I reckon she'll feel a mite better if you're with her."

"I can help you talk to this Dakota."

"I'll make him see the straight of things," Preacher said.

Tall Dog hesitated a moment longer, then nodded and walked toward the trees where Betsy, Audie, and Nighthawk waited.

Preacher stood there while the Dakota chief dismounted. When they were facing each other, the mountain man said, "You know how I'm called, but I didn't get your name when we talked earlier."

"I am Man in the Cloud."

"I'm honored to know you, Man in the Cloud. And I would never lie to a man who has trusted me with his true name. I don't know what happened at your village this mornin', but I give you my word my friends and I didn't have anything to do with it."

"Some of the people were watching the young men at sport," Man in the Cloud said. "There were shots from a ridge near our village. A young woman, Brown Robin, fell dead. The shots also struck two of our warriors and injured them greatly. I do not know if they will live. Just before the shots, one of the men on the ridge cried out your name and tried to stop you from firing."

Preacher shook his head. "Anyone can say a name. I wasn't there. Neither were any of the people with me. We haven't been out of each other's sight all morning."

"Who would know your name? Who would try to make us believe you attacked us?"

"Those are mighty good questions." Preacher scraped his thumbnail along his jawline. "And I've got a pretty good idea what the answers are. I'm not sure it'll make sense to you when I explain, though."

"Go ahead," Man in the Cloud said.

For the next few minutes, Preacher tried to tell the Dakota leader about Decker Galloway, Skarkavik, and the man Galloway had sent south to prevent any help from reaching the village of Tall Dog's grandfather. Putting it in terms that Man in the Cloud could understand proved to be a challenge, but as Preacher talked, he began to get the impression that the man understood enough of what he was saying.

"After trying to ambush us on our way upriver and failing, this man must have been following us, waiting for another opportunity to kill us . . . or trick someone else into killing us."

"He tried to use the Dakota to do this evil thing?"

"That's sure my hunch, yeah."

Man in the Cloud scowled darkly. "The Dakota do not like to be tricked."

"I don't blame you for feelin' that way. I don't like it, neither."

"Where can I find this man?"

"I don't have any idea. I wouldn't be surprised if he's somewhere close around here, watchin' us, waitin' to see what's gonna happen." Preacher smiled. "And if I'm right, I'd bet a hat that he's mighty disappointed right about now!"

Gabe Simon cursed bitterly as he watched through the spyglass while Preacher and the Indian chief clasped wrists in a gesture of friendship.

"What is it?" McNair asked. "What's goin' on?"

"It didn't work, that's what's going on," Simon snapped. "It looks like Preacher and that damned redskin have made friends."

"How's that possible?" asked Brendle. "We shot up their village and killed some of the filthy savages and made sure they'd blame Preacher for it!"

"All I can figure is that somehow he talked them out of believing that." The bitter taste of disappointment filled Simon's mouth. "The way things were going, I figured they'd fight him one or two at a time until he was dead, then massacre the rest of the bunch." Simon cursed again. "I should have known when they didn't charge in and slaughter the whole bunch right away that it wasn't going to work!"

McNair said, "What do we do now?"

"I think maybe we should head back to Fort Snelling," Brendle said.

Simon jerked around and glared at him. "You can give up if you want to," he snapped, "but if you do, you won't get paid."

"Now, hold on—"

"My job is to stop Preacher, and I'm going to do it, one way or another."

"Shoot him from a distance," McNair suggested. "Him and that tall blond Indian."

"There are four of them and three of us," Simon pointed out. "We can't kill all of them with one volley. And there's no guarantee that none of us would miss our shot. We might have two or even three of them left to deal with." Simon shook his head. "From what I've seen of them, I don't want to be looking over my shoulder for any of that bunch, including the giant redskin and even that little fella. We need to wipe them out all at one time."

"So we keep following them?" Brendle said, obviously trying not to sigh.

Simon scowled at him again. "I thought you were talking about quitting."

Brendle shrugged and said, "I'll stick with you a while longer. They still have quite a ways to go before they get where they're goin', don't they?"

"Yeah, they do."

"Well, maybe we'll get lucky between now and then. You'll figure out a way, Gabe."

Simon nodded. Even though he was disappointed in how things had worked out today—those savages were riding off and leaving Preacher's bunch to go on their way unmolested—there was still plenty of time to carry out the task Decker Galloway had assigned to him.

As long as Preacher and the others died before they reached the lake, everything would be fine.

Surviving the encounter with the Dakota seemed to be a turning point for Preacher and his companions. For the next week and a half, they enjoyed a trouble-free journey, with the exception of a couple of days when rain made the traveling slower and unpleasant.

Most of the days were gorgeous, however, warm and

breezy with white clouds towering in the deep blue sky. The group was able to move at a good, steady pace over the rolling hills and plains that were broken up by stretches of forest. The hunting was good, and they usually had fresh meat.

Going by the directions in Axel Gunnarson's letter to Tall Dog, they had left the St. Peter's River and followed one of the tributaries, a route that led them almost due north. They reached the head of that small river and continued north. Enough creeks flowed through this land that they were in no danger of running short of water.

They hadn't seen another human being since Man in the Cloud and the rest of the Dakota rode off. That solitude might bother some people, but Preacher thrived on it. He enjoyed having good companions such as Tall Dog, Audie, and Nighthawk, but if he had been out here alone except for Dog and Horse, he would have been fine with that, too.

One day while Preacher and Audie were riding in the lead together, Preacher said, "You reckon we're across the border by now?"

"If not, we must be getting pretty close. Can you look around and tell that we're in territory claimed by Great Britain instead of the United States?"

Preacher chuckled. "Not one damn bit. I never paid too much attention to lines on maps."

"They can be important," Audie said. "The world has to have some sort of system of organization."

"Why?" Preacher asked. "If everybody just tended to their own business and got along, I don't reckon we'd even need maps. If somebody wanted to go somewhere, you'd just tell him which rivers to follow and which mountain passes to use."

"In an ideal world, perhaps. That is, after all, the way our Indian friends live. They have no need of maps and borders, at least in the formal sense. But the Crow know where their hunting grounds end and those of the Blackfeet begin. Even in such simple cultures, the concept of *yours* and *mine* exists . . . and men will kill over the idea."

As usual, Audie was right. Preacher said, "So the short answer is, you figure we've crossed the border."

"Don't you?"

"Yep," Preacher said.

A range of low, rounded mountains appeared on the western horizon. Later in the day, Preacher pointed them out to Tall Dog and said, "Accordin' to what your grandpa said, we stay east of those, don't we?"

"Yes, there are hills around the lake where Skarkavik is located, but it lies east of that range, which runs farther to the north than my grandfather's people have ever been. They have heard stories that a land of never-ending ice and snow can be found in that direction."

"I'd think a place like that would be where a bunch of Vikings would want to go."

Tall Dog shook his head. "It is true that the winters are harsh in the homelands of my father's people, but they do not last all the year around. There is time for hunting and fishing and even a bit of farming." He smiled. "And perhaps one of the reasons the Vikings roamed so much is because they were looking for some place where the weather was nicer!"

Preacher had to laugh at that. What the youngster said made sense, all right.

* * *

Gabe Simon grunted with effort as he pulled himself to the top of the ridge. The slope was steep but not sheer. A man could climb it if he was willing to work hard enough.

Simon was willing. He saw this as his last, best chance to carry out Decker Galloway's orders and stop Preacher.

Breathing hard, he stood with his hands on his hips and looked along the rimrock. Several large boulders perched at the edge, and more boulders littered the slope below.

The trail ran along the base of the bluff, and a short distance beyond it lay a brush-choked ravine. On the other side of the ravine, the spruce forest grew so thickly that horses would find it impossible to get through.

This place was Simon's ace in the hole and had been ever since he'd set out on this mission. He would have preferred to catch up to Rolf Pedersen, kill him and take that letter away from him before the man ever reached St. Louis, but things hadn't worked out that way.

Stopping Preacher and his companions before they headed north would have been better, too, but fate and bad luck had conspired against Simon there, just as they had in every attempt to stop Preacher since then.

But in the back of Simon's mind had lain the trap he was going to spring here. This was the best route to the lake where Decker Galloway's timber operation was located. Simon had had no guarantee that Preacher and the others would come this way, but as he and McNair and Brendle followed the bunch and spied on them, Simon had become more and more convinced they were headed this direction.

Finally, he'd been sure enough of that to race ahead, pushing their horses to the utmost so they could reach this spot first.

Those horses were down below, heads drooping and

sides heaving as they puffed for breath while McNair and Brendle held them. McNair called up the slope, "How's it look?"

"Just like I remembered from when I saw it coming south," Simon replied. He nodded decisively. "This is where Preacher and the rest of those blasted troublemakers die at last."

CHAPTER 14

The forests of spruce, pine, and birch were even thicker now, covering much of the landscape so that the vast open stretches they had crossed farther south were gone. In some places, the trees stood so close together that Preacher and the others had to ride around them, rather than trying to go through those areas of dense growth.

The terrain was more rugged, too, criss-crossed by deep gullies and ravines where narrow streams ran swiftly. Because of that, the travelers had to detour back and forth instead of heading due north as they had been ever since leaving the St. Peter's River.

Despite those obstacles, Preacher found this to be beautiful country. It reminded him of places he had seen in the Rockies, even though there weren't any massive, snow-capped mountains looming over the landscape.

"I wonder how the fur trappin' is around here," he mused to Tall Dog as they rode side by side with Dog loping out ahead of them.

"Probably good," the young warrior said, "although with the decline in the market for beaver pelts, the effort required might not be worth it. You would have to transport the pelts a long way to sell them and probably wouldn't get a very good price."

"Yeah, the Hudson's Bay Company used to have fur tradin' posts all over up here, but I've heard that they closed most of 'em down and have gone more into the mercantile business in the settlements." Preacher spat to one side. "These days, fellas would rather be shopkeepers instead o' fur trappers and traders. What's the world comin' to?"

Tall Dog laughed and said, "You sound like one of the elders of the Crow, Preacher, always complaining about how things are now compared to the way they used to be."

"I ain't changed all that much since I was a younker. Don't see any reason why the world has to change."

"And yet it does."

A resigned sigh was the only response Preacher could make to that.

A short distance farther on, the forest became dense enough that they had to veer to the left alongside a ravine carving a deep but narrow gash through the landscape. That put the ravine to the riders' right, and to their left, a steep bluff rose about a hundred feet and ran for several hundred yards. The game trail along the bluff's base was wide enough for two riders to travel alongside each other.

Preacher caught Tall Dog's eye and angled his head behind them. Tall Dog understood that the mountain man was telling him to fall back and ride with Betsy.

Tall Dog wasn't going to argue with that suggestion.

Audie was next in line, leading the extra mounts, with Nighthawk and the pack animals bringing up the rear.

Even though they hadn't run into any trouble for quite a while, Preacher hadn't forgotten about the earlier efforts to kill them. He knew there was a chance whoever wanted to stop them from reaching Skarkavik was still lurking somewhere nearby, so he didn't let down his guard.

Anyway, after surviving so many years of hard, dangerous living, he was in the habit of being careful. His eyes never stopped moving. His keen gaze flicked back and forth between the thick forest, the ravine, and the rugged bluff alongside which they rode.

About twenty yards ahead, Dog came to a sudden stop. The big cur stiffened and the hair on his back bristled. His ears pricked up as his sharp snout lifted and pointed up the slope.

Dog had heard or scented something unusual, Preacher realized. Maybe both. And the cur's reaction told him that whatever it was, Dog didn't like it.

"Dog!" Preacher called in a low, penetrating voice. "Hunt!"

Dog tried to leap up the slope, but it was too steep for him. His paws scrabbled against the rocky ground for a second, then he slid back down. Clearly agitated, he began running back and forth on the trail, a short distance each way, as he looked up at the top of the bluff and bared his fangs.

That was enough for Preacher. He twisted in the saddle, waved an arm at the others, and yelled, "Get back!"

Tall Dog reined in sharply and reached for the reins of Betsy's horse as well. The trail was too narrow for both mounts to turn around easily, though.

Beyond them, Audie and Nighthawk began struggling with the same dilemma. None of the group hesitated even a second in trying to follow Preacher's order, but circumstances made it difficult for them to do so.

Movement at the top of the bluff caught Preacher's eye.

He saw one of the boulders perched on the rim suddenly lurch forward. The boulder's weight shifted enough to topple it. With a growing rumble, it began to roll down the slope. It crashed into smaller rocks and started them falling, too. Dust shot into the air in billowing clouds.

Before Preacher and his companions could do more than start trying to turn their horses around, they were caught in the path of the avalanche that thundered down at them.

The ravine was the only place they could go.

Preacher waved his arm at the brush-choked defile and shouted, "Go! Get down in there!" but he didn't know if the others could hear him over the growing roar of the rockslide.

The ravine's sides were steep, too steep for the horses to descend. Preacher slipped out of the saddle and slapped Horse on the rump as he yelled at the big gray stallion. Horse bolted ahead. He might be able to outrun the worst of the avalanche, especially without the mountain man's weight on his back.

From the corner of his eye, Preacher saw that Tall Dog was already off Skidbladnir. The paint lunged ahead, following Horse. Betsy's mount was right behind it.

Betsy herself was in Tall Dog's arms, cradled against his body as he leaped into the ravine. His back and shoulders were hunched as if he were trying to wrap himself around her to protect her.

Preacher couldn't see Audie and Nighthawk. He had no time to worry about them. Rocks almost as big as he was were already tumbling around him. He leaped as far out into the ravine as he could.

The thick brush was the only thing that gave them a chance. Otherwise the desperate leaps would leave them with broken legs or arms or necks. That might wind up happening anyway. Preacher crashed into the growth, felt the branches claw at him, heard the crackle as the vegetation gave way.

The heavier branches that didn't break pummeled him like viciously wielded clubs. But enough of the vegetation gave way to slow his fall. He sank deep into the brush before stopping.

As soon as his plunge halted, he began trying to pull himself upright and force his way closer to the trail so the ravine's bank would protect him from the falling rocks. He heard some of them smashing through the brush not far from him.

It was like trying to fight his way through a million clutching hands. The rumble got louder and louder and he felt the ground trembling underneath him. The ordeal seemed like it lasted a long time, but he knew that in truth it was only a minute or so before the rumble trailed away and left an echoing, dust-filled silence behind it.

The shrill scream of a horse in pain shattered that silence. The awful sound came from Preacher's left, back where Audie and Nighthawk had been. He hoped his friends had escaped the avalanche . . .

But even more so, right now his mind was filled with anger and the thirst for vengeance on whoever had started that slide. Dog's reaction just before all hell broke loose, combined with the way that first boulder had lurched forward so abruptly, told him that the avalanche had been no accident.

Preacher paused long enough to take stock of himself. He knew that once things calmed down, he would realize how battered and bruised he was. Several ugly scratches inflicted by broken branches stung his flesh.

But he could tell that no bones were broken, and when he reached down to the holsters on his hips, he felt the walnut grips of the Colt Patersons. Both irons were still where they were supposed to be, held in place by rawhide thongs over the hammers that he now thumbed free.

With grim resolve on his face, Preacher began to climb the side of the ravine.

The ravine's wall was rough enough to provide him with footholds and handholds. Some protruding rocks and roots helped, too. He pulled himself up out of the brush, and when he was in the open again, he stopped and looked back to the left, the direction that had been behind him when the avalanche began. Dust still swirled in the air but was beginning to clear. He didn't see any sign of his companions.

If they were all dead, he would settle the score, he vowed. And then he would go on to Skarkavik, somehow, and kill Decker Galloway, because he had no doubt that the timber baron was ultimately responsible for what had happened here.

Preacher was almost at the top, within moments of pulling himself back onto the trail, when he heard voices.

"I don't see any of them, damn it!" a man called harshly. "Where are they?"

"Buried under all that rock, I expect, Gabe," another man answered. "They didn't have time to get out of the way. I don't think we'll ever find them, to tell you the truth."

A third man spoke up. "They're bound to be smashed flat. It's a damn shame for such a pretty girl to wind up that way."

"Yeah, it would've been better if we could've found a way to grab her and then kill the others. We could've had ourselves a fine old time with her."

The first man, the one called Gabe, said, "The important thing is that they're dead and they won't cause my boss any headaches. Let's go get the horses and get out of here."

Preacher had pretty well located all three of them by the sound of their voices. Gabe was the closest, with the other two being farther away along the trail.

One of them commented, "I think that big stallion and the paint might've got clear. It was hard to tell for sure with all the dust in the air. But if they did, we can round them up and take 'em along. That'll be a nice little bonus."

Preacher hoped the man was right, that Horse and Skidbladnir had indeed escaped from the avalanche. If that was true, Horse would come to his whistle, and more than likely Skidbladnir would come with him.

He would see about that when he was finished with Gabe and the other two skunks prowling around up there.

He heard their footsteps as they started to walk away and knew their backs were turned toward him. He seized the chance to pull himself the rest of the way onto the trail, which was almost completely covered with rocks in places.

Gabe was about thirty feet from him, the other two maybe a dozen feet farther on. As Preacher straightened to his feet, he called, "Hold on there, boys. I ain't finished with you."

All three men cursed and whirled around, their eyes big with surprise.

Each man held a rifle. As the barrels came up, Preacher's hands dipped to the Colts and came up with the big revolvers bucking and spouting flame.

He could have drawn the Colts and gunned down the

three killers before they knew what was going on, but that wasn't the sort of man he was. He didn't mind shooting a varmint in the back when it was necessary and had never lost a second's sleep after doing so, but he preferred to give a man an even break when he could, even lowdown ones like these.

His first two shots smashed into Gabe's chest and knocked him backward out of the way, making the other two clear targets. Preacher fired the left-hand Colt and drilled one of the men, who spun off his feet from the impact.

The third man actually got a shot off, but he hurried and the rifle ball hummed well wide of Preacher. The mountain man's right-hand Colt blasted again and the last man rocked backward as the shot tore through his throat. Bright crimson blood fountained from the wound. He dropped the rifle and fell, landing with his arms stretched out to the sides.

The second man had gone to a knee and dropped his rifle, as well. He pressed his left hand to his chest where Preacher had shot him. His right fumbled at the pistol stuck in the waistband of his trousers. He jerked it loose and raised it.

His hand was shaking so much that the barrel danced around, and he probably couldn't have hit anything even if he managed to pull the trigger.

Preacher didn't give him the chance to try. He shot the man in the head instead. The man flopped backward, landing in the spray of blood, brain matter, and bone fragments that exploded out the back of his head along with the round from Preacher's Colt.

Gabe was still writhing around a little, so he wasn't dead yet. Preacher kept him covered as he approached, even though Gabe wasn't making any attempt to reach the rifle he had dropped. A lot of men had died from making the mistake of thinking a fight was over too soon. Preacher didn't intend to be one of them.

As he loomed over Gabe, he nudged the man's rifle even farther away with his foot and then said, "What's your name, mister? I know the Gabe part. What goes with it?"

Preacher's voice broke through the haze of agony that must have been clouding the wounded man's brain. His head jerked a little toward the sound. It took his eyes a couple of attempts before he was able to focus on Preacher.

Realizing who stood over him prompted some cussing. Preacher let it continue for a moment, then said, "You're wastin' what little breath you got left, mister. Forget tellin' me your name. Tell me who you work for."

"You . . . you can go . . . straight to hell, you . . ."

The weak voice trailed off into more curses.

"You'll be in hell first," Preacher told him, "and so will your boss, Decker Galloway. When he gets there, he'll probably want to know how come you didn't kill me like you were supposed to."

The flash of surprise in the man's eyes was enough confirmation for Preacher. It had been remotely possible that the man had some other reason for wanting him dead, but Galloway was the simplest answer and Preacher remembered Audie telling him about something called Occam's Razor that said the simplest answer was usually the best. Preacher never had been able to figure out what it had to do with shaving.

Gabe had time to look surprised by Preacher's mention of Decker Galloway, and then the life faded from his eyes.

He was dead, just like the other two, and now it was time for Preacher to find out if any of his companions had survived the avalanche.

He had just pouched the two irons when he heard someone call urgently, "Preacher!"

CHAPTER 15

Turning quickly, Preacher spotted Tall Dog weaving around the boulders in the trail, stepping over the ones that were small enough for that. He had Betsy in his arms, holding her with his left arm under her knees, his right arm around her shoulders. Her arms, legs, and head all hung loosely.

Preacher hoped she was just knocked out, not dead. Tall Dog appeared to be all right, just upset. As fast and spry as he was moving, he couldn't be badly injured.

Preacher hurried to meet them. He waved a hand toward an open spot at the edge of the trail and said, "Lay her down over there. How bad is it?"

"I don't know," Tall Dog replied as he carefully lowered Betsy to the ground. "Her head is bloody."

Preacher knelt beside her and said, "She's alive, though. Her heart's beatin'. You can tell because the blood's still comin' from that scratch. Looks like one of those flyin' rocks walloped her." With his fingertips, he probed gently around the wound on Betsy's forehead. "Don't feel like her skull's busted. I'd say she just got knocked cold. She'll probably wake up with a headache but be all right other than that."

Tall Dog still looked worried. "There is so much blood."

"Head wounds generally make folks bleed like stuck pigs," Preacher told him. "You ought to know that, as many fights as you've been in."

Tall Dog nodded slowly and said, "I suppose you are right. But somehow this seems worse."

"That's because you're sweet on the person doin' the bleedin'."

"What?" Tall Dog seemed to be trying to feign surprise but not doing a very good job of it. "I am not sweet on—"

"Don't waste your breath denyin' it. The rest of us got eyes, you know."

Beside him, Betsy stirred a little and let out a low, breathy moan.

Tall Dog instantly knelt on her other side. Preacher straightened to his feet and told the young warrior, "You tend to her. I'm gonna have a look around. I don't reckon you saw any sign of Audie or Nighthawk?"

"No," Tall Dog replied as he gingerly lifted Betsy's head and pillowed it in his lap. He glanced along the trail at the sprawled bodies. "Those are the men who started the rockslide?"

"Yeah. They won't give us any more trouble."

"Good," Tall Dog said with a grim note of satisfaction in his voice.

Preacher started back along the trail, going around the piles of rock when he could, clambering over those he couldn't. The avalanche's path was about fifty yards wide. As he neared the other side of it, he called, "Audie! Nighthawk! You boys back here somewhere?"

"Umm!"

The familiar deep voice of the giant Crow made Preacher hurry even more. He spotted Nighthawk's head sticking up above a slab of fallen rock and moved around it quickly to see the warrior kneeling beside Audie, who was stretched out on the ground.

"I tell you, I'm all right, Nighthawk," Audie said as he started to sit up.

Nighthawk planted a massive hand in the middle of his chest and held him down. "Umm!"

"Very well, I'll rest, but I tell you, it's not necessary. I'm a bit shaken up, of course, but otherwise unharmed."

Preacher said, "I see the two of you made it through all right."

"Thanks to Nighthawk. He grabbed me and leaped into the ravine. It was rather a rough landing, of course, but the vegetation broke our fall enough so that no real damage was done. You appear to be equally unharmed, Preacher, so I assume you followed that same tactic."

"Yeah. Wasn't time to do anything else but jump and pray."

"What about Tall Dog and Miss Kingsley?"

"They're all right. The gal got a knock on the head from one of those flyin' rocks but don't appear to be hurt bad. Tall Dog's lookin' after her." Preacher realized the horse that had been making noise earlier had fallen silent, probably because it had died from its injuries. Despite his relief that all of his human companions had survived, practical matters had to be faced. "Did any of the horses get away?"

"I don't know," Audie said. "We started them running back along the trail just before we leaped. That was the only chance they had. I'm sure they didn't all make it, but a few might have."

"If you're all right, I'll go see what I can find."

"I'm fine, as I continue trying to convince this gigantic nursemaid here."

"Umm," Nighthawk said.

"Preacher . . ." Audie's voice stopped the mountain man as Preacher started to turn away.

"Yeah?"

"That avalanche was no accident, was it? This was another attempt on our lives?"

"No, it weren't no accident. I'm certain of that."

"What about the men who started it?"

Preacher told him the same thing he'd told Tall Dog. "They won't trouble us no more."

"Good," Audie said fervently. He added, "I don't suppose you were able to interrogate any of them."

"I talked to one fella enough before he crossed the divide to know that Galloway's the one who sent 'em after us. Seems like he's afraid somebody's gonna come along and interfere with his plans for that village where Tall Dog's grandpa and them other Vikings live."

"We are going to interfere, aren't we?"

"We're gonna interfere up one way and down the other," Preacher promised as his eyes narrowed in anger and determination.

By the time another hour had passed, Preacher had taken stock of the situation. All the saddle horses had escaped the avalanche except for one of the spare mounts that had been caught in the falling rocks.

Dog had also made it out of the disaster's path. Preacher had felt a huge surge of relief when Horse had come in response to his whistle and the big cur was loping alongside the gray stallion. He and his trail partners had been together for a long time.

Skidbladnir and Betsy's mount had followed along behind Horse and Dog, and Preacher was glad to see them, too.

All three pack horses were dead, swept into the ravine by the avalanche. Preacher salvaged as many of the supplies as he could, assisted by Nighthawk once the giant Crow was convinced that Audie was all right and didn't need to be watched over constantly.

A couple of the spare saddle horses could be pressed into service as pack animals. The supplies they had lost would be missed, but Preacher, Tall Dog, Audie, and Nighthawk were all accustomed to living off the land anyway, so they would be fine. Betsy might miss some of what passed for luxuries out here on the frontier, like sugar and salt, but she would survive.

Betsy was awake and, as Preacher had predicted, had quite a headache. Tall Dog had soaked a cloth in a nearby stream and used it to clean most of the blood from the gash on her forehead, then bound the cool, wet rag around her head. That helped some with the pain.

"I'm going to have a terrible scar," she complained as she sat on one of the rocks and held a hand to her head. "I'll be ugly."

"A scar will not make you ugly," Tall Dog assured her. "Nothing could do that, but certainly not a scar. Such marks are signs that we have survived troubles, and we should look upon them with pride and honor. My body is covered with scars. You should see them."

Then he blushed fiercely as he realized the implications of what he had said. His reaction was enough to bring a slight smile back to Betsy's face, at least.

Nighthawk dragged the three corpses to the edge of the trail and tossed them into the ravine. Preacher nodded in approval and said, "I heard one of 'em mention their horses. Reckon we ought to find them, since those old boys don't need 'em anymore, and take 'em to replace the ones we lost."

Audie, who was also looking on, nodded in agreement. "That's an excellent idea, Preacher. If they have any supplies, we'll take those as well. Under the circumstances, I think we'll be well within our rights to do so. We're going to be back almost to full strength. Their trap didn't work out so well for them."

"The varmints sure got what they had comin'," Preacher said.

It took time to move the horses that had wound up behind the avalanche's path through the obstacle formed by the fallen rocks. They had to lead the animals through one at a time and move some of the fallen rocks to make the path wider. With everything that had happened, it was late in the day before the group got started moving again.

No one wanted to make camp here, though. They wanted to put the scene of this attempt on their lives behind them, even Betsy, who rode without complaint even though her head hurt and she had to be bruised and sore all over.

All of them would stiffen up by the next morning, Preacher knew. There might be plenty of moaning and groaning going on as they moved around . . .

But at least they would still be alive to moan and groan. That was more than ol' Gabe and his two cronies could say.

Preacher didn't know if anyone else was left to try to stop them from reaching Skarkavik. It seemed unlikely, yet he wasn't ready to rule out the possibility. Because of that, he remained watchful as they continued working their way north toward the great lake where the village was located.

Fortune favored them during this last leg of the journey. They didn't run into any more trouble as another week passed on the trail. The bruises and the sore muscles healed, and a scab formed on the cut on Betsy's forehead so that she didn't have to keep it bandaged. It was going to leave a scar, as she had feared, but not a big one, Preacher thought.

Then, at midday of another bright, clear day, they rode out of some trees and stopped short at the breathtaking sight before them. A few yards away, a rocky bluff dropped down a short distance to water of a deep blue shade that stretched away into the distance as far as they could see. The wooded shoreline curved gradually away from them in both directions.

This appeared to be the southern end of the lake, because thickly wooded banks were visible to east and west, although they lay a good distance away. The lake was several miles wide here, and Preacher could tell that it widened more by the way the eastern and western banks fell away until they couldn't be seen anymore.

According to Axel Gunnarson, Tall Dog's grandfather, it took more than a day to row a boat from one side to the other at the lake's widest point, and several days to go from the south end to the north end. Preacher could believe that now as he gazed out over the vast sweep of water.

He nudged Horse forward and rode to the edge of the bluff. A dozen feet below, gentle waves washed up on a narrow, rocky beach.

Tall Dog, Betsy, Audie, and Nighthawk joined him. Each of them wore the same sort of awed expression that Preacher did.

"It's as if we've come to a vast ocean," Audie said.

"Umm," Nighthawk added.

"Indeed. It does look almost like the Pacific along the western coast of this continent. And yet, of course, we know logically that this lake is nowhere near that large. It's even considerably smaller than the so-called Great Lakes southeast of here."

"Yeah, but from where we're sittin', it's mighty big," Preacher said. He turned to Tall Dog. "Where's your grandpa's village from here?"

"According to his letter, three days' ride up the eastern side of the lake."

"We'd best get started then, since we've still got a ways to go."

Audie gestured at the water and said, "You don't want to take in this magnificent view for a few moments longer?"

"I don't reckon there'll be any shortage of pretty scenery where we're goin'."

"Yes, Grandfather said that the country here is as beautiful as our homeland," Tall Dog said. "Of course, Norway isn't actually my home. The Rocky Mountains are. Still, I seem to feel something drawing me to it, even though I have never set eyes on it and probably never will."

"You feel an atavistic, ancestral connection to the land your father's people came from," Audie told him. "It's something you were born with, a part of you that will always be there. That's true of everyone. Our past is inescapable and a part of it stays with us forever whether we want it to or not, echoing down through the centuries."

Betsy said, "All I know is, I've never seen any place as pretty as this one."

"We can appreciate it while we're on the move," Preacher said as he lifted Horse's reins and turned the big stallion to follow the shoreline to the east.

The land around the lake was fairly flat and made for easy traveling except in the places where the trees grew right down to the edge and were too close together for the horses to get through them. When Preacher and his companions came to one of those barriers, they had to ride away from the water until they reached a spot where they could turn north again and circle around the dense forest.

"Is there no end to these trees?" Tall Dog asked during one such detour.

"You can see why that fella Galloway wants to start cuttin' 'em down and turnin' 'em into lumber," Preacher said. "Just to look at 'em, you'd think he could fell trees for the next hundred years and never make even a little dent in 'em."

"But we know that's not the case," Audie said. "Every natural resource is finite, and once man's greed comes into play, that end is usually much closer than we realize. With proper management, these forests could last forever. But that would require Galloway not making quite as much money, quite as quickly."

The little man shook his head and went on, "Too many men aren't willing to compromise even that much of their ambition. Judging by the fact that he was willing to send killers after us, I very much doubt that Decker Galloway cares about anything other than money."

"He's fixin' to find out just how wrong he is," Preacher said.

Keeping the lake to their left, they made steady progress up the eastern shore that afternoon. The western shore receded into the distance as the lake widened, and by the time they stopped to make camp that evening, it was no longer visible. The lake really did look like an endless ocean now.

As they continued up the lake the next day, the western shore reappeared and gradually came closer the farther north they went.

Preacher pointed that out and said, "Looks like we're gettin' to the north end. Either this lake's a lot smaller than we thought it was, or else we're in the wrong place."

"Perhaps," Tall Dog said, shaking his head with a worried frown on his face. "I thought we had followed my grandfather's directions correctly. But I suppose all we can do is keep going the way we are."

They did so, and by nightfall, Preacher realized that while the lake narrowed quite a bit through this stretch, it wasn't ending at all. In fact, it had already begun to get wider again by the time they made camp.

"We're still going the right way," Tall Dog said with relief in his voice. "We should reach Skarkavik sometime the day after tomorrow."

"We'd best start keepin' our eyes open for Galloway's men," Preacher advised. "There ain't no tellin' where we might run into them around here."

They hadn't seen anyone else since the avalanche, although Preacher had felt eyes watching them from time to time. He checked with Tall Dog, Audie, and Nighthawk and found that they had experienced the same sensation.

All of them were in agreement that the watchers were most likely Indians who lived in the areas through which they were passing. Those watchers had stayed out of sight, not wanting a confrontation, and were content to know that the group of strangers was moving on.

After making camp another time, Preacher expected to reach the village by the middle of the next day, if Axel Gunnarson's letter was correct.

After a peaceful night, while they were eating breakfast before sun-up the next morning, the mountain man swallowed some hot, strong coffee and said, "We've been pushin' pretty hard for a long time now. Why don't the rest of you wait a spell before you ride out this mornin'? That'll give the horses a chance to rest a mite longer."

And Betsy, too, although he didn't say that because he knew she would argue if he did and claim that she didn't need any extra rest. She always wanted to carry her share of the load, without any special treatment.

Tall Dog had noticed the way Preacher phrased the suggestion. He said, "What will you be doing if we wait to depart?"

"Figured that'd give me a chance to scout out ahead some."

"I could come with you—"

Preacher knew that Tall Dog didn't really want to leave Betsy, so he interrupted, "No, I'd rather you stayed here. I ain't had a chance to get out on my own for a long time now. I like all you people, but I'm a solitary sort of cuss by nature. Y'all just take it easy, and I'll be back in a spell."

"A most gracious offer, indeed," Audie said. "We'll take you up on it, won't we, Nighthawk?"

"Umm."

As the sky lightened more, Preacher saddled Horse and swung up onto the stallion's back. He rode with his rifle across the saddle in front of him and the keeper thongs undone on the Colts.

Everything he'd said back there was true, he reflected as he moved out of sight of the camp. The horses would benefit from some extra rest, and so would the humans.

But now that he was riding alone, he realized just how much he actually had missed that solitude. In the past, he had spent weeks or even months at a time in the mountains, just him and Horse and Dog, and had been perfectly fine with that.

Audie and Nighthawk were his best two-legged friends in the world, and Tall Dog wasn't far from joining that circle. But Preacher was his own best company.

As he rode, he mulled over the circumstances that had brought them here to the north country. Maybe the problem with Decker Galloway had been resolved and when they reached Skarkavik, they would find that everything was peaceful in the village again. In that case, Tall Dog could enjoy a visit with his grandfather and see what the Viking side of his heritage was like.

Yeah, maybe, Preacher thought . . . but he wouldn't have bet a hat on things turning out peaceful. They never did.

He was riding alongside the lake with the trees close at hand on the right and the water to the left. The sun was edging above the tops of the spruce and pine, casting orange light out across the lake, which was so tranquil it looked like glass at this time of day.

Up ahead, several large trees had fallen at some time in the past, forming a barrier. When the others got here, there might be room to lead the horses around the end of the deadfall, Preacher thought as he slowed the stallion, but they'd need to be careful doing so and would have to take it one animal at a time.

Padding along beside him, Dog growled. Preacher glanced down and saw that Dog's hackles had risen again.

Preacher was about to tell the big cur to hunt so that Dog could flush out whatever had him on edge, when that became unnecessary.

A scrawny figure in a long leather coat and some sort of funny-looking metal hat jumped up from behind the deadfall to stand on top of one of the logs. The sunlight reflected from the blade of the sword he thrust into the air above his head as he cried out in a language that didn't make a lick of sense to Preacher, even though something about it seemed vaguely familiar.

But as he heard the answering cries from the trees, he knew he didn't have to understand the words to realize that he might be in a heap of trouble.

CHAPTER 16

The fella standing on the log didn't attack. He seemed content to stay where he was, waving that sword around and yelling at the top of his lungs.

Half a dozen men ran out of the trees and formed a half-circle around Preacher so that he was pinned against the lake. He turned Horse so that he was facing them and let the rifle barrel drift in their direction. Some had swords, while others brandished odd-looking axes with short handles that had strips of leather wrapped around them. He didn't see any guns among the men.

"Dog, stay," he told the big cur quietly but firmly. He didn't want Dog starting a ruckus until he knew for sure what was going on here.

Dog obeyed the command, but he stood tense and ready to spring. Deep growls still rumbled in his throat.

As the men closed in slowly around him, Preacher took a better look at them. Some wore buckskins, while the others had on leather trousers and tunics or long coats like the man standing on the deadfall. A couple sported metal hats while the others were bareheaded. All of them had beards down to their chests and long hair. Some wore it hanging loose, others had twisted and knotted it into braids. Most were fair-haired while one man had red hair and another brown.

Preacher relaxed slightly. He had a pretty good hunch that he was looking at some of Axel Gunnarson's people.

He could make himself understood in just about any Indian language, but he didn't speak a word of that Scandihoovian lingo. If the fella on the log ever ran out of breath and stopped yelling, Preacher figured he would ask for Axel Gunnarson, explain that he was a friend of Bjorn Gunnarson, and hope that at least one of these wild-looking varmints understood English.

He didn't get a chance to do that because just then the man on the deadfall pointed the sword at him and yelled something that sounded like a command.

A particularly big member of the group shouted back and charged Preacher as he whirled the axe he held over his head. He had one of those metal hats crammed on his blond head, which looked really strange considering that he also wore buckskins much like Preacher's garb.

Preacher could have shot him, of course, but he still hoped to be friends with this bunch and blowing a hole through one of them likely would ruin any chances of that.

So instead he kicked his feet free of the stirrups, swung a leg over Horse's back, and dropped to the ground. As his boots hit the grass, he tossed the rifle aside, yanked his tomahawk from behind his belt, and yelled right back in the attacker's face.

That took the varmint by surprise and made him hesitate for a second. That was long enough for Preacher to get himself set. As the man swung the axe at him, Preacher blocked it with the tomahawk. The weapons came together with a jolting impact that shivered all the way up Preacher's arm to the shoulder.

Tomahawk and axe locked together as the two men

strained against each other, strength versus strength. Then the attacker's right foot suddenly shot out and tried to hook behind Preacher's left knee. Preacher twisted to avoid the move, and while the man was slightly off-balance, Preacher struck with his left fist, hammering it into the man's ribs. As the man grimaced and bent to his right from the blow, Preacher slid his tomahawk free of its tie-up with the axe and slammed the flat of it against that metal hat.

The resounding *clang!* rang out loud and clear. Preacher could have slashed the tomahawk's keen edge across the man's throat just then and opened it up, but he refrained. He threw another punch with his left, hooking that fist against the bearded jaw with enough power behind it to knock the man off his feet. While he was still stunned, Preacher stepped on his right wrist, bent down, and tore the axe out of his grip.

When Preacher stepped back to face the others, he had the tomahawk in his right hand, the leather-wrapped handle of the axe in his left.

The others were just watching him with surprised looks on their faces. Evidently, they had expected the man with the axe to cut him into little pieces.

Now that he had demonstrated his prowess, they might decide it was best to rush him all at once.

From the looks of the way they hesitated, their pride wouldn't allow them to do that. The one on the deadfall yelled some more. He was so mad he jumped up and down on the log as he frantically waved the sword in the air.

If he wasn't careful, the crazy little varmint might fall off and run himself through.

The biggest of the others advanced slowly toward Preacher. He appeared to be the oldest, too. A few gray streaks were visible in his long brown beard. He wore no helmet. His long hair was pulled back into a single thick braid. He had a furry vest made from what looked like bear hide over his buckskin shirt.

The sword he carried had such a long, heavy blade that he had to grip the handle with both hands. As he came closer, Preacher saw that an assortment of different shapes were carved into the blade, giving the metal an ornate, decorative look.

There was nothing decorative about its edges, though. Preacher figured they were razor-sharp and could cut through flesh and bone like butter.

Since the fellow was advancing steadily toward Preacher but not getting in any real hurry to launch an attack, the mountain man took advantage of the opportunity to speak up.

"I'm lookin' for Axel Gunnarson," he said. "I'm a friend of his grandson Bjorn."

That made the big man facing him frown. He might not understand English, but he was bound to recognize the names Preacher had thrown out there.

Before Preacher could say anything else, the man on the log screamed, jumped up and down some more, and cried, "Galloway! Galloway! Galloway!"

The others knew that name, right enough. All of them snarled, and the one closest to Preacher spat some furious-sounding words, whirled that big sword up, and sprang toward him with a grimace distorting the heavily bearded face.

Preacher crossed the tomahawk and the axe into an X shape to catch the blade as it swept down toward him. That kept the sword from splitting his skull, but the blow's impact knocked him back a step. He tried to recover as the man swiped the sword at him with more speed and agility than seemed possible from someone wielding such a long, heavy weapon.

Since Preacher was falling backward anyway, he let himself go and rolled into a somersault that brought him up on his feet again. He spotted the sword coming at him and batted it aside with a swing of the axe.

While he had that split-second opening, he leaped in and struck with the tomahawk, once more using the flat of the head. It smashed against the attacker's left shoulder.

Even though Preacher's opponent was taller and heavier than the mountain man, he felt the tremendous power Preacher packed into that blow. He grunted, grimaced, and lurched back. His left arm sagged, probably because it had gone numb from his shoulder being hit like that.

The sword was more awkward to use one-handed. The man slashed wildly at Preacher with it anyway, but Preacher darted aside, avoiding the swing with relative ease. He took a quick step that brought him just past his attacker and rammed his right elbow into the small of the man's back.

The man didn't go down. He arched his back and yelled in pain but stayed upright and swung the sword at Preacher again in a roundhouse swipe. Preacher had to dive under it. Since he was down that low anyway, he threw himself against the man's knees.

That finally brought him down. As the man rolled onto his back, Preacher sprang on top of him and pressed the axe under the beard and against his throat.

"Best settle down, friend," Preacher told him. "It wouldn't take much pressure to open up that throat of yours."

Preacher didn't expect the man to understand what he'd said, but the fella surprised him by looking up and grating in English, "Arne Winterborn does not surrender! Do your worst, vile minion of the evil Galloway! Cut off the head of Arne Winterborn if you dare!" The man's mouth twisted into a snarl in the middle of the bushy beard. "It will come to you in the dark of the night and chew your throat until its mouth fills with your hot blood!"

Preacher stared at him for a moment, then couldn't help but burst out laughing. That just seemed to make the man even more angry.

"My friend Audie's gonna love you," Preacher said.

He took the axe away from the man's throat and stood up. He backed away a couple of steps and tossed the axe onto the ground next to Arne Winterborn, if that was the fella's name.

"I know you understand what I'm sayin', so listen to me. I don't work for Decker Galloway. I know who the damn varmint is, but we ain't friends. He's my enemy, even if I ain't ever laid eyes on him. I came to help the people of Skarkavik, and I'm assumin' that's you."

The other men muttered among themselves in their language. The first man who had charged Preacher, the one he had taken the axe from, had gotten back to his feet and rejoined them. He cast a sullen glare toward the mountain man and gestured emphatically as he spoke. He seemed to be trying to convince the others to attack all at the same time.

Arne Winterborn sat up, reached under his beard, and brought his hand out with a few drops of blood staining his thick, strong fingers.

"Could've been a whole heap more of that red stuff spilled out if I'd pushed a little harder with the axe," Preacher told him. "I just nicked you so's you'd know I meant business."

"Aye, Arne Winterborn knows how close he was to death. Close enough to spit in its face! You may be sorry you did not kill Arne Winterborn when you had the chance."

"I doubt that, because like I keep tryin' to tell you, I

want to be your friend, you big, stubborn galoot! Where's Axel Gunnarson?" Preacher nodded toward the scrawny man still standing on the log. "That ain't him, is it?"

"That one?" Arne Winterborn laughed. "Odgar Haugstad? Who could mistake Odgar Haugstad for the leader of our people?"

"Remember, I just got here. I don't know anybody in these parts. I only know about Axel Gunnarson because I'm friends with his grandson Bjorn, also called Tall Dog back where we come from."

Arne Winterborn extended a hand. "You knocked me down, you can help me up," he said.

Preacher was willing to do that, especially since the fella had stopped calling himself by name, at least for the moment. Before reaching out to clasp Arne's hand, though, he said, "You try to trick me and pull me down and I'll slap this tomahawk alongside your head."

"Trick?" Arne bellowed, evidently offended again. "You think I am Loki, the trickster?"

"No, I reckon you're Arne Winterborn, the way you kept spoutin' that name. Folks call me Preacher, and I'm glad to meet you . . . I think."

"Arne Winterborn is no trickster."

"There you go again with that funny way of talkin'. Does everybody up here speechify like that?"

"Like what? What is this . . . speechify?"

"Never mind," Preacher said as he took hold of Arne's wrist. He heaved, and the big man came up on his feet.

The fella on the deadfall—Odgar Haugstad, Arne had called him—started yelling and hopping around again like a crazed rooster.

"Does he do that all the time?" Preacher asked.

"What Odgar lacks in stature, he makes up for in volume and enthusiasm. Or at least he tries to. He is the record-keeper and tale teller of our people. He assists Axel, so we try to go along with what he wants."

Even though Arne Winterborn had been trying to kill Preacher a few short minutes earlier, the mountain man couldn't help but feel an instinctive liking for the grizzled old cuss. Good humor lurked in the man's blue eyes.

"You mean he's sorta puffed up with his own impor-tance and feels like he can boss the rest of you around."

Arne shrugged. "As I said, we try to accommodate him . . . and he did order us to kill you because you are one of Galloway's men."

"Only I ain't one of Galloway's men. We're here to help you and your people deal with that problem, in fact. Axel Gunnarson wrote to his grandson askin' him to come up here and lend a hand. Tall Dog brought a few friends along with him."

"This Tall Dog you speak of . . . you say he is Bjorn Gunnarson?"

"That's right."

"Where is he?"

"Right here," Tall Dog called as he stepped out of the woods behind the other men from Skarkavik. He had an arrow nocked on his bowstring and was ready to draw and fire. Audie and Nighthawk emerged from the trees, too, and leveled rifles at the villagers.

More screeching came from Odgar Haugstad, who could see the newcomers plainly from the deadfall. The other men, having heard Tall Dog's voice, looked around quickly and nervously to see that Preacher's friends had the drop on them.

"Thought you fellas were gonna wait back along the trail until I rejoined you," Preacher drawled.

"Did you really believe that would happen?" Audie asked. He looked at the men with their mixture of Viking and frontier garb and their distinctive weapons and added, "This is amazing. It's almost like we stepped right into the pages of one of the eddas."

Tall Dog spoke up again, this time in what Preacher recognized as Norse, the language of his father . . . and his father's people. These men seemed to understand what he was saying.

Preacher didn't savvy much of it, but he heard the names Bjorn Gunnarson, Olaf, Axel, and Rolf Pedersen. He was sure Tall Dog was explaining his relationship to the patriarch of this group and also mentioning the letter his grandfather had sent by way of Rolf Pedersen. All that certainly seemed like enough to establish their bona fides.

Whether these latter-day Vikings would accept the explanation or not, Preacher didn't know.

Odgar Haugstad didn't seem inclined to. He pointed a bony finger at Tall Dog, bounced up and down on his toes, and yelled another bunch of what might as well have been nonsense words to Preacher.

But then Arne Winterborn let out a loud and explosive "Bah!" and lifted his sword. His left arm had started working again, Preacher noted.

Instead of attacking, Arne turned the sword and slid the blade into a leather scabbard that was hung from rawhide thongs on his back. He strode toward Tall Dog, extended his hand, and said something in their tongue.

Tall Dog lowered the bow, unnocked the arrow, and slipped it back into the quiver that hung behind his head. He put the bowstring over his shoulder.

Then he took Arne's hand, and the two of them embraced

in a rough hug that culminated in such heavy pounding on the back by both of them that it was a wonder they were able to stay on their feet.

Tall Dog turned toward Audie and Nighthawk and introduced them. Arne stared at Audie and exclaimed in English, "Never have I seen such a little man! Or are you a boy?"

"I'm a fully grown man," Audie replied coolly.

"So I thought by the silver in your beard and hair. All-Father Odin may not have blessed you with height, but Arne Winterborn recognizes a fellow warrior when he sees one!" He held out his hand. "It is my honor to meet you."

"And mine to meet you," Audie replied as he shook with the man towering over him. Arne's ham-like paw enveloped Audie's hand.

Tall Dog said, "Audie is the smartest man I know. He can talk for hours about many things and knows something about everything under the sun."

"You mentioned the eddas," Arne said. "You have read them?"

"I've studied them in translation, as well as some of the original versions," Audie said. "And the sagas, also."

"We must discuss them when there is an opportunity." Arne turned to Nighthawk, who was even taller than he was—but not by much. "All-Father Odin must have carved you from a mountain!"

"Umm," Nighthawk said.

"Aye!" Arne responded without waiting for a translation from Audie. Perhaps he didn't need one.

They clasped hands, embraced, and again big hands pounded on backs with tremendous force.

Over on the log, Odgar Haugstad was quivering with what appeared to be rage, but he had ceased his magpie screeching as if realizing that it wasn't doing any good.

When Arne waved his friends over and started to introduce them to Tall Dog, Audie, and Nighthawk, Odgar jumped down from the deadfall and raced into the woods, heading farther north along the lakeshore.

Preacher figured the little fella was taking word of their arrival to the rest of Skarkavik's people. That was all right. Now that they had won over Arne Winterborn and appeared to be in the process of doing so with the others, Preacher wasn't worried that the rest of the villagers would attack them when they showed up.

He picked up his rifle and walked over to join Audie and Nighthawk, who were standing slightly to one side as the others clustered around Tall Dog and talked to him in Norse. Quietly, Preacher asked Audie, "You have any idea what all that palaverin' is about?"

Audie shook his head. "I have a smattering of Old Norse, which seems to be the dialect they're using. I can read it fairly well, given time to work on a translation, but understanding it in speech is totally different. They're going much too fast for me, although I can catch a word here and there."

"They've decided to be friendly, though?"

"That appears to be the case. Except for the little fellow who ran off as if his trousers were on fire."

It sounded slightly odd for Audie to refer to someone else as little, but the former professor had a point. Odgar Haugstad was taller than Audie, but he was so scrawny he might not weigh much more, if at all.

"How long did you wait before you followed me?" Preacher asked.

"A while." Audie shrugged. "Long enough for the horses to rest a bit more, as you suggested. But Tall Dog ran out of patience fairly quickly. He knew we might be getting close to our destination, and he's eager to meet his grandfather."

"Umm," Nighthawk put in.

"Yes, and he didn't want to miss out on any excitement if you happened to run into trouble, that is correct. Which, of course, is exactly what happened. I have to admit, Nighthawk and I felt the same way. He hates to miss out on a fight, and I'm very intrigued by the prospect of learning more about Viking culture first-hand. Although it appears these gentlemen have adopted some of the customs of the frontier, as well, instead of maintaining their homeland's traditions unaltered. It's a strange amalgamation, the likes of which may not be found anywhere else."

"Yeah, from the looks of it, they're sort of half mountain man, half Viking." Preacher changed the subject by asking, "Where's Betsy?"

"In the woods with the horses, perhaps a hundred yards from here."

"You left her alone?"

"We heard the commotion," Audie explained, "and not knowing how much trouble you might be in, we decided to investigate in force. It was possible that all three of us might have been required to extricate you from your predicament."

Preacher grunted. "I was doin' just fine . . . not that I wasn't happy to see you boys show up when you did. I was makin' progress with ol' Arne Winterborn there. It helped a heap when it turned out he savvys English."

"I really look forward to talking with him. For now, however, we'd best fetch Miss Kingsley and the horses. Come along, Nighthawk—"

Then they heard the sharp crack of a gunshot.

CHAPTER 17

Tall Dog reacted instantly. He broke off the conversation he was having with Arne Winterborn and the other men from Skarkavik and dashed toward the trees. As he entered the woods, he grabbed the rifle he had leaned up against the trunk of a spruce when he, Audie, and Nighthawk had arrived on the scene.

Preacher and Nighthawk weren't far behind the young warrior. Whatever was going on, they wouldn't let Tall Dog face it by himself. Dog bounded along beside them, weaving around the trunks, bursting through gaps in the undergrowth, and gradually gaining ground on them.

Because of that, the big cur reached the scene of the trouble first. Preacher heard growling and snarling ahead of them, followed by angry shouts. Concern for Dog made him move even faster, risking a bash on the head from a low-hanging branch.

He burst out into a clearing just a couple of steps behind Tall Dog. Nighthawk, who hadn't been able to get through the dense growth as quickly because of his massive size, was a few steps behind Preacher. But the giant Crow emerged only a couple of heartbeats after the mountain man did.

Preacher came to an abrupt halt gripping his rifle, ready

to fire if he needed to. Tall Dog was a step to his left, and Nighthawk loomed up on his right.

The clearing was about twenty feet wide and fifty long. On its far side, to the right, Horse, Skidbladnir, and the other horses stood. Horse and Skidbladnir, along with Audie and Nighthawk's mounts, were accustomed to trouble and didn't move, but the other animals were a bit skittish from the sound of the shot and the smell of powder smoke.

Directly in front of Preacher and his companions, Dog crouched, ready to spring. Facing him was a man with blood on the leather leggings he wore, probably where Dog had clamped his jaws a few moments earlier. The man clutched at the wound with one hand, waved one of those short axes in the other hand, and yelled what were probably Norse curses at Dog.

Beyond them were half a dozen more men, all dressed in the same mixture of frontier and Viking garb that marked the men of Skarkavik. One of them was a tall, brawny man with white hair and a long beard worked into a pair of braids. He wore a leather vest that left his powerful chest and muscular arms bare except for brass rings with symbols engraved on them that encircled both upper arms.

Just below the ring on his right arm was a bloody streak where something had gashed the flesh. The wound didn't keep him from holding a short-bladed sword in his right hand. He pressed the weapon to Betsy's throat as he kept his left arm clamped tightly around her waist.

The man shouted something in Norse. From the corner of his mouth, Tall Dog said quietly, "He orders us to stay back, or the girl will die."

Preacher spotted Odgar Haugstad among the other men.

He said, "You reckon that big white-haired fella is your grandpa?"

"He might be," Tall Dog allowed. "I have never seen him before. I will find out. But first . . ."

He yelled something angry-sounding.

"What'd you tell him?" Preacher asked.

"I asked him if he is the sort of man who makes war on women. I told him that Betsy is no shield-maiden and is not a suitable opponent for a true man."

The white-haired man shouted back at Tall Dog.

Audie had reached the clearing by now, having hustled after the others as quickly as his short legs would carry him. He said, "It seems that these people prefer to negotiate at the top of their lungs."

"They're an enthusiastic bunch, all right," Preacher agreed.

Some loud crackling in the brush made him glance over his shoulder. Arne Winterborn and the rest of the original bunch were pushing into the clearing, as well. The place was getting a mite crowded.

And he and his friends were caught right between those forces, Preacher realized.

Tall Dog and the white-haired man were still glaring at each other. Arne Winterborn strode forward and waved his arms as he spoke up. He pointed at Tall Dog and said, "Bjorn!"

The white-haired man leaned back a little as his eyes widened. "Bjorn?" he repeated.

Tall Dog answered in Norse. Preacher heard the names Bjorn and Olaf. The white-haired man let go of Betsy. She dashed across the intervening space, past Dog and the man the big cur had bitten earlier, and threw herself in Tall Dog's arms as he lowered his rifle.

Preacher, Audie, and Nighthawk kept their rifles trained

in the general direction of the group in front of them. If it was going to come to a fight, they would give a good account of themselves. With the Colts spitting fire in his hands, Preacher figured he could lay waste to quite a few of the varmints, if the situation got that dire.

But it might not, because now that he wasn't holding Betsy prisoner anymore, the white-haired man struck his bare chest with the hand holding the sword and declared loudly, "Axel Gunnarson!"

Betsy looked up at Tall Dog and said, "That's your grandfather? The man we've come all this way to find?"

"It would appear so," Tall Dog said.

"Oh, no! I . . . I'm so sorry. I shot him!"

Tall Dog glanced down at her in surprise. "You shot him?"

In English, Axel Gunnarson said, "It was my fault, grandson. I surprised the maiden and handled her roughly, thinking she might be a foe. She had a small pistol and fired it at me." He moved the arm that had the bloody crease on it. "Thank the gods she is not a very good shot, even at such close range."

Then he put back his head and bellowed in laughter.

"Well . . . well . . ." Betsy looked slightly offended. "Like he said, I was surprised. I mean, the way he grabbed me, I thought he must be one of Decker Galloway's men."

The mention of Galloway's name put an abrupt end to Axel Gunnarson's amusement. He spat some of those words that Preacher took to be Norse curses and then said, "I thought you might be a . . . how do you say it? . . . a woman who travels with Galloway's men?"

Betsy's face turned red. "I am not!" she said. "And I don't appreciate that you took me for one!"

"Everyone should stop arguing now," Arne Winterborn said. "We are all friends here. Bjorn and the others have come to help us, Axel." He shook his shaggy head. "They had no way of knowing that it is too late."

"Too late!" Tall Dog repeated. "What do you mean, it is too late?"

"Come back to camp with us," Gunnarson said. "We will talk there."

Preacher noticed that he mentioned returning to camp, not to the village of Skarkavik. That didn't bode well, the mountain man thought.

The man Dog was growling at said something in Norse. Preacher figured the man was asking for the big cur to be called off, so he said, "Dog, come."

Dog turned away from the man, but as he came over to Preacher, he looked back and gave the fella a disdainful look.

"Your dog's name is Dog?" Arne asked the mountain man.

"That's right."

"And he calls his horse Horse," Audie put in.

"Arne Winterborn likes it!" Arne said. "Simple and impossible to forget."

"That's what I've always figured," Preacher said dryly.

Arne jerked his head toward the north and said, "Come."

The whole bunch set off in that direction on foot, with Preacher and his companions leading their mounts and the pack animals. Preacher took note of the fact that some of the villagers were in front of them and some were behind, so his party was still effectively surrounded.

But the tension had eased and the atmosphere was friendlier now, with the exception of Odgar Haugstad and a few of the other men who still cast hostile, suspicious glances at Preacher and the others.

Obviously, some of Axel Gunnarson's people were mistrustful of outsiders, and probably with good reason.

Until he knew exactly what was going on, Preacher wasn't going to hold that attitude against them.

Gunnarson motioned for Tall Dog to fall in alongside him. Tall Dog hesitated, evidently unwilling to leave Betsy.

Audie said, "Go ahead, lad. Nighthawk and I will look after the young lady."

"Umm," Nighthawk agreed.

Preacher said to Tall Dog, "Your grandpa's more likely to tell you about what's goin' on around here. See what you can find out."

"Yes, that is a good idea," Tall Dog replied with a solemn nod. He lengthened his stride and caught up with his grandfather in the lead. The two of them immediately began talking in low tones. Preacher figured the conversation was in Old Norse, more than likely, so he wouldn't have understood any of it anyway.

He found himself walking next to Arne Winterborn. Giving in to curiosity, he asked, "Are you Axel Gunnarson's segundo?"

"Se . . . gun . . . do?" Arne shook his head. "Arne Winterborn is a very intelligent man and knows much English, but he does not know this word."

"Well, it ain't exactly an English word. It comes from Spanish. Means second in command."

"Ah! Arne Winterborn understands!" He turned his head and spat to the side. "That for the Spaniards! My ancestors raided their homelands, many years ago. But one thing I will say for them: They are not the Franks."

They strode on, following Gunnarson and Tall Dog as the party made its way through the woods along the eastern side of the lake. Arne continued, "To answer your question, Axel Gunnarson is our *jarl*. Our leader. Other than that, all men are equal. There is no . . . segundo." He thumped his chest with a closed fist. "But Arne Winterborn is known and respected far and wide as a mighty warrior."

"After our little tussle, I don't doubt it a bit."

"Why are you called Preacher?" Arne asked. "You look like no mewling priest Arne Winterborn has ever seen!"

"I ain't a real preacher," the mountain man replied. "Never claimed to be. My real name is Arthur, or Art, and that's how folks knew me when I first went west. But I kept tanglin' with a bunch of fellas called the Blackfeet—"

"Yes! I have heard of them. Fierce warriors, but cruel and ruthless."

"That's a good description of 'em," Preacher agreed. "After a while, them and me got to be mortal enemies, I reckon you'd say. So when they up and captured me one time, it looked mighty bad for me. They tied me to a post they set up in the ground, and when it got to be mornin' again, they planned to pile up wood around my feet and set it on fire."

"Like a funeral pyre! When a warrior of my people dies, his body is put on a boat and we launch it out into the water and set it on fire, so that the flames consume his remains and cleanse his soul and send it winging to Valhalla!"

"I can see doin' that," Preacher said, "but I wasn't dead at the time. They was gonna burn me alive, the varmints. I done everything I could to get loose, and I just couldn't. So I got to thinkin'."

Arne watched him intently, eager to hear the story.

"I thought back to a while earlier, when I'd been in St. Louis, a big town on the Mississippi River, and I'd seen a fella standin' on a street corner preachin'. He was lettin' loose with a real stemwinder, too, that just went on and on. The way he carried on, he seemed plumb crazy."

"Yes, yes, go on," Arne urged when Preacher stopped to take a breath.

"Thinkin' about that got me to recollectin' how Injuns feel about crazy folks. They believe anybody like that is touched by the spirits and is under their protection."

"The protection of the gods, you mean?"

"Yeah, I reckon that's what you'd call it. So I figured it'd be worth a try if I started preachin' my own self. I let loose with it, repeatin' everything I could remember that I'd heard that fella back in St. Louis say, and I threw in some things that I'd heard other hellfire and brimstone preachers spout, and I just plumb made up some stuff of my own. The important thing was to keep talkin' long enough and crazy enough that those Blackfeet'd be convinced I was pure-dee outta my mind."

Arne slapped him on the back and said, "A clever deception, worthy of Loki himself! Did it work?" He laughed. "What is Arne Winterborn saying? Of course, it worked! You are here, are you not?"

"Yeah, I am. After I'd been preachin' the rest of that night, they didn't set me on fire the next mornin'. But they didn't turn me loose just yet, neither. That took preachin' for most of that day, until they finally decided I was so loco I just had to be under the protection of the spirits. That was when they let me go." Preacher paused. "They've had occasion to regret that a heap of times since."

"Oh, ho! You have taken your vengeance on them, you mean?"

"We still ain't friends, that's for damn sure."

"And that is how you got the name Preacher."

"Yeah, I made the mistake of tellin' a few folks about it, and the story got spread around. Things like that travel fast on the frontier. Somebody started callin' me Preacher and the name stuck." The mountain man shrugged. "I been Preacher for so long now, sometimes it seems like I ain't ever been called anything else."

"It is a good story," Arne Winterborn said. "Would have been better with some slaying in it. Do you have any stories with slaying in them?"

"A few," Preacher said.

Before Arne could ask him anything else, the group came to a place where the bank rose into a broad, rocky shelf about thirty feet above the water. A number of temporary shelters made from tree branches and pieces of animal hide were scattered around, as were several campfires. Fifty or sixty people were there, among them quite a few women and children.

They all assembled quickly and came forward to greet the new arrivals. Some of the men carried rifles or pistols. The others had swords or axes.

These were what was left of the people of Skarkavik, Preacher thought suddenly. The realization was a grim one.

Axel Gunnarson lifted his voice and spoke to the camp's inhabitants. He half-turned toward Tall Dog, lifted an arm, and said something about Bjorn and Olaf. That eased the tension that had gripped the people when they saw strangers in the midst of the group.

But their expressions were still troubled, and most of the faces had gaunt, hungry, skittish looks, like wild animals that had been hunted for too long.

One of the women came forward and spoke to Gunnarson and Tall Dog. She was tall, broad-shouldered for a woman, with thick, honey-colored hair in a braid down her back. The gray woolen dress she wore hugged an ample bosom and trim waist.

Seeing Preacher looking at her, Arne leaned over and

quietly informed him, "That is Alfhild. She was married to my friend Halvor and bore him four fine children, two sons and two daughters."

"Was married?" Preacher repeated.

"Aye. Last year a storm caught him on the lake while he was fishing, and he drowned. The gods were angry that day. Since then Alfhild has mourned Halvor, but her time for mourning will soon be over."

"And then maybe you and her . . .? Or are you already married to somebody else?"

"Arne Winterborn has no wife. Alfhild will go with Axel Gunnarson, or perhaps Arne Winterborn, or perhaps someone else. It will be her choice."

"It usually is, one way or another."

Alfhild nodded to Axel Gunnarson, turned to Preacher, Audie, Nighthawk, and Betsy, and said in English, "Come with me. There is hot food, and you can rest from your journey."

Audie said, "We greatly appreciate your hospitality, madam."

If his diminutive size came as a surprise to her, she didn't show it. She just nodded and held out a hand in a graceful gesture for them to follow her.

Arne clapped a hand on Preacher's shoulder and said, "We will speak again later, friend."

"Lookin' forward to it," Preacher told him.

As they followed Alfhild toward one of the larger hide shelters, their route took them past Tall Dog and Axel Gunnarson. Tall Dog caught Preacher's eye and said, "There is much for us to talk about. After you have eaten and rested, my grandfather wishes to hold counsel with you."

"Don't wait too long about it," Preacher said. "Looks

like your grandpa and his people have plenty of trouble on their hands, and the sooner we get started puttin' things right again, the better."

"I only hope," Tall Dog said with a sigh, "that things can be put right again. But it may be too late for that . . ."

CHAPTER 18

Alfhild ushered them into the shelter, which was a rough square with posts on each corner, hides hung to form walls, and pine boughs laid across poles to make a roof. At this time of year when the weather was pleasant, it would provide plenty of shelter, but it wouldn't be much good when winter came roaring in. Folks needed good sturdy cabins to survive those long, cold, snowy months.

A rough-hewn table stood in the center of the room with benches on both sides of it. Heaps of fur robes and blankets were scattered around, much like in an Indian lodge.

Alfhild nodded toward the table and told the visitors, "Sit. I will bring food and drink. Then you can sleep if you wish."

"I don't reckon we need to turn in just yet," Preacher said. It was still the middle of the day, and he was eager to hear what Axel Gunnarson had to say. "But somethin' to eat would be mighty welcome."

"We have venison stew."

"Sounds good."

"And mead."

Preacher frowned in puzzlement. Seeing that, Audie said, "Mead is a type of liquor made from honey. It's a traditional drink of the Vikings. Their gathering places were sometimes known as mead halls."

"Well, bring it on," Preacher said. "And we're obliged to you, ma'am."

"My name is Alfhild," she told him with a stern expression. "Not ma'am."

"Yes, m—Alfhild. That's a pretty name."

She snorted and turned away.

With a smile, Audie said, "I think you'll have to put quite a bit of effort into it if you hope to impress that one, Preacher."

"Who said I was tryin' to impress her?"

"I'm just saying that she strikes me as very much a no-nonsense type. You know, practical and level-headed."

"Umm," Nighthawk said.

"Yes, and most likely rather opinionated, too, old friend. But, as you say, she really is a very handsome woman."

Preacher just shook his head and placed his rifle on the table. "She's a widow woman. Husband drowned in the lake last year, accordin' to Arne Winterborn. She's gettin' to the end of the mournin' period, though, and is liable to be lookin' for a new husband."

"Which eliminates you from consideration," Audie said, "since the chances of you ever settling down anywhere are non-existent."

"You got that right," Preacher said. "Anyway, I got the feelin' ol' Arne has his eye on her. I just met the fella and it's true he tried to kill me, but he seems a likable sort other than that. I wouldn't want to cut in on his plans."

Audie, Nighthawk, and Betsy sat down at the table, as well, and a few moments later, Alfhild returned with a couple of the other women from Skarkavik. They brought bowls of stew and mugs of drink. The four visitors dug in, enjoying the thick, savory stew.

After sampling the mead, Preacher licked his mustache and said, "That's a mighty fine brew. Potent, I expect."

"Of course," Audie agreed. "The Vikings made quite an art out of drinking and celebrating. I know these people don't follow all of the old traditions faithfully, but they seem to have kept some of the best ones."

Nighthawk, being an Indian, didn't drink liquor. Alfhild must have known that, because she brought him water, as well as water for Betsy.

"Would you like to go to the hall where the women are?" she asked the auburn-haired girl.

Betsy shook her head. "No, I'd rather stay here, if that's all right."

Alfhild nodded gravely and said, "You can be wherever you are comfortable."

The other women departed, but Alfhild remained, sitting at the far end of the table. Preacher figured Axel Gunnarson must have appointed her to take care of the guests . . . and keep an eye on them.

The visitors enjoyed the meal. After consuming the large bowl of stew and drinking a couple of mugs of mead, Preacher was beginning to reconsider what he'd told Alfhild about not needing to rest. He was getting a mite drowsy.

That feeling disappeared instantly when Tall Dog and his grandfather walked in through one of the openings in the hide walls. Axel Gunnarson's upper right arm was bandaged where Betsy had creased him with that pistol shot.

Tall Dog and Gunnarson sat down on the bench on the other side of the table from Preacher, Audie, Nighthawk, and Betsy. Both men wore solemn expressions, and Preacher was ready to hear what they had to say.

"My grandfather and I have had a long talk," Tall Dog began. "He has told me everything that has happened to him and his people in the past year. He wishes for me to explain it to you because even though he speaks English well, he feels I am more comfortable with the language."

"Go ahead, youngster," Preacher told him gruffly. "We're listenin'."

"Some months ago," Tall Dog began, "a group of men approached the village of Skarkavik, which is located about five miles farther up the lake from where we are now. Men of the village who were out hunting saw them coming and brought word back to Skarkavik. My grandfather and his people had been living there in peace for several years, so they expected no trouble. Even so, they were cautious."

"That's only wise," Audie put in.

Tall Dog nodded. "They were ready when the strangers arrived and met them outside the village with a well-armed delegation. The leader of the group introduced himself as Decker Galloway. He said that he owned sawmills back in the eastern provinces and had come west to investigate the forests in this region to see if it would pay to establish a logging operation here."

Preacher said, "When he saw these forests, he must've figured right away that it would be."

"No doubt," Tall Dog agreed.

"What did your grandfather think of the idea?" Audie asked.

"The people of Skarkavik exist by hunting and fishing and a bit of farming. They use the trees to build their homes and boats and wharves for those boats, and the forest provides shelter for the game they hunt. But there are trees beyond number, and my grandfather did not believe it would hurt anything for Galloway and his men to cut some of them down."

Preacher nodded and said, "Yeah, it seems like there would be room for a loggin' operation in these parts, too, without botherin' your grandpa and these other folks."

"That is what Grandfather Axel and the other men of Skarkavik thought. And Decker Galloway seemed very friendly. He said he wanted to get along with everyone in the area and cause trouble to no one."

"But he was lyin'."

"At first it did not seem so. Galloway went away for a time and then came back with more men. They began cutting down trees, but closer to the village than he had said they would come. My grandfather went and asked him about this, and Galloway claimed these were the best trees. He promised not to take too many of them or crowd the villagers too much, though."

Audie said, "I'd wager that didn't last long."

"No, unfortunately not. Galloway's men began dragging the logs to the lake using mule teams they had brought with them. They took the logs through areas where crops had been planted because that was the closest way to go.

"Naturally, that caused hard feelings. My grandfather went to Galloway to complain. Galloway said there was nothing he could do about it, that he had to carry on his business in the way that would make him the most money."

"Yes, that's what it comes down to, all too often," Audie said. "How are they transporting the logs once they get them to the lake?"

"They float them down to the mouth of a river that runs to Hudson's Bay and load them onto boats to take them on from there," Tall Dog explained. "At least, that is what they did for a while . . . until Galloway decided to build a sawmill in Skarkavik."

"Actually in Skarkavik?" Preacher repeated. "Not just close by?"

"The harbor where the village is located is the best place for boats to come in and have the lumber from the sawmill loaded on them. Then they go back down the lake and follow the river to Hudson's Bay, as before."

Audie said, "I assume that disrupted life in the village quite a bit."

Axel Gunnarson spoke up, saying bitterly, "It ruined everything. The sawmill runs all the time and the terrible noise drives away all the game in the area. The sawdust fouls the harbor and drifts out into the lake and makes the fishing bad. Several families lived in the place where Galloway decided to build. His men ran them off and tore down their cabins." The old man clenched a fist and slammed it down on the table. "We had enough! We tell them to leave. Galloway and his men, they laugh at us. So we try to make them leave."

"It was terrible," Tall Dog said. "Galloway got wind of what was going to happen. He had men waiting for the group that came to the sawmill. They had guns and were hidden, and when the villagers arrived, Galloway gave them no chance. His men opened fire."

Anger welled up inside Preacher. "I never did cotton to ambushers," he said. "What happened?"

"A dozen men were killed. More than that were wounded. The ones who were still alive retreated into the village, but Galloway's men followed them. They killed more men, burned cabins, took women and girls prisoner . . ." Tall Dog's face was drawn into bleak lines as he recounted the atrocity.

"Eventually the people had to flee or stay and be killed. The ones who got away are the ones you saw outside."

Betsy spoke up, asking, "What about the women you mentioned, the ones who were captured?"

"There are still twenty women and girls being held prisoner in Skarkavik. It is feared they are being abused by Galloway's men."

Preacher figured that was pretty likely. And it just increased the score against Galloway that had to be settled.

"How long ago did this happen?" Audie asked.

"Several months. Soon after the people were driven out of Skarkavik, my grandfather sent Rolf Pedersen to find me and give me the letter asking for help. He and my father have been in contact now and then over the years, sending messages back and forth with fur trappers who come through the area from time to time." Tall Dog summoned up a faint smile. "Evidently my father has told stories about what a great warrior I am and how I have friends who are known far and wide as fighters. My grandfather thought I might be able to do something."

"We'll do somethin', all right," Preacher said. "We'll teach that lowdown skunk Galloway he can't get away with what he's done."

"He has a hundred men and many rifles."

Gunnarson burst out with an angry spate of Old Norse. He must have been too mad to compose his thoughts in English. Tall Dog listened, nodding, and then told the others, "The men of Skarkavik are good fighters. They have attacked Galloway's men and done what damage they could, but they are too outnumbered to drive the invaders away. Meanwhile, Galloway continues to cut down trees, saw them into lumber, and send the lumber back east so he can become richer and richer. Sometimes, groups of his men come into the woods and hunt my grandfather's people. Galloway wants to drive them away completely . . . or wipe them out. Whatever it takes for him to rule the lake and all the land surrounding it."

"Settin' himself up as a little emperor, eh? Varmints have tried that before. It usually don't work out well. Folks'll only take so much before they rise up and strike back."

Audie said quietly, "But as outnumbered and outgunned as they are, our new friends may not be able to strike back effectively, no matter what sort of fighters they are."

"Well," Preacher said as he looked around the table, "they're outnumbered by four less now, and we'll just have to hope that makes a difference."

Since there were still several hours of daylight left, Preacher figured it might be a good idea to go ahead and get a look at the problems facing them. They left Betsy with Alfhild and headed north along the lake toward Skarkavik.

Betsy protested a little at being left behind, but not too strenuously. Preacher figured she was still tired and shaken up from what had happened earlier.

The group heading for Skarkavik consisted of six men: Preacher, Tall Dog, Audie, Nighthawk, Axel Gunnarson, and Arne Winterborn.

"You said you've been tryin' to cause what trouble you can for Galloway and his bunch?" Preacher asked Gunnarson.

"We attacked them whenever we could find a small enough group out away from the village. We stole their axes and saws. Two of our men tried to burn down the sawmill, but they were caught and killed. Then a group tried to reach Galloway himself and kill him."

"Cut off the head of the serpent, and the rest dies," Arne put in.

"I reckon they didn't succeed, or we wouldn't be here," Preacher said.

"They were caught, as well. Five men made the attempt. Two were killed outright. Two more were taken prisoner and tortured to death." Gunnarson's voice hardened. "The fifth man was tortured, too, but not quite to the point of death. Then he was taken into the woods and left where we would find him. He lived long enough to pass along a message from Galloway: We were to stop trying to interfere with his operation, or our women who are still in the village would suffer."

"That monster," Audie said. "Did you cease your efforts against him?"

"Mostly," Gunnarson said. "We had no choice. Since then, we have caught a few of his men in the woods alone." He scowled. "They never returned to Skarkavik. But their bodies were never found, either. Galloway cannot lay their deaths at our feet."

Preacher said, "He don't sound like the sort who needs a lot of evidence before he strikes back at his enemies. He may have punished those gals anyway."

Arne raised a clenched fist and shook it. "The blood of Vikings runs in their veins!" he said. "They would not want us to cease fighting our enemies because of them!"

"Probably not," Gunnarson agreed. "But at the same time, we must try not to do anything that will cause them all to be killed. Some are the wives and daughters of men who still fight at our side."

An idea stirred in the back of Preacher's mind. These

folks were in a bad fix, but he might have a way to start getting them out of it.

They circled away from the lake so as to approach Skarkavik from the east. A thickly wooded ridge overlooked the village and provided a good view of it, Gunnarson said. He led them to it, and then the six men worked their way through the brush until they could peer through narrow gaps at the log structures below.

Skarkavik was laid out on three sides of a small but deep harbor, Gunnarson explained, with Tall Dog helping him out on some of the words that weren't familiar to him. The north and south banks of that harbor were rocky and steep, rising fifteen or twenty feet above the water. The eastern end had a narrow, gravelly beach along it, and wharves had been built out far enough from the beach that boats could tie up at them.

Gunnarson talked to Tall Dog in Old Norse for several moments, then the young warrior translated, "The boats that carry the lumber and bring in supplies have a shallow draft, so they have no trouble getting into the harbor. The fishing boats of my grandfather's people could manage it as well. You can see them, pulled up on the shore to the north of the wharves. Some of Galloway's men still use them, pushing them out into the lake so that they can catch fish for the loggers and millers."

Not far from the wharves stood a large building made of logs and crudely sawn planks. Smoke rose from a couple of chimneys that stuck up from its roof. A loud, clanking, clattering noise came from inside the building.

"That must be the sawmill," Preacher said.

"Yes, three families lived in that space," Gunnarson replied. "Their homes were destroyed to make way for Decker Galloway's greed."

"You have any idea where the women and girls are being kept?"

Arne Winterborn pointed and said, "There, in the mead hall, or the feasting hall as some call it. We have seen them from time to time while watching the village."

The structure he indicated was the second-largest building in the village, after the sawmill. If not for that, it would have been the largest. Its sides were made from vertically arranged logs, and its roof sloped to a high peak and was covered with wooden shingles. A thick door framed with heavy beams opened into one end.

The other buildings were cabins such as might have been found in any frontier settlement. Audie studied them for a moment and then asked, "Why didn't you build your dwellings in the form of traditional Viking longhouses?"

"We are not in the old land," Axel Gunnarson answered. "When we came here, we decided to adopt the customs of this new land that we found favorable. The smaller dwellings are easier to heat in the winter. We are descended from the Vikings, but in truth, we are not exactly the same."

"Fascinating," Audie murmured. "When we finish dealing with this Galloway problem, I look forward to spending more time with you and your people, Jarl Gunnarson."

"You do not have to call me by the traditional title. You are not one of us."

"I believe in giving a man the respect he deserves. You are known as the jarl of Skarkavik, and that is how you should be addressed."

Arne Winterborn grinned and clapped a hand on Audie's shoulder. "I believe a true Viking's spirit may be housed in this diminutive form," he declared.

Preacher asked, "Where does Galloway live?"

"In my former quarters at the rear of the mead hall," Gunnarson said.

About a dozen men were moving around the village below. Preacher said, "What does Galloway look like? Is he one of those fellas down there?"

Gunnarson shook his head. "I do not see him. From his looks, he could almost be a Viking himself. He has red, bushy hair and a beard. But he is short and wide, not tall as most of our men are."

"An Irishman," Arne added with contempt dripping from his voice. "Our ancestors fought the Irish from time to time. They fight well and can hold their strong drink, but they are as much beast as human, I believe."

"I've known plenty of Irishmen," Preacher said. "I agree with you about the fightin' and drinkin' parts, but some of them are fine fellas."

"I suppose anything is possible," Arne muttered. "At least they are not Franks. Or Danes."

Tall Dog had been watching and listening in silence. Now he said, "Are there guards posted around the village?"

"Aye," his grandfather replied. "Galloway has had men watching the place night and day ever since he ran us out of our homes. It is difficult to get close without being seen. That is why our raids have been unsuccessful."

"I reckon he's probably especially careful about protectin' the sawmill and the mead hall," Preacher said.

"Yes. There are always armed men looking for signs of trouble."

Tall Dog looked intently at the mountain man and asked, "What are you thinking, Preacher?"

"Galloway's got the advantage as long as he has those prisoners. Without those gals as hostages, it'd be a lot easier to strike back at him."

"That is what we thought, as well," Gunnarson said. "But our attempt to free the women failed."

"Well, I don't mean no offense to you or your men, Axel . . ." Preacher smiled.

"But Decker Galloway has never had to deal with the man called Ghost Killer," Tall Dog finished for him.

CHAPTER 19

"What is this Ghost Killer?" Arne asked when they had returned to the current camp of Skarkavik's survivors. "It sounds like a story Arne Winterborn would enjoy! Lots of slaying!"

They were sitting at the table where they had eaten earlier. Betsy and Alfhild were off somewhere else.

"You remember them Blackfeet Injuns I was tellin' you about earlier?"

"Preacher's mortal enemies," Arne said with an enthusiastic nod.

"Well, when I was a younger man, sometimes I'd slip into one of their camps at night. I was pretty good in those days at movin' around without anybody knowin' I was there. So I'd wait until those Blackfeet were good and asleep, and then I'd crawl up to 'em in their bedrolls and cut their throats. I'd kill 'em so quick they didn't have a chance to make any noise."

Arne slammed a fist down on the table. "Yes! You would slay an entire band!"

"Well, not usually. I'd send five or six of those blood-thirsty varmints across the divide, and then I'd slip back out of the camp without any of the others knowin' I'd been there."

Arne guffawed and said, "Now Arne Winterborn understands. The Blackfeet did not know you had been there until they awoke in the morning and found their comrades dead!"

"That's about the size of it," Preacher agreed with a nod.

"And then they would be terrified that death had crept among them like a phantom and slew their friends and brothers. A Ghost Killer!" Arne reached over and pounded Preacher on the back. "What a wonderful story!"

Tall Dog said, "Sometimes they call him the White Wolf, too, because he is white and hunts and kills with the ferocity of a wolf. They all hate and fear him. Blackfoot mothers tell stories about Preacher to frighten their children into obeying."

Preacher said, "You got to remember, I was a heap younger when I started doin' those things. I've gotten a mite rusty since then. I ain't sure I could do any of that now."

"Don't believe him," Audie said with a chuckle. "He's still as capable as he ever was."

"Umm," Nighthawk agreed.

Axel Gunnarson leaned forward, clasped his hands together on the table, and asked, "What do you think we should do about Galloway, Preacher? I welcome your counsel."

Preacher understood the implication of what Gunnarson said. Gunnarson was the leader here, the jarl, as these folks called it, and he wasn't going to concede that position to anybody.

But at the same time, the survivors from Skarkavik

needed help, and Gunnarson was glad to accept any that Preacher could provide.

"Those prisoners are the key," the mountain man said. "If we can get them out of there and take them somewhere safe, then we'll have a free hand to fight back against Galloway."

"They are heavily guarded."

"That's why we need a distraction to draw some of the attention away from the place where they're bein' kept. Then Tall Dog and Nighthawk and me can go in there and turn 'em loose."

"Arne Winterborn shall go with you!" Arne declared.

Preacher shook his head. "No offense, Arne, but this is a three-man job, and I'm used to fightin' alongside Tall Dog and Nighthawk."

Arne scowled. "Am I not a good enough warrior?"

"I'm sure you are, and that's why we'll be countin' on you to help with the distraction."

Arne looked like he wasn't convinced of Preacher's sincerity, but he stopped arguing, at least for the moment.

Tall Dog asked, "What sort of distraction did you have in mind?"

Instead of answering directly, Preacher asked Gunnarson, "How often do those boats come to pick up the lumber and take it back east?"

"There is a boat every few days. Every three or four, I would say. The sawmill never stops running unless some of the machinery breaks down, and Galloway's men can have a load ready in that time."

"When was the last one here?"

Gunnarson looked at Arne and frowned. "Do you recall? It has not been long."

"The day before yesterday, I believe," Arne replied.

Preacher said, "So the next one will be due tomorrow or the next day."

Gunnarson nodded. "That is right. You are going to attack one of the boats?"

"Once it's loaded, we're gonna set it on fire."

"Of course!" Audie exclaimed. "Earlier, Arne spoke of Viking funerals. I've read about them. They put the body of the honored dead on a boat, push it out into the water, and then set it ablaze with burning arrows fired from the shore."

"And that's what we're gonna do," Preacher said, "only we'll have to have a mighty good archer handlin' that part of the job, since the arrows will have to be fired from farther away than the shore."

Arne bolted to his feet and bellowed, "That is a job for Arne Winterborn!"

Axel Gunnarson smiled, which slightly relieved the grim cast of his features. "My friend speaks the truth. Arne is the best bowman among us. The strongest and the most accurate."

"See, I told you we'd have an important job for you," Preacher said to Arne with a grin.

Audie said, "When Galloway's men see that the boat is on fire and the load of lumber is threatened, they'll all flock down to the harbor to help put out the fire."

"Umm," Nighthawk said.

"Yes, the guards at the mead hall may be reluctant to disobey Galloway's orders and abandon their posts," Audie said, "but at least they won't have any reinforcements close at hand. That will make it easier for you and Preacher and Tall Dog to handle them."

Preacher said, "We'll need a force of men waitin' near the village so that we can turn the gals over to them, once we get 'em away. It'll be up to them to protect the women on the way back here." He looked at Gunnarson. "Does Galloway know where this camp is?"

"I do not know. He has not attacked us here."

"He's liable to if we're able to get the prisoners away from him. Even more likely if we burn up one of his ships and a bunch of lumber while we're doin' it." Preacher shook his head. "I hate to ask you folks to do it, but you might want to think about packin' up and movin' somewhere else. Some place there ain't no chance Galloway would know where to find you."

Gunnarson scowled but then slowly nodded. "You are right. We must do what is the safest and best for our people." He looked at Arne Winterborn. "Will you begin spreading the word?"

"Of course, jarl. The people will be unhappy, but they will do as you say. This camp is not home . . . but it is the closest thing we have to it now."

"Someday soon, things'll be different," Preacher promised them.

Even though it was fairly late in the day by now, Axel Gunnarson told Arne Winterborn to start scouting for a new location to which they could move the survivors' camp. Arne took a couple of men from the village with him, and Audie and Nighthawk tagged along, too.

Preacher sat with Tall Dog and Gunnarson and discussed the details of the rescue attempt.

"We may need to wait until the boat after the next one arrives," Gunnarson commented. "I do not know if we can move our camp in time to strike tomorrow or the next day."

Preacher nodded. "That makes sense. I know you're eager to free those gals and to settle the score with Galloway, but sometimes it don't pay to rush things."

"I will put Arne in charge of moving the camp. He is a good man, full of words but a valiant warrior who would give his life to help our people. And as I said, the best archer among us."

"He'll need to be. That bluff we were on a while ago, spyin' on the village, looked to be the best place to shoot those flamin' arrows from."

Tall Dog said, "I saw that you have used pitch on the roofs of your shelters to make them more waterproof. Is there a place not far from here where you can get more?"

"Yes, there is a seep a few miles east of here, but we have a number of buckets of the stuff on hand already." Axel Gunnarson frowned. "Why do we need more pitch?"

"We will wrap the arrowheads in cloth soaked and covered with pitch," Tall Dog explained. "It will help them burn hotter and longer and make it more likely the lumber boat will catch on fire."

Gunnarson nodded. "I see. This is something you learned from your Indian relatives?"

"That's right."

Gunnarson rested a hand on the young warrior's shoulder. "It is good that you have come to help us, grandson, you and your friends. For the first time in months, I feel hopeful that we will drive out the invaders and reclaim our home."

"You will if we have anything to say about it," Preacher told him.

A short time later, Alfhild came back to the shelter with Betsy. The girl's auburn hair was twisted into braids now, and she wore a clean woolen dress instead of the dress she'd been wearing earlier. A belt of plaited rawhide was tied around her waist.

Tall Dog grinned at her and said, "You look like a Viking woman now."

"I told Alfhild I wanted a shield and a sword so I can be a shield maiden like her."

Alfhild snorted. "It takes much experience and strength to fight with a sword and be a shield maiden. You will stay here in the village and help the other women and girls."

"While you go and fight against Galloway and his men?"

"I have fought many battles," Alfhild declared with a defiant thrust of her chin.

"Aye, she is a fine shield maiden," Gunnarson said. "I would fight with her at my back any day . . . if we were fighting enemies who did not wield rifles and pistols." He nodded toward Betsy and patted the bandage on his arm. "From what I have seen so far, this one could be a gun maiden."

"Gun maiden," Betsy repeated with a smile. "I like that." Then she quickly turned solemn as she went on, "But I really am sorry about shooting you, Mr. Gunnarson. You took me by surprise and I didn't know who you were."

"I understand, girl. I will not surprise you again." He looked at Tall Dog. "You should remember that, too, grandson. Do not come up on this one from behind if you value your life."

"I will remember, Grandfather," Tall Dog said as he looked toward the ground.

Preacher wasn't sure which of them got redder in the face, Tall Dog or Betsy.

* * *

Audie, Nighthawk, and Arne Winterborn returned at dusk and reported that they hadn't yet found a suitable location for the new camp. They would resume their efforts the next morning.

The shelter where Preacher and the others had discussed the situation would also serve as living quarters for the visitors. Since it reminded Preacher of an Indian lodge, that was just fine with him. He had spent plenty of nights in such places and had always been comfortable.

Alfhild and another woman brought supper for them. Alfhild remained and ate with them. When the meal was over, Audie and Nighthawk wandered off to talk more with Arne, while Tall Dog and Betsy stepped out to walk around the camp.

That left Preacher with Alfhild.

The mountain man wasn't completely alone with the woman. Dog lay at his feet as he sat turned around on the bench, away from the table, and stretched his long legs out in front of him. Alfhild sat on the bench as well, several feet away.

"When I first saw him, I thought he was a wolf," Alfhild said with a nod toward the big cur.

"That tends to be most folks' reaction."

"But then I saw how he walked beside you, proud and strong like a friend. A wolf would not act like that with a human."

"Well, I reckon he's got some wolf in him," Preacher allowed. "Enough so that he's mighty good at huntin' and trackin' and fightin' when he has to be."

"Arne says you call him Dog."

"That's right. He answered to it right off." A faraway look came over the mountain man's rugged features. "You know, he ain't the first Dog I've had. The others have always been pretty similar, but I get to where I can see the little differences in 'em. The things that never change are how smart and loyal they are, and how they seem to understand the things I say to 'em. The exact same qualities are true of Horse, too. It's almost like as time goes on, each of 'em is the same critter as before, or as close to it as they can get, what with bein' born from different sets of parents. Audie told me once about some folks who believe that nothin' really dies permanent-like, that the spirit in every livin' thing passes on but then comes back in some other form. I don't know if there's any truth in that, but I know that with Dog and Horse, I feel like I got friends that'll never truly leave me."

"The little man seems to know a great many things."

"He ought to. He was a professor for a long time at one of them fancy schools back east. Then he got to where he couldn't stand bein' cooped up no more, so he left it all behind and headed for the mountains, sort of like I did when I was a youngster."

"My people know about being restless. That is why they built their longships and sailed all over the world."

"That and the plunder that was waitin' for 'em, eh?"

She sat up straighter and said, "Battle is in the blood of my people. Yet there comes a time when we want to have a place of our own where we can live in peace and raise our families. Skarkavik was such a place."

"Until Decker Galloway came along, that is."

Alfhild nodded. "Yes. You speak of Vikings and their plunder, but Galloway wants to plunder this land until there is nothing left of value. He would strip it down to the rock and dirt and cares nothing for those he harms."

"And that's why he's got to be stopped."

They sat there quietly for a moment, then Alfhild changed the subject by asking, "Would your dog allow me to pet him?"

"Sure. He looks fierce, but he's a friendly ol' galoot at heart, as long as folks treat him friendly-like. Or until I tell him not to be."

As Alfhild moved closer on the bench, Preacher continued, "Dog, be on your best behavior now. Sit up."

The big cur pushed up from his reclining position and sat there placidly as Alfhild came close enough to reach over and scratch his ears. His tongue lolled out and he looked like he was grinning.

"He is a fine dog," she said.

"None finer," Preacher agreed.

"I hope you always have such a friend."

"So do I."

"One thing I wonder about . . . If what your small friend says is true and the spirits of all things return to live again in a different form . . . what will you return as, Preacher?"

He looked at her for a moment, frowning slightly, and then broke out with a hearty laugh.

"Ma'am, that might not do to think too much about, because Audie says that how you act in this life has somethin' to do with what you come back as in the next one, and I ain't exactly been what you'd call saint-like. Far from it, in fact."

"And yet I sense that you are a good man."

Preacher grew serious as he said, "Seems like death has always followed me around, ma'am. I try to be a peaceable man, but then things happen so that I just can't keep from fightin' and killin'. I reckon that's why I could never settle down. Folks might want me around for a spell when they need the kind of help I can give 'em, but when it's time for peace and quiet again, nobody wants some ol' lobo wolf prowlin' around where they are. That day comes, it's best I'm movin' on."

"Perhaps you have not yet found the right place."

She had slid still closer on the bench until Preacher could have reached out and touched her arm. If he lifted his hand a little higher, he could brush the back of his fingers along her strong jawline. Could slide his hand around to the back of her neck under that thick mass of honey-colored hair . . .

He did none of those things. Instead, he said, "You know, this is probably the most I've talked in a month of Sundays. I don't normally sit around flappin' my jaws like ol' Nighthawk does. My mouth's a mite dry. Got any more of that mead?"

She stood up, fetched a pitcher from the other end of the table, and filled the empty mug sitting at his place. She handed it to him and he took a drink, then licked his lips in satisfaction.

"That's what I needed, all right."

She stood there in front of them, her head held high, and said boldly, "If you would like, I will stay here with you tonight."

Preacher pushed his lips out, took another long swig of the mead, and in the light from the flames in the fire ring to one side of the shelter studied the lines and curves of the body hugged in that woolen dress.

"We only met each other today," he pointed out.

"How long must two people know each other before realizing the truth of what is between them?"

"Well, it generally takes longer than that, or so I've been told. There's another thing: you're a widow still in mourning for the husband you lost."

"I am a widow, but the mourning ends when I say it ends."

Preacher couldn't argue with that. He downed the rest of the mead in the mug and said, "Tall Dog and Audie and

Nighthawk will be comin' back before long. I don't know where Betsy's gonna spend the night—"

"She will stay with the unmarried women."

"Maybe so, but the other three will be here."

"You act like what I suggest is something to be ashamed of."

Preacher came to his feet and growled, "Damn it, woman, this ain't the way I do things. I'm generally the one who does the pursuin'."

"Yes, but soon there will be much fighting. None of us know what the future will bring." Alfhild's broad shoulders rose and fell in a shrug. "I would not go to my grave never again knowing the touch of a man."

"You make it mighty hard to say no . . ."

"Then do not say it."

Preacher hesitated a heartbeat longer, then said, "Dog, go guard the door. When Tall Dog and Audie and Nighthawk get back, don't let 'em in until I tell you it's all right."

Dog stood up, trotted to the entrance that was covered by a flap of animal hide, and pushed out into the night.

"He really does seem to understand what you say," Alfhild commented as she lifted her hands and rested them on Preacher's chest.

"Yeah, and that comes in mighty handy sometimes, too," Preacher said.

CHAPTER 20

The next morning, as the people of Skarkavik began taking down the temporary camp and packing what they could carry with them, Preacher and Tall Dog left with Arne Winterborn to scout for a new location.

Audie and Nighthawk stayed behind this time to watch over the camp and help protect it in case Decker Galloway's men attacked the place. There was no real reason to think that would happen; Galloway hadn't made a move against the survivors so far. But there was no guarantee it wouldn't, either, and Preacher knew it was always best to be prepared for trouble.

None of Preacher's friends had said anything to him about returning to the shelter the night before and finding Dog standing guard at the entrance. Audie and Nighthawk claimed to have talked so late with Arne Winterborn that when the time came to turn in, they had rolled up in blankets and robes at his place. Tall Dog said that after walking Betsy back to the dwelling of unmarried women, he had been seized by the desire to sleep under the open sky as he often did at home back in the mountains.

Preacher figured they were all just being discreet and had chosen not to acknowledge what they must have known happened. He was grateful to them for that although he certainly wasn't ashamed of anything he had done.

To his way of thinking, a man always owned up to his actions whether they turned out to be right or wrong. Either way, they were his choices and nobody else's.

He hadn't decided yet whether going along with what Alfhild wanted was a mistake. It sure hadn't seemed like it at the time.

But he began to wonder about that as the morning went on and Arne mentioned several times how much he admired Alfhild. Arne had his eye on her, that was for sure. But he was waiting for the widow's period of mourning to be over.

Clearly, he had no idea that Alfhild had already decided that it was.

Tall Dog kept his face expressionless every time Arne brought up the subject. Again, Preacher was grateful for his discretion.

Preacher had made it clear that he wasn't the type to settle down. When this mess with Decker Galloway was cleaned up, he would be heading back south again, back to the American Rockies. Alfhild couldn't honestly claim anything else.

And Preacher just wasn't the sort to brood or second-guess anything he'd done. Those thoughts passed through his mind quickly and then he put them aside to concentrate on the task at hand.

Late in the morning, they found a rugged canyon several miles east of the lake. A quarter of a mile wide at its mouth, it stretched for at least a mile between rocky cliffs. Pine and spruce grew inside the canyon, but not as thickly as they did in other areas.

"Have you been up in there?" Preacher asked Arne.

"One day while I was hunting, a long time ago, I followed

a wounded elk in there so I could finish it off and take the meat back to Skarkavik. As I recall, there is a small spring at the far end that forms a pool."

Preacher had noticed that when there weren't many folks around, Arne talked more normal-like and didn't have the habit of referring to himself by his full name. Nor was he as boastful and bombastic when there was no audience.

"It sounds like a good place," Tall Dog commented.

"Aye. Not as nice as Skarkavik, of course. There is not enough water for so many people to live here permanently." Arne scratched at his beard. "But as a place to stay for a short time, it would be good enough. I had forgotten about it until just now."

Preacher nodded. "We need to get back to the camp and let folks know about it so they can start haulin' their goods over here. Is there a way out at the other end?"

"A small trail up the cliff, easily defended. This end, though . . ." Arne shook his head. "It would be better if it were narrower. But we are unlikely to find any place better. At least the trees provide cover, if we are ever forced to fight to defend it."

"Let's head back, then, and let folks know where they're gonna be stayin' for a while."

Audie was waiting for them with news when they got back to the camp.

"Galloway's boat is at Skarkavik now, taking on a load of lumber. Nighthawk and I reconnoitered earlier and saw it there. As you can see, we're not ready to move . . ." He waved a hand at the beehive of activity going on in the camp as people gathered their belongings and disassembled the shelters and packed up what they wanted to take with them.

"That's all right. We'll wait for the next boat to rescue

those gals. I know these folks are eager to have them free and to get back to their real homes, but a few more days shouldn't make any big difference."

"You found a good place for them to relocate temporarily?"

"Yeah, there's a canyon a ways east of here. It ain't perfect, but Arne says it's likely the best we'll find, and he knows the country hereabouts."

"Indeed. So for now, we continue with the move and refine our plans to strike at Galloway."

"That's right. This delay might even be a blessin' in disguise."

Decker Galloway always donned a white shirt, a brown tweed suit, and a silk cravat with a ruby stickpin when he got up in the morning. His high-topped boots were always polished.

When he was a boy in the workhouse in Dublin, dressed in rags and wearing shoes that were more holes than leather, he had sworn to himself that if he ever had money, he would dress like the gentlemen he saw in the streets and in passing carriages. The gentlemen who glanced at the stocky little redheaded urchin, curled their lips and sneered in disgust, and then looked away, dismissing him from their thoughts as if he were no more than a bug to be squashed underfoot.

That goal had stayed with him when he ran away from the workhouse, when he endured the hardships and indignities of the ocean crossing as the lowest of crew members on the ship, when he labored in the mills in the eastern provinces, carrying out the backbreaking tasks that added layer upon layer of hardened muscle to his frame.

Determination and a native cunning had lifted him

out of that menial existence. So had a willingness to do whatever was necessary, such as following the mill foreman one night as the man stumbled home drunkenly from a tavern and planting a knife in the fool's back, creating the need for a new foreman—a job for which Decker Galloway was well-suited by then.

Eventually there was marriage to a mill owner's daughter. Galloway was not, by any stretch of the imagination, a handsome man, but he possessed a raw, forceful power in his personality that drew women to him. And to be honest, the mill owner's daughter was not much to speak of when it came to looks, either.

So it was a good thing that wasn't the reason he married her.

She was back east now in the mansion in Toronto, still married to him, doing whatever it was she did to fill her days. Galloway didn't know or care. He had been busy for years now with other things, things that were actually worthwhile.

He had discovered fairly quickly that no matter how much money he made, it wasn't enough. He had the respect of the gents and the swells, oh yes, the wealth and power gave him that, but he found that it didn't matter. Those foppish fools he had envied back in Dublin knew nothing of real life. They didn't know what it was like to work for a goal and crush anyone stupid enough to get in your way.

Those were the things that made life worthwhile.

Just sitting in an office and crushing his enemies also wasn't sufficient to satisfy the drive inside him, though. Galloway wanted to be up and out, moving around, doing things, meeting every challenge head on and smashing it to bits.

But even so, there was no reason why a man couldn't be well-dressed while he was doing that.

So he pulled on the expensive clothes, combed his hair and beard, and went to the curtain that separated his living quarters from the rest of the mead hall. He paused there with the curtain pushed back and looked over his shoulder at the four-poster bed he'd brought in from Toronto on one of the boats.

The woman who lay there, a lump under the thick comforter, was one of his favorites, a brunette named Gerda. But just because he enjoyed her company didn't mean she was excused from her other responsibilities.

"Get up and join the others at chores," he growled. Gerda moaned but pushed the covers back. She knew better than to disobey.

Galloway walked through the mead hall, ignoring the hostile looks sent in his direction by the women and girls being held here. Some had been put to work mending clothes and doing leatherwork, while others just sat on the robes and blankets spread on the floor where they slept. His boots clumped on the thick planks that formed the floor as he went to the entrance and strode out to survey his domain.

Skarkavik looked like what it was, a wilderness village built and inhabited by primitives. The cabins, although constructed of logs, reminded him of the mud and wattle hovels where the farmers lived back in Ireland. He had spent his first few years in a place like that before his father died of a fever and his mother took him to Dublin, where she survived by selling herself on the streets until she disappeared. Galloway assumed she had either been killed by one of her customers or succumbed to disease.

It didn't really matter. Dead was dead, whatever the cause. And by then he had already learned not to waste time mourning when he had his own existence to worry about.

That was how he'd wound up in the workhouse, but he had never forgotten the farm . . . or lost the hatred all those memories of childhood stirred up in him.

He swallowed that feeling now as he hooked his thumbs in his coat pockets and continued his usual morning look around.

The cabins might be squalid, but the mill was a thing of beauty, at least to him. It loomed huge, by far the biggest structure in the village, with a high-peaked roof and large double doors standing open at both ends of its rectangular shape. The shutters on the long sides were raised and propped open to let air circulate. That kept the heat and smoke generated by the fire under the huge metal boiler from becoming oppressive.

The side openings also allowed some of the racket from the constantly moving shafts in the heavy engine to escape, otherwise it would be deafening in there. Galloway didn't care whether his men lost their hearing, but he had learned that if you at least pretended to care about the well-being of those you employed, they tended to work harder for you. That was why he was so good to them, only insisting that they toil for twelve-hour shifts.

The shafts in the engine drove the broad leather belts that powered the conveyors and the saws. The mill was large enough to accommodate two production lines. The trimmed and debarked logs were lifted onto the conveyors at the eastern end of the building, then carried along and sawed into long pieces of thick lumber by the series of spinning blades along the way. Men waited at the western end of the lines to stack that lumber in the long shed where it would be stored until the next boat arrived.

From where Galloway stood, he could see some of the

activity going on, but he didn't have to witness the mill in operation to be familiar with what went on there. He knew every inch of the operation, was familiar with every detail of every job that had to be carried out, because in his time he had worked every one of them. And not for just twelve hours at a time, either. No, he had worked sixteen, eighteen, even twenty hours a day, worked well beyond the point of sheer exhaustion until he was just blind, staggering tired.

Men who reached that point sometimes got careless and lost fingers, hands, even whole arms to the saws. Galloway remembered seeing one man faint and fall face first into one of the spinning blades. A sight such as that would make a man wide awake and fully alert again, that was for damn sure.

Galloway walked down to the wharf and watched for a while. The supplies brought in on this trip had already been unloaded, and men were loading and stacking lumber on the long deck of the flat-bottomed boat. It was a stern-wheeler, well-suited for navigating not only the lake but also the river that led into the interior from Hudson's Bay.

Galloway spotted Cecil Judson supervising the loading. Judson was a tall, burly, balding man who was Galloway's chief assistant. He wore canvas trousers with suspenders over a flannel shirt. A broad-brimmed black hat was thumbed back on his head.

"Cecil, any sign of those men I've been expecting?" Galloway called to Judson.

"Sorry, boss, not on this boat," Judson replied with a shake of his head. He came over to the edge of the deck and rested one booted foot on the low rail that ran around it. "Who are these fellas, if you don't mind me askin'?"

Galloway did mind. He didn't like sharing his decisions with anyone. That was too much like being asked to justify them, and he was long past the point where he was going to bother justifying anything he did.

"Never you mind about that," he snapped. "When they show up, you just let me know right away, understand?"

"Sure, Mr. Galloway. Don't you worry about that."

Galloway jerked his head in a nod and turned to walk back toward the mead hall. He wasn't worried, but he was eager for the men he'd sent for to get here.

Once they did, he could put an end to the problems plaguing him, once and for all.

The villagers worked all that day and most of the next transporting their personal belongings, supplies, and the hides and posts they had used to build their shelters to the new encampment in the canyon.

Audie and Nighthawk helped with the move, while on the second day, Preacher, Tall Dog, and Arne Winterborn returned to Skarkavik to keep an eye on the village and figure out exactly how they would attempt to rescue the prisoners being held in the mead hall.

They watched as Galloway's men took lumber from a shed and carried it to the boat, three workers to each long, thick piece of wood. When they reached the wharf, they passed the rough boards to other men waiting on the deck, who stacked the lumber in neat piles.

Preacher nodded toward the boat and asked, "Can your arrows make it that far, Arne?"

"Aye! My bow is the best in all Skarkavik. In the past, I have shot arrows that carried even farther than that. And my aim is always good."

"It'll need to be," Preacher said. "I reckon you'll have time to send three or four flamin' arrows flyin' down there before those fellas figure out what's goin' on and start shootin' back. But they'll be using rifles, not bows."

Tall Dog said, "Some of them may try to charge up here after you."

"So much the better if they do! Any men who attack Arne Winterborn will not be in position to stop the rescue of the prisoners." Arne scratched his beard and frowned in thought. "I will bring several warriors with me. If Galloway's men come after us, we will be ready for them. We will fight, and if the gods smile on us, we will kill them all!"

Tall Dog pointed to an area of trees behind the mead hall and said, "We will need to have men waiting there, too, to take charge of the captives once we have freed them. They can protect them and get them back to the new camp as quickly as possible."

"While you and me and Nighthawk stay here and do as much damage as we can to Galloway's operation," Preacher said. "Maybe even do some damage to ol' Decker Galloway himself, if we get lucky."

"There he is now," Arne said, leaning forward as an angry glare settled over his face.

A man had just walked out of the mead hall. He was short and broad, just as Decker Galloway had been described to Preacher, but the mountain man could tell by the way Galloway moved that he wasn't fat. There was nothing soft about the man. That was pure muscle giving him his hefty shape.

"Dressed up mighty highfalutin, ain't he?"

"He always wears those fancy clothes," Arne said with a dismissive gesture. "But inside he is as much a barbarian as all his Irish kind."

They watched as Galloway walked down to the wharf and talked to a man on the boat that was tied up there.

Preacher let his hand slide over the smooth stock of his rifle and said, "I could put a bullet in his head right now and end this."

"But that would leave the prisoners at the mercy of the other men, and the three of us would not be able to rescue them," Tall Dog pointed out. "As hard as it is to wait, that is the best thing we can do."

"Oh, I know that," Preacher agreed. "It's just a mite frustratin' is all." He looked at Decker Galloway and added, "There are some varmints in this world that just need killin', and that's all there is to it."

CHAPTER 21

When Preacher, Tall Dog, and Arne Winterborn got back to the canyon that evening, they found that most of the shelters had been set up and a number of cooking fires were burning around the new camp.

Axel Gunnarson, along with Audie and Nighthawk, met the three men as they came in.

"This is a good place you found," Gunnarson declared. "It will make a fine place for us to stay until we have defeated Galloway and can return to our homes."

Audie pointed to three places on the higher ground around the encampment and said, "We have sentries posted there, there, and there, Preacher. If Galloway decides to send men against us, we'll at least see them coming."

"Umm," Nighthawk said.

"I agree, if our plan is successful and we're able to free the captives, he'll almost certainly attack us. Although I've never met him, Decker Galloway doesn't strike me as the sort of man who'll take a defeat like that lying down. He'll feel compelled to strike back."

"Let him," Preacher said curtly. "Tall Dog, Arne, and me watched the village for quite a while today and learned some things. Galloway has a bunch of men workin' for him, all right, but most of 'em spend their time cuttin' up logs and loadin' and unloadin' cargo. I'm sure some of them can put up a scrap, but they ain't real fightin' men."

"Not like the men of Skarkavik," Gunnarson said as he clenched a fist. "We may be outnumbered, but we will never be outfought."

"And that is why, in the end, you and your people will triumph, Grandfather," Tall Dog said.

"Your people, too, grandson," Gunnarson said as he clapped a hand on Tall Dog's shoulder. "When Skarkavik is ours again, there will always be a home for you there."

Tall Dog smiled and nodded, but Preacher noticed that he didn't say anything, certainly didn't commit to staying in Skarkavik. All along, the plan had been for the visitors, including Tall Dog, to return to the American Rockies when their work here was done. Preacher didn't figure that had changed.

That evening, Gunnarson gathered all the survivors and explained the rescue plan to them. Men whose wives or daughters were being held prisoner immediately clamored to join the daring effort.

Gunnarson shook his head. "It will be better for you men to stay here and protect the other women and children in case of trouble. Seeing your loved ones in danger might be too distracting. A man must keep a clear head in the midst of battle if he hopes to survive and achieve his objective."

Preacher agreed with that decision. Not only would those men worry about their wives and daughters, when they saw how the prisoners had been abused they might also be filled with such rage that they couldn't control themselves. They might want to go after Galloway and his men and seek bloody revenge, rather than concentrate on getting the women and girls back to the camp safely.

The time for vengeance would come later. Preacher would see to that.

When the question of which men were staying behind was settled—although not without some grumbling from those who wouldn't be going along—Gunnarson began splitting up those who would take part in the raid on the village. Some would accompany Arne as he fired the flaming arrows at the lumber boat. Others would go with Preacher, Tall Dog, and Nighthawk to wait in the nearby woods while that trio freed the prisoners. Then they would take charge of the women and girls and get them back to the new camp as quickly as possible, protecting them from any dangers along the way.

One of the men spoke up, asking, "When will we go after the prisoners?"

Preacher recognized him as the man who had been bitten by Dog the day he and his companions had first encountered the people of Skarkavik. His name was Einar Lindholm. He still had a bandage wrapped around his leg where Dog had sunk his fangs, and more than once Preacher had seen him limping around the camp and casting sullen, resentful glances at the big cur.

Preacher wasn't sure he liked the idea of having Lindholm along on the rescue attempt. He would talk to Axel Gunnarson about that later, he decided, but for now, he didn't want to start a ruckus.

Keeping his voice neutral, the mountain man said, "We'll have to wait until the next boat arrives. That'll be two or three days from now if things go like they have in the past. But just to be sure, startin' first thing tomorrow mornin' we're gonna post scouts where they can keep an eye on the village. They'll bring word as soon as the next boat shows up, or if anything unusual happens."

Lindholm nodded. He was a burly fellow with dark

blond hair and would be one of the group assigned to escort the prisoners back to the camp once they had been freed.

"Because we may not get much warnin' when we have to make our move, all of you fellas need to be ready to go on short notice," Preacher continued. "Have your weapons with you at all times, and make any other preparations you need to. When the right moment comes, we'll be hittin' that varmint Galloway hard and fast."

A cheer went up from the assembled men, led by Arne Winterborn, who drew his sword from its sheath and thrust it high above his head as he shouted with enthusiasm and battle lust that all the other men of Skarkavik echoed.

Decker Galloway just hadn't had any idea what he was letting himself in for when he decided to make war on these folks, Preacher thought.

After the group had broken up for the night, Preacher and Tall Dog headed for the shelter they shared. Preacher hadn't seen much of Alfhild the past couple of days during the hectic move to the new camp, so he was happy when he spotted her waiting by the entrance to the tent-like structure.

"Food will be ready soon," she told them. "It is only a pot of elk stew."

"Stew sounds mighty good to me," Preacher assured her. "You're a fine cook."

Alfhild scoffed at that compliment and declared, "Like any true shield maiden, I prefer fighting to cooking."

"Both are important," Preacher said.

"A man must eat well in order to fight well," Tall Dog added.

"And so must a woman," Alfhild said curtly.

Tall Dog looked like he was going to say something

else, but Preacher caught his eye and gave him a cautioning look. Tall Dog must have understood because he kept his mouth shut after that except to shovel in spoonfuls of the stew that was indeed tasty, Preacher thought, even though it was a mite skimpy on the meat.

Alfhild ate with them as if this were her dwelling, too, and Preacher wondered if she intended to spend the night. He thought that might be a little awkward with Tall Dog here, but then he decided he didn't actually care. He had never been one to worry over-much about what anybody else thought of him, although he wouldn't want anybody looking down on Alfhild.

After they had eaten, Preacher sat at the table nursing a mug of mead as he reached down with his other hand to scratch Dog's ears. He asked Alfhild, "What do you know about that fella Lindholm?"

"Einar Lindholm? I know who he is, of course, but I've never really had anything to do with him." Alfhild's mouth twisted a little in a grimace. "However, I think he would like to have something to do with me. I have seen him looking at me with fire in his gaze more than once, even before my husband died. And he has a wife of his own."

After hearing that, Preacher disliked Lindholm even more. He looked down at Dog and said, "You knew which of those fellas was the one that needed bitin' the most, didn't you, boy?"

"Why did you ask me about Lindholm?" Alfhild wanted to know.

"He's goin' along on the raid when we try to rescue the prisoners," Preacher explained. "Nothin' special about that, of course, since all the able-bodied men are goin' except the ones who have wives and daughters there. I just don't think Lindholm likes me and Tall Dog and

Audie and Nighthawk very much. And he sure don't like ol' Dog here. You reckon we can trust him?"

"He is one of us," Alfhild said simply. "Whether I like him or not, I cannot believe he would ever betray his own people."

Preacher hoped she was right about that.

During the next couple of days, Preacher made a point of talking individually to each of the men who would be going along on the rescue attempt. He wanted to get to know them, to get a sense of how dependable they were and how much they could be trusted to follow orders quickly and without a bunch of foolish questions.

Often you didn't have a chance to get to know the men with whom you'd be going into battle. But it wasn't a bad thing to do so when the opportunity presented itself.

He found that all of them were likable and seemed trustworthy. Many possessed the same tendency toward being bombastic in their speech that Arne Winterborn did. That must be part of the Viking life they led, Preacher thought.

He talked to Einar Lindholm last. He was going to follow his instincts about Lindholm. If his gut told him not to take the man along on the raid, he would leave Lindholm behind. He was confident that Axel Gunnarson would back him up on that decision if necessary.

Preacher thought about telling Dog to stay with Audie and Nighthawk while he talked to Lindholm, figuring there was no need to antagonize the man unnecessarily.

Then he remembered that Dog would be at his side during the rescue attempt, of course, and Lindholm needed to be able to accept being around the big cur. There was no better time to find out about that than now.

He found Lindholm using a whetstone to sharpen the head of a battle axe. Lindholm sat on a stump and ran the stone along the axe's keen edge. He barely glanced up as the mountain man approached.

Then he looked at Dog and scowled. He set the whetstone aside and gripped the axe handle with both hands.

Dog stopped beside Preacher. His hackles rose slightly. Preacher heard the start of a rumbling growl deep in the big cur's throat.

"Dog, rest," he said, not raising his voice or speaking sharply.

Instantly, Dog relaxed . . . but not completely. The hair on his neck lay down slowly and he made no sound, but he remained standing tense and ready for trouble.

Lindholm stood up, still gripping the axe. "What do you want?" he asked.

"You've probably seen me talkin' to the other fellas who are goin' along on the raid."

Lindholm jerked his head in a nod.

"I'm tryin' to talk to everybody," Preacher went on. "I need to make sure we all understand who's in charge of this mission."

"Axel Gunnarson is my jarl," Lindholm replied in a sulky voice. "I take my orders from him."

"If you're gonna be part of that rescue attempt, you take your orders from me. Your jarl's put me in charge of things, and that's the way it is."

"I do what Jarl Gunnarson tells me." Lindholm glared stubbornly at Preacher for a moment, then added, "If he says to follow your orders, then I will do it."

"You know good and well that's what you're supposed to do."

Lindholm didn't say anything, so Preacher let it go at that.

"One other thing . . . If you're holdin' any grudges against Dog here, you'd better forget about 'em, because he'll be right with me the whole time."

Lindholm grimaced. "The beast attacked me for no reason."

"He wouldn't do that. You must've made a threatenin' move of some sort."

"You call me a liar?" Lindholm opened and closed his fingers on the axe handle. Preacher saw the eagerness to fight shining in his eyes.

"I'm sayin' you're wrong. Dog wouldn't jump somebody without a good reason. I've trained him better than that, and he's too smart to go against what he's been taught."

Lindholm sneered and said, "Perhaps you are not as good a teacher as you think. Or perhaps the beast is just a dumb brute as stupid as he is ugly."

Dog growled before Preacher could tell him not to.

"I reckon he's smart enough to know when he's been insulted," Preacher said.

Lindholm brandished the axe and said, "Back away, beast, or I'll split your skull!"

Preacher stiffened. Lindholm's threat was loud enough that some of the other people in the camp were bound to have heard it. They would spread the story. The people of Skarkavik liked to gossip just as much as any other group of human beings.

What Lindholm had just done was a direct challenge . . . and Preacher couldn't allow it to go unanswered.

"Put that axe down," he said quietly.

Lindholm switched his glare from Dog to Preacher. "What?"

"I said for you to put that axe down."

As the mountain man spoke, his hands went to the buckle of the belt holding the two holstered Colt revolvers. He unfastened it, took it from around his waist.

He heard a step behind him but didn't look around. Wasn't a wise move to take your eyes off a man who hated you while he was holding a deadly weapon.

"Preacher, what are you doing?" It was Alfhild who asked the question.

"Glad you're here." Without turning around, he held out the gunbelt behind him. "Hang on to these for me, will you?"

Lindholm was starting to get the idea now. He looked past Preacher at Alfhild, and his sneer turned into a leer. In a dismissive tone, he said, "This is none of your affair, woman. Go away and come back after I have dealt with this interloper." The leer got even uglier. "Then perhaps you will have put your grief behind you and will be ready for the arms of a real man to hold you again."

Preacher heard the hiss of the sharply indrawn breath Alfhild took. Then the weight of the guns went away as she lifted the belt from his hand.

"You will never be man enough to hold me, Einar Lindholm," she said with contempt dripping from her voice.

Fury glittered in Lindholm's eyes. He half-turned, lifted the axe in one hand, and brought the weapon down so that the head embedded in the stump where he had been sitting a few minutes earlier.

He turned back toward Preacher but didn't stop to set himself. Instead, he yelled and charged at the mountain man.

Preacher halfway expected a sneak attack like that.

He yelled, "Dog, stay!" and tried to twist out of the way of Lindholm's lunge.

Lindholm was a big man but quick on his feet. He covered the distance between himself and Preacher faster than Preacher figured he would. His right shoulder rammed into Preacher's right shoulder.

The impact staggered Preacher but didn't bowl him over, as it would have if Lindholm had run into him head on. Preacher was able to reach out, grab the leather vest that Lindholm wore over his shirt, and heave on it.

That impetus added to Lindholm's momentum made him unable to control it. He stumbled, lost his balance, and fell, rolling over several times before he came to a stop sprawled on his stomach.

Preacher considered advising him to stay down but then discarded the idea.

He wanted Lindholm to get up. He wasn't ready for this to be over yet.

Lindholm didn't waste any time getting his hands and knees under him and then pushing to his feet. He didn't appear to have been hurt by the fall as he swung around to face Preacher again. This time he approached with more caution, holding his hands out in front of him and moving them around as if he intended to grapple with the mountain man.

By this time, more people were approaching from the camp. Preacher saw Dog sitting beside Alfhild, and looking beyond them he spotted Tall Dog, Audie, Nighthawk, Axel Gunnarson, and Arne Winterborn among the spectators gathering to watch the battle.

Preacher wasn't trying to impress anybody. He planned to either beat the hostility and resentment out of Einar Lindholm or else confirm that the man couldn't be trusted to go along on the raid.

Getting a little of his own resentment out was just an added benefit. Preacher hadn't liked the way Lindholm talked to Alfhild and Dog.

Lindholm charged again. Preacher was set this time. The two men came together, reaching swiftly for wrestling holds, swaying back and forth as strength worked against strength.

Then Preacher suddenly found himself in the air, heels flying overhead, his hat sailing away. The perfectly executed throw sent him crashing to the ground.

If Lindholm hadn't yelled in what he took to be triumph, he might have succeeded in landing on Preacher with both knees and pinning him to the ground, maybe even doing some real damage.

But that strident shout prodded the mountain man into action. Despite being half-stunned and his muscles not wanting to work, Preacher forced himself to move. He came over on his left side. Lindholm's dive narrowly missed him. Preacher rocked back and drove his right elbow into Lindholm's left side, aiming for the ribs.

That knocked Lindholm away from him. Lindholm slumped on the ground and wasn't so quick to get up this time. He groaned as he struggled back into a sitting position. With a grimace, he grabbed at his left side with his right hand.

Preacher didn't think he had broken any of the fella's ribs. He hadn't felt any of them go. But they would surely be bruised. The pain and the growing stiffness would slow Lindholm.

Preacher stood up. He had recovered from the shock of being thrown down, and everything was working again. Maybe this was enough, he thought. Depended on how Lindholm handled it.

"We can let this go and call it good—" he began.

Lindholm snarled something in Norwegian that Preacher had to figure was decidedly uncomplimentary to his ancestry. With an effort, Lindholm made it to one knee.

Preacher was about to warn him not to try anything else when Lindholm launched himself at the mountain man's knees in a flying tackle.

Preacher darted out of the way and thought he had made it, but Lindholm got a hand on his right ankle and jerked that leg out from under him. Preacher went down and Lindholm scrambled after him.

As Lindholm dove at him again, Preacher jerked both legs up and caught Lindholm's weight on his feet. Preacher snapped his legs out and drove Lindholm backward. Lindholm's feet actually came off the ground as he waved his arms desperately.

That didn't stop him from smashing against the stump where he had stuck the axe.

Lindholm lay beside the stump for a couple of heartbeats as his chest rose and fell deeply, then he reached up, caught hold of the stump, and used it to brace himself as he struggled up again.

Then he seemed to notice the axe for the first time, and with a shout, he grabbed hold of it, wrenched it from the wood, and whirled toward Preacher. In a continuation of the same movement, he threw the axe at the mountain man.

CHAPTER 22

Preacher's eyesight was almost supernaturally keen, his reactions blindingly fast. He saw the axe spinning through the air toward him as if it were moving a lot slower than it actually was. The axe was perfectly thrown with such skill that Preacher had to give Lindholm credit for his ability. Its revolutions would end with the razor-sharp head cleaving Preacher's skull.

That was what would have happened if he hadn't reached up and caught the handle, stopping the axe dead in mid-air about a foot from his face.

"Einar!" Axel Gunnarson bellowed as he strode forward, obviously unable to hold in his anger. "Such treachery is not fitting for a man of Skarkavik!"

Lindholm pointed a shaking finger at Preacher and shouted, "This is no man of Skarkavik! Would you take his side? He is lower than a Dane!"

"He came hundreds of miles to help us," Gunnarson barked back. "And he is friends with my grandson. Watch your tongue, Einar."

Alfhild took a step forward and said, "You spoke with great disrespect to me as well, Einar Lindholm. You are fortunate that I do not fetch my sword and shield and challenge you to fight to the death."

"I do not make war on women," Lindholm responded with a snarl.

"Enough!" Gunnarson slashed the air with his hand. He turned to Preacher. "What would you have us do?"

"Everybody's got a right to be a lowdown skunk if that's what they want, I reckon," Preacher said. "But I don't want Lindholm goin' along with us. I wouldn't trust him."

Lindholm's eyes widened with rage. "I would never betray my people!"

"Maybe not, but I still don't want you at my back."

Gunnarson hesitated. Preacher could tell it went against the grain for him to side with an outsider against one of his own people, no matter what the circumstances. But Gunnarson had placed his faith in Preacher, and he didn't want to go back on that, either.

Finally, he said, "Einar, you will remain here with the others and guard the encampment when we attempt to rescue the prisoners. This will be for the best."

Lindholm glared at him, but he wouldn't go against his jarl's decision. He jerked his head in a nod and then came toward Preacher with his hand out.

"I would have my axe."

Preacher started to ask if Lindholm still intended on splitting his skull with it, but then he shrugged and tossed the weapon toward the man. Lindholm plucked it out of the air.

"Stay away from Dog," Preacher warned.

"I have no intention of getting near the filthy beast."

That was almost enough to prod Preacher into starting the fight all over again, but he controlled the urge and nodded.

"The same goes for Alfhild."

She said, "I can speak for myself, Preacher." With a

defiant toss of her head common to women all over the world, not just those descended from Vikings, she went on, "I have no interest in you, Einar Lindholm. You should pay more attention to your own wife instead of trying to seduce widows."

Lindholm scowled at her but didn't say anything else. Instead he turned on his heel and stalked away without looking back.

Preacher picked up his hat, slapped it against his leg a couple of times, and put it back on his head as Alfhild came over to him, carrying the belt and the holstered Colts.

He took them from her as she held them out and buckled them around his hips. The crowd that had gathered was breaking up now that the fight was over. Tall Dog, his grandfather, Audie, and Nighthawk came over to join Preacher, as well.

"I am sorry that one of my people acted toward you with such disrespect, Preacher," Gunnarson said. "Einar Lindholm is not a bad man, but he is a very proud one. He is ashamed of himself for the fear he showed when your dog attacked him."

"Then he needs to figure out a way to get over that." Preacher forced his own anger aside and went on, "Sorry for puttin' you in a bad spot, Axel. I know you didn't want to have to take sides in that ruckus. But I've got to do what I reckon gives us the best chance of rescuin' those prisoners, and that means leavin' Lindholm behind."

"As much as I hate to say it, I agree with you." Gunnarson took a deep breath. "But it is over now. He will cause no more trouble. He will accept my ruling."

Preacher hoped Gunnarson was right about that.

Fighting Decker Galloway and his men was going to be enough of a chore.

* * *

If things went as they had in the past, Galloway's lumber boat was likely to arrive at Skarkavik the next day. Figuring that it wouldn't hurt to have as much warning as possible, Preacher sent Tall Dog a couple of miles back down the lake to watch for the boat. If it got past Tall Dog somehow, which Preacher considered pretty much impossible, he had sentinels posted near Skarkavik, too. They would bring word when the boat arrived.

Arne Winterborn had prepared half a dozen arrows, winding cloth soaked in pitch around their heads. He had a bucket of pitch ready, too, and one of the men going with him would carry it when the time came to launch the attack. Another man would carry a candle lit from one of the cooking fires. The arrows would be dipped in that pitch and then set ablaze before Arne sent them winging toward the boat.

"We want to wait until Galloway's men have finished loadin' this shipment of lumber," Preacher told Arne, even though they had already gone over the plan several times. "The bigger the potential loss, the more of Galloway's men will come runnin' to try to put the blaze out."

"Yes, I understand," Arne nodded. "I will fire all six of the arrows onto the boat."

"If there's time. Those varmints are liable to start shootin' at you as soon as they figure out what's goin' on and where you are . . . and they'll be usin' rifles, not bows."

"Arne Winterborn can launch all six arrows before they realize the fires of Muspelheim are raining down upon them!"

Preacher didn't know anything about that Muspelheim

place Arne was talking about, but it didn't matter. He nodded and clapped a hand on the big man's shoulder.

"Sounds like that's gonna be one hell of a blaze."

"Aye!"

Now all they had to do was wait, Preacher thought. And sometimes that was mighty hard.

Tall Dog found a bluff covered with trees and boulders that overlooked the lake and settled down to wait. There were plenty of places where he could keep out of sight, and he was close enough to the water that he knew he would hear the boat's engine as it approached. There was no way he could miss it unless he was dead.

Perhaps that was exactly what someone had in mind, he thought as he listened to the unknown person moving closer to him. He had heard the skulker approaching a full two minutes earlier.

Whoever it was had no talent for stealth. Tall Dog heard nearly every step, every faint crackle of brush, every rattle of a dislodged rock.

He was sitting with his back to one of the boulders. In this position, the rock was taller than his head, so he was confident that the skulker couldn't see him and didn't know he was there. Soundlessly, he set his rifle aside and drew the tomahawk from its loop at his waist.

If the man trying to sneak up on him was one of Decker Galloway's minions, Tall Dog would show no mercy.

Another quiet scrape of a footstep, this one close by. Tall Dog's muscles tensed for action. He saw a shadow move on the ground to his right. With an explosive movement, he lunged up, reached across with his left hand, and caught hold of an arm. He jerked the surprised figure down to the ground and loomed above the skulker, tomahawk lifted and poised to strike.

But even as he went into action, he realized he had made a terrible mistake. He picked up a familiar scent, but by then it was too late to stop what he was doing. His muscles carried out the attack automatically.

Betsy Kingsley stared up at him and screamed.

Tall Dog let go of her and stood up so quickly that he almost fell from unaccustomed clumsiness.

"Betsy!" he exclaimed. "I . . . I am sorry! I did not know it was you—"

She choked the scream off quickly. With a look of horror on her face, she interrupted him.

"You almost killed me!"

"I am sorry," Tall Dog began again, even though he knew that in truth, he actually hadn't come that close to killing her. He had stopped the tomahawk blow well before it fell. When it came to life and death, even split-seconds could be a long time.

Betsy closed her eyes and breathed hard for a moment as she made an obvious effort to control the emotions coursing through her. Tall Dog could tell that she was terrified, and he felt anger at himself for being responsible for that.

Of course, that near-miss never would have happened if she had just let him know she was there instead of trying to sneak up on him . . .

Maybe she hadn't been trying to do that, he reasoned. Maybe she hadn't seen him sitting behind the boulder and hadn't known he was there. He had selected the spot for its cover, after all.

And she hadn't been raised on the frontier, he reminded

himself. It hadn't occurred to her to sing out and warn him of her presence.

This was just an unfortunate accident, one that could have been a lot more unfortunate.

Tall Dog slipped the tomahawk back through its loop and extended his hand to her.

"Let me help you up," he offered.

Betsy opened her eyes and blinked a couple of times before she slowly raised her hand and took the one Tall Dog held out to her. His grip was firm but gentle as he lifted her to her feet.

When he let go of her, she stood there brushing off and straightening the wool dress she wore. It was dyed blue and looked very nice on her, especially with her auburn hair loose and falling around her shoulders today instead of being braided the way it had been much of the time since they'd come to Skarkavik.

"I should be apologizing to you," she said. "I should have known better than to surprise you."

That was true, but Tall Dog didn't see that agreeing with her would serve any purpose. Instead, he said, "I should not have reacted so violently."

"Nonsense. What if I'd been one of Galloway's men? You had every right to protect yourself."

Tall Dog was relieved that she felt that way. He wasn't particularly surprised by her reaction, though. Betsy had a strong practical streak in her personality, as well as the stubbornness that had brought her along on this expedition to start with.

"What are you doing out here?" he asked.

"I overheard what Preacher told you about coming down here to watch for Galloway's boat. I thought you might like some company."

Tall Dog nodded and said, "Indeed, I would," although he had been perfectly content being alone. He had always enjoyed the solitude of the wild places. But Betsy didn't have to know that, either.

Instead, he gestured toward a fairly flat slab of rock nearby and went on, "Why don't we sit down? We can watch the lake from here."

She frowned slightly and asked, "Shouldn't we get out of sight, just in case the boat comes along? We wouldn't want them to see us and realize that somebody is spying on them. That would just alert them to the possibility of trouble waiting for them."

"The boat won't come in sight without us being aware of its approach well before that," Tall Dog said confidently. "Sound travels well over the water, and steamboat engines are loud. We'll hear it while it's still a mile away."

"That's true, I suppose." Betsy reached back and swept the dress against her legs as she sat down on the rock. Tall Dog sat down beside her.

"I have not seen you much since we got here," he commented.

"You've been busy with Preacher and the others, figuring out where to move the camp and then how to rescue those prisoners, and I've been helping Alfhild and the other women with their chores. I want to pitch in, too, you know."

"Of course. Do you like it here?"

"Well . . . I don't like the situation. All the trouble your grandfather and his people have had. It's just not fair. But the country . . ." She sighed and then smiled. "It's so beautiful here, Tall Dog! The woods, the lake, the mountains . . . it's all so magnificent. Nothing at all like where I grew up."

"It is very nice here," Tall Dog agreed. "I still prefer the mountains where my mother's people live, but I understand why the place means so much to my grandfather and the others. From what I know, it is much like their homeland back across the sea in Norway."

"You don't want to stay here? I know it would please your grandfather if you did." Betsy paused, then added, "I think he'd like to turn the leadership of these people over to you when he's gone." She laughed softly. "You could be Jarl Tall Dog."

He shook his head. "It will be many years yet before Grandfather Axel needs a successor. He is still in the prime of his life. And although he is family . . . this is not my home."

"I suppose I understand that. So when the trouble here is taken care of, you'll be going back to St. Louis and then to the mountains?"

"That is my plan. You can go back to St. Louis with us and resume your life there."

Betsy surprised him for the second time today. She shook her head vehemently.

"I'm not going back to St. Louis," she declared. "There's nothing waiting for me there. I like this place, and I like the people." Her chin lifted. "I'm going to stay, if they'll have me as one of them."

Tall Dog didn't know what to say to that. He hadn't expected such a decision from Betsy.

But when he thought about it, he could understand. She had no friends or family in St. Louis. She had been working in a tavern just to survive, and in time that easily could have led to an even worse situation.

She had already made friends among the people of Skarkavik. Probably many of the young men admired her.

She would have no trouble finding a suitable husband among them.

For some reason, that thought made Tall Dog's chest feel as if an iron band was tightening on it. He forced that feeling aside. He needed to be as practical as Betsy was.

"I think that is a good idea," he said. "For you to remain in the village once it is again in the hands of its rightful inhabitants, I mean."

"But you're not going to stay." It wasn't a question.

He shook his head anyway and said, "No."

What either of them might have said next, Tall Dog was fated never to know. Because at that moment, a faint rumbling and chugging sound came to his ears, drifting through the cool, clear air, and his head lifted sharply in response.

"I hear it, too," Betsy said a little breathlessly. "The boat's coming, isn't it?"

"Yes. We should move back in the trees."

Without thinking, he grasped her upper arm and helped her stand. The warmth of her flesh through the woolen dress made him catch his breath. So did the way the sunlight splashed her hair and struck red highlights off it. Even though the air was thick with the scent of pine and spruce, he had no trouble catching the scent of those clean auburn tresses, as well.

But he couldn't think of any of that now. Instead he hustled her into the trees, where they stopped and gazed back at the lake's placid blue surface, listening as the sound of the boat's engine got louder as it approached.

After a few minutes, the vessel came into view, moving smoothly along the surface as the paddlewheel at its rear churned the water behind it. Smoke rose from its stacks, and the engine chuffed. The smell of woodsmoke from the fire in its belly drifted ashore and reached the two watchers in the trees.

"We need to go tell Preacher the boat is on the way," Betsy said. "Today is the day those poor women and girls will finally be freed."

Tall Dog nodded and hoped that her words turned out to be true.

CHAPTER 23

Decker Galloway had already taken his morning constitutional around the village, so he headed back toward the mead hall. He expected the next boat today, but it likely wouldn't arrive until later in the morning. And it was always possible, due to unforeseen delays, that it might not come in at all.

Everything seemed to be running smoothly this morning. The chug of the engine in the mill blended with the whine of the saws to make beautiful music in Galloway's ears. Every minute of it meant more money in his pocket.

He nodded to the two men standing guard at the mead hall door. They were there to keep the prisoners from escaping, but it was also their job to keep the men out. Where women were concerned, Galloway believed in keeping a tight grip on his workers, allowing them to enjoy female company only at certain specified times. If they could avail themselves of the pleasures of the flesh any time they wanted to, it would be a terrible distraction from work.

Anyway, the prospect of having the men visit their quarters if they met the goals Galloway set in their work served as a powerful incentive. Galloway believed in using whatever was necessary to get the job done.

And the job was carving a timber empire out of these endless forests.

He stepped past the guards into the hall and was conscious of the apprehensive looks the prisoners cast his way. He had another reason for not allowing the men in here. This was his home now; he wasn't going to allow a bunch of lustful loggers to turn it into a den of iniquity.

And although he didn't like to think about it too much, Galloway had another reason for not allowing any debauchery in here. He didn't believe for a second in those old pagan gods . . . but he didn't want to tempt them into taking vengeance on him for defiling the center of the community, either.

He went into his quarters. Gerda was gone, probably out there in the hall somewhere with the other women. Galloway sat down in a comfortable armchair he'd brought out from Toronto and began going over the numbers he had entered carefully in a thick, leather-bound ledger.

He had an actual office elsewhere in the village, but he liked to keep this ledger with him for just such moments as this. With his lumberman's instincts, he already knew that production was up in recent weeks, but it was nice to be able to see that in black and white.

Those numbers translated in his head into other numbers—dollars and cents—and he was sunk so deep in that pleasant reverie that he didn't hear the boat at first. Besides, the racket from the mill made it difficult to hear anything else.

But then the sternwheeler's captain blew a long blast on the vessel's steam whistle to announce its arrival, and Galloway looked up from the ledger with a smile on his bearded face. He closed the book and got to his feet.

When he stepped outside, he saw that the boat was already tied up at the wharf. Cecil Judson was on his way toward the mead hall. He stopped when he saw Galloway striding toward him.

"Morning, boss," Judson said. "That fella you've been waiting for came in on the boat today."

Galloway drew in a breath but suppressed the sigh of relief that almost escaped. He never showed any sign of worry around the men, only complete, utter confidence.

"Jack Hargett?"

"Yeah, that's what he said his name was."

"How many men does he have with him?"

"Looked like about a dozen," Judson said.

Galloway nodded in satisfaction. A dozen men didn't sound like many, but he knew he could trust Hargett to pick men who could handle the job.

In this case, that job was to be ruthless, cold-blooded killers.

"Where are they now?"

"I pointed out your office to them and told them you'd probably be along in a while, once you knew the boat was in."

"All right. Get back to work. There are supplies to unload and lumber to send on its way."

Judson nodded and said, "Sure thing, boss."

Galloway headed for the cabin he had taken over to use as an office. As he approached, he saw the men lounging outside it as they waited for him.

Roughly dressed in workingmen's clothes, the most striking thing about them was that each man carried either a rifle or a shotgun. They all had pistols tucked in their waistbands and several wore sheathed knives. A pair who bore a family resemblance to each other—brothers, more than likely—had axes canted over their shoulders in addition to the firearms they carried.

The craggy, unshaven faces turned toward Galloway as he approached. Some of the men scowled. Others were impassive.

One man stood with his thumbs hooked in the gunbelt around his hips as he propped a shoulder against the door jamb. He straightened from that casual pose when he spotted Galloway coming toward him.

"Hello, Decker," he drawled.

"Jack," Galloway responded with a curt nod.

He allowed such informality with a man who worked for him only because he and Jack Hargett had known each other for a long time, from all the way back in Toronto.

Hargett had never been a regular employee of the Galloway Mills. Instead, he handled special jobs from time to time . . . such as when Decker Galloway needed someone to stop troubling him and disappear.

Unlike most of the other newcomers Hargett wasn't an impressive physical specimen. He was medium height and had a lean, wolfish build. His narrow, high-cheekboned face had dark stubble on cheeks and jaws. Above a hawk-like nose were two of the coldest eyes Galloway had ever seen . . . including his own. Jack Hargett was a killer with ice in his eyes and in his veins.

"I'm glad to see you," Galloway said. "Come on in."

Hargett stepped aside to let Galloway go first and then followed him into the office, stepping up onto the puncheon floor. The other men remained outside.

There was no desk in the room, but a solidly built table served the same purpose. The only decorations were a couple of bearskins hanging on the walls. Galloway liked them. Other than that, it was a simple, functional room, just as Galloway was a simple, functional man.

Galloway went behind the table, motioned Hargett to a chair on the other side. Hargett sat down and Galloway asked him, "Want a drink?"

"A little early in the day, isn't it?"

"Did that ever stop either of us?"

A humorless chuckle came from the lean man. "Not that I can recall."

Galloway got a jug and two tin cups from a shelf and poured the drinks. "Good Irish whiskey," he said as he slid the cup across to Hargett.

Galloway sat down behind the table and the two men drank, not bothering with any sort of toast, just tossing the liquor back. As Galloway dropped his empty cup on the table, he said, "You took your damned sweet time about getting here."

"I started rounding up men as soon as I got the word from you that you needed me," Hargett responded. "Sometimes that takes a while."

"Is a dozen enough?"

"That depends on what you need done." Hargett put his cup on the table, too. "But I can tell you this much . . . When it comes to trouble, those fellows are pretty damn capable."

Galloway grunted. "Good."

"So what is it you want us to do?"

Galloway clenched both hands into fists on the table in front of him and said, "You're going to kill a bunch of bloody Norwegian troublemakers who like to run around pretending to be Vikings."

For the first time since he'd gotten here, a genuine smile appeared on Hargett's face.

"Now this is starting to sound interesting," he said. "Tell me all about it."

Preacher looked across the encampment and watched Arne Winterborn talking to Nighthawk. He couldn't hear what Arne was saying, but judging by the way the big man waved his arms around and burst out laughing from time to time, he guessed that Arne was regaling Nighthawk with some sort of story about his adventures. Nighthawk nodded gravely in response.

"Those two certainly have become fast friends," Audie said from beside Preacher. "Perhaps because both of them like to talk so much."

"Yeah, I reckon that's it, all right," Preacher said dryly.

"I've asked Arne to come visit us sometime when all this trouble is over," Audie went on. "I don't know whether he'll do it or not, but I think he would enjoy making a journey such as that. The Viking blood seems stronger in him than in many of these people, and I think he gets restless and would like to see more of the world."

"Payin' a visit to our neck of the woods sounds like a good idea, all right. Hope he gets a chance to do that someday."

"Perhaps someone else would like to visit," Audie said. "Or even stay."

He nodded in another direction, and when Preacher looked that way, he saw Alfhild moving gracefully across the camp, bound on some errand.

"Now, don't you go to matchmakin'," he cautioned Audie sharply. "You'd be plumb wastin' your time. Alfhild ain't gonna go nowhere but right there in Skarkavik, once we've took it back from that varmint Galloway. That's her home and always will be."

"Are you sure about that? She's ended her period of mourning. She might be ready to move on to something completely different in her life."

Preacher shook his head. "I'd have to see it to believe it, and I don't expect to see it."

Whether Audie would have persisted in his efforts, Preacher didn't know, because at that moment he spotted Tall Dog running toward the canyon. Betsy hurried along beside him, with the young warrior holding her right hand to help her keep up. She used her left hand to pull her dress above her ankles and give her legs room to run faster.

Audie saw them coming as well and exclaimed, "The boat must be in!"

"That's the only reason Tall Dog'd be rattlin' his hocks like that," Preacher agreed. "I'll go meet 'em. You find Axel and let him know. Arne, too."

"Indeed!" Audie hustled off as quickly as his short legs would carry him.

Tall Dog and Betsy stopped to catch their breath just inside the canyon, where several sentries were posted. The men gathered around the newcomers to ask excited questions. They fell silent when Preacher arrived and asked, "Is the boat at Skarkavik?"

"It should be by now," Tall Dog replied with a nod. "It passed us on the lake a short time ago and was moving rapidly. But we know from watching the last one that it will take more than an hour for Galloway's men to unload the supplies it brought and load the next shipment of lumber."

"We ain't takin' no chances on that chore goin' quicker than usual," Preacher said. "If we don't make our move before that boat heads back down the lake, then we'll have to wait until the next time."

Grim expressions appeared on the faces of the sentries when he said that.

"These folks have waited long enough to get their loved ones back," the mountain man went on. "We're puttin' a stop to that today. Come on."

The encampment was bustling with activity. Alfhild took charge of Betsy while Preacher and Tall Dog formed a hurried council of war with Audie, Nighthawk, Axel Gunnarson, and Arne Winterborn.

"All is in readiness," Arne reported. "I and the men accompanying me will head for the village."

"Find yourselves a good spot and lay low while you wait. Don't let any of that no-good bunch spot you. We'll give you the signal when we're ready, and after that it'll be up to you to determine the right time to make our move."

Arne nodded, scowling with eagerness and anticipation.

"The rest of the men going on the raid are assembling," Gunnarson said. "They had their weapons ready, just as you ordered, Preacher. We can leave whenever you say."

"Reckon we don't have any time to waste. It'll take a while to slip up into the trees behind the mead hall. We can't afford to tip Galloway off on what's about to happen. Tell everybody who's goin' to report to the mouth of the canyon. The women and children need to gather in one spot to make it easier to protect them while we're gone. The men who'll be doin' that need to form a wall in front of them, leavin' a couple of fellas posted out a ways to keep watch for anybody comin' this direction."

"A shield wall, just as our ancestors did!" Gunnarson proclaimed. He hurried to put the plan into action. Preacher,

Tall Dog, Audie, and Nighthawk went to the canyon mouth to join up with the rest of the rescue party.

The men of Skarkavik were well-disciplined, and Preacher had made sure that each of them knew what his job would be when the time came for action. Arne Winterborn and his three companions departed first, hurrying away toward the village on the lakeshore. Arne grinned at Preacher and pumped his fist in the air as he trotted past, carrying the long bow that would launch the flaming missiles toward the boat.

A short time later, the fifteen men who would form the escort for the prisoners had gathered, all of them grim-faced and armed with rifles and pistols. Several of them had swords and shields slung on their backs, as well, in case they had to do any close fighting.

Preacher looked them over and was glad to see that Einar Lindholm was not among them. The man was going to abide by Gunnarson's order and stay behind with those who were charged with protecting the camp.

As he glanced toward the canvas-walled shelters, Preacher spotted Alfhild and Betsy standing in front of one of them. Each of them held a rifle. Preacher nodded to them, knowing they would fight if necessary. So would most of the other women.

Not for the first time, Preacher thought about how badly Decker Galloway had underestimated these people.

Then he said, "Let's go," and broke into a trot toward the village with Tall Dog on one side and the big cur loping along on the other.

Arne Winterborn knelt in the undergrowth beneath the pines and watched the bustling activity in the village below. Burly men in wool shirts, canvas trousers, and work boots carried long, thick lengths of lumber from the storage shed to the wharf and passed them across to the members of the boat crew who piled them on the open cargo deck.

Arne couldn't imagine a worse fate than to be forced to carry out such menial tasks day after day. A man ought to spend his days hunting and fishing, and the rest of the time was for drinking and lovemaking and fighting.

The other three men waited in the brush behind him. Arne could smell the sharp reek of the pitch in the bucket. It had been placed near enough to one of the campfires to soften the sticky black stuff without setting it ablaze. It would remain in that state for a while so that Arne could dip the arrowheads in it.

"Is it time?" one of the men asked in a whisper.

"Not yet," Arne told him. "Preacher said we should wait until all the lumber is loaded on the boat. He suggested that I fire the arrows as soon as they cast off, so that is what I will do."

He was willing to go along with Preacher's instructions. But the urge to fight was strong in Arne Winterborn. He hoped that Galloway's men wouldn't take too long getting the rest of that lumber put on the boat . . .

Jack Hargett had listened with great interest as Galloway told him about the former inhabitants of the village he had taken over. When Galloway was finished, Hargett said, "They sound like they've lost their minds. Do they think they're really Vikings?"

"I don't know what they think," Galloway said disgustedly. "But they were in my way, so I forced them out. If they'd had any sense, they would have moved on and found somewhere else to live." He waved a hand vaguely to take in not only their surroundings but the entire area. "Lord knows there's plenty of room out here in the western provinces. There's nothing but empty country for hundreds of miles."

"But they want this spot."

"So do I," Galloway snapped. "And they're still lingering in the vicinity and causing trouble for me. That was their choice. Whatever happens next is on their own heads."

"You want me and my boys to get rid of them . . . permanently."

"That's right. Whatever it takes. I'm tired of their interference."

"I don't reckon a bunch of crazy people will pose much of a problem," Hargett commented with a shrug.

"Don't underestimate them," Galloway cautioned. "They may be insane, but they're good fighters. It may not be as easy as you think it will be."

"No offense, Decker," Hargett drawled, "but no matter how they stack up against a bunch of axemen and sawyers, they won't be any match for men like the ones with me."

"I hope that's true." Galloway reached for the jug again. "Don't waste any time finding out."

In the deep shadows under the dense growth of trees, Preacher raised his hand in a signal to stop. The group of would-be rescuers came to a halt behind him.

Preacher had moved out slightly ahead of Tall Dog. From where he was, he could see the rear of the mead hall about fifty yards away and slightly to the right. To the left, a hundred yards away, rose the thickly wooded bluff where Arne Winterborn and his companions should be waiting for Preacher's signal.

Past the mead hall, Preacher had a narrow view of the wharf where the lumber boat was tied up. Men were still loading the cargo of roughly sawn boards on it. The raiding party had arrived in time.

No one in the village was looking in this direction. Preacher tied the piece of red cloth he had gotten from Alfhild onto the end of his rifle barrel and thrust it up above the brush for a brief moment. He had to trust that Arne was watching for the signal and had seen it. That would tell Arne that Preacher's group was in position.

Preacher withdrew the rifle and took the cloth off the barrel. Tall Dog eased up beside him and said quietly, "Now we wait."

"That's right. It's in Arne's hands now. He has a better view of the wharf, so he'll decide when the raid's gonna start." Preacher turned, caught Axel Gunnarson's eye, and motioned the jarl forward. When Gunnarson had joined them, Preacher said, "You're in charge of this bunch, Axel, but if you need any help figurin' out what to do, you can always count on Audie. He's just about the smartest fella I've ever known."

"Yes, I agree," Gunnarson said. "I feel better having him along. I have told my men to follow his orders, as well."

Preacher nodded. "Just get those gals back to the camp, and when you do, everybody hunker down and get ready for a fight. I'm hopin' Galloway will be so shook up he won't come after us right away, but we can't count on that. This could be the showdown."

Nighthawk had drifted up beside them, moving with

unnatural grace and silence for such a huge man. He said, "Umm."

"Yeah, we're gonna do as much damage as we can," Preacher agreed. "Maybe cripple Galloway's forces so much he can't come after us right away."

"If the gods have other plans and it is our destiny to die in battle today, it will be a glorious death," Gunnarson declared.

Preacher grinned. "Down where we come from, when the Indians are goin' into battle, they sometimes say this'll be a good day to die. I reckon you fellas have got a lot in common with them folks."

Tension gripped the men waiting in the trees as the minutes crawled past. Preacher hoped Arne hadn't missed the signal. This wasn't the best vantage point, but from what he could see, Galloway's men weren't loading lumber on the boat anymore. If the shipment was ready to go, the boat would be pulling out soon. They couldn't afford for Arne to miss his chance.

Preacher waited on one knee. Dog was right in front of him, sitting on his haunches with his tongue lolling out. Tall Dog and Nighthawk flanked the mountain man, the young warrior on Preacher's right, the giant Crow on the left. All of them watched the sky between the bluff and the lake shore.

Axel Gunnarson, Audie, and the rest of the men were spread out through the woods to the right, ready to take charge of and defend the prisoners if they successfully made their escape.

"Umm," Nighthawk breathed.

Preacher knew just what he meant. He felt the same way himself.

Then Tall Dog gripped Preacher's arm and said, "There!"

Preacher saw it, too. The flaming arrow arched out from the bluff, not really that noticeable against the blue sky. The shaft flew and flew, carrying what seemed to be an impossible distance . . .

Then plunging down unerringly to land in the stacks of lumber on the boat's deck.

CHAPTER 24

"Dog, go!" Preacher snapped as he surged to his feet. "Hunt!"

Tall Dog and Nighthawk bolted up, as well. The three men ran toward the mead hall as Dog raced in front of them, low to the ground, legs flashing.

Shouts of alarm rose in the village. Preacher saw more flaming arrows raining down from above. He didn't know how many Arne had launched so far but was glad to see that the big man was keeping up the barrage.

Dog charged past the mead hall. Preacher slowed and pressed his back against the wall as he neared the corner. Tall Dog and Nighthawk followed his example. When Preacher reached the corner, he leaned around it to take a quick look.

Flames leaped up in several places on the heavily loaded boat. The crew ran around, scooping up buckets of water from the harbor and flinging the liquid on the fires, but although they were keeping the blaze from spreading as quickly as it might have otherwise, they weren't making any actual progress in putting it out. They were just fighting a holding action.

Dozens of Galloway's men ran toward the wharf, filling

the air with shouted curses and questions. Most of them seemed to be pouring out of the big sawmill building.

Two men armed with rifles still stood in front of the mead hall entrance. They looked like they wanted to join the others in fighting the fire, but their devotion to duty—or their fear of disobeying Decker Galloway's orders—kept them rooted to their spots.

Preacher turned back to his companions and said quietly, "Two men at the door. You and me, Nighthawk."

The giant Crow nodded, reached to the quiver on his back, and drew an arrow that he fitted onto his bowstring. Preacher gripped his tomahawk, raising it as he wheeled around the corner.

"Hey!" he called to the guards, quietly enough that they could hear him without attracting the attention of anyone else in the village.

The guards jerked toward him and tried to bring up their rifles. Preacher's arm whipped forward. The tomahawk turned over once in the air and its keen edge thudded home in the middle of one guard's forehead, splitting the man's skull and cleaving into his brain.

At the same time, the arrow flew from Nighthawk's bow and struck the second guard in the chest with such force that the head ripped all the way through the man's body and emerged bloody from his back. The shaft stuck out a good six inches.

Both men crumpled, dead by the time they hit the ground.

Preacher glanced across the village toward the lake. Like the predator he was, Dog had taken down one of the stragglers, knocking a man down from behind. The big cur had his jaws locked around the unfortunate man's throat, and as he lifted his head and tore out the flesh, blood sprayed in the air.

"Come on!" Preacher told Tall Dog and Nighthawk.

More guards might be waiting inside the mead hall; Preacher didn't know. Decker Galloway's living quarters were here, too, so it was possible the man himself might be there.

If he was, Preacher would seize the chance to deal with him—permanently. Taking women and girls prisoner the way he had, likely subjecting them to all manner of degradation, had done away with the possibility that the mountain man might show him any mercy.

By the time the three men reached the door, a woman was waiting there, a big-bosomed brunette with a determined thrust to her jaw. She gripped what looked like a leg that had been broken off a chair. As Preacher appeared in the doorway, she started to swing it at his head.

He caught her wrist in his left hand, stopped the blow before it could finish falling, and said, "Hold it, ma'am! We're friends! We've come to get you and the other gals outta here."

He figured she spoke at least some English. Everybody they had met from Skarkavik so far did.

Over Preacher's shoulder, Tall Dog added, "We are helping the people of Skarkavik. Jarl Gunnarson waits nearby." He threw in a few words of Old Norse to make sure he got his point across.

The woman cried out in surprise and apparent joy. Her hand opened and the chair leg fell to the ground, so Preacher let go of her wrist. She turned and called to the other women and girls, who were edging tentatively toward the entrance. When they heard that they were being rescued from their captivity, they stopped hesitating and rushed forward.

Preacher and Tall Dog stepped back to let them out of the mead hall. They were so frantic that they jammed up the doorway as several tried to force their way through at once. That delay resolved itself quickly, though.

Preacher bent to wrench his tomahawk out of the dead guard's skull. Nighthawk put his foot on the chest of the other man and pulled his arrow out with a further ripping and rending of flesh that the man was too dead to feel.

While they were doing that, Tall Dog hurried to the corner of the mead hall and waved the former prisoners around the building. He pointed and told them where his grandfather and the other men from Skarkavik were waiting in the woods. The women ran desperately toward safety.

"Tall Dog!" Preacher called. "Some of 'em spotted us! Here they come!"

The shouts of "Fire! Fire!" from outside made Decker Galloway lurch up from his chair. Nothing was more feared in timber country than an out-of-control blaze.

Jack Hargett was on his feet, too. He knew as well as Galloway how dangerous fire was. He spun toward the door as Galloway charged out from behind the desk.

The men Hargett had brought with him were still standing just outside the cabin, staring toward the harbor where smoke had started to billow up from the boat floating a short distance from the wharf. One of them asked Hargett, "What do we do, boss?"

Galloway answered instead. "Go help my men put that fire out, you fools!" he yelled. "Go!"

As the men ran toward the lake, Hargett said, "My boys don't take kindly to being talked to like that, Decker, but I reckon under the circumstances, it's all right."

Galloway was about to make some angry retort when

one of the men, who had lingered behind the others, said, "Jack, I saw something you need to know about."

"What is it?" Hargett snapped.

"That fire didn't just break out on the boat by accident. Somebody up on that bluff was shooting flaming arrows at it. You didn't say anything about there bein' Injun trouble around here!"

Galloway grabbed the man's shoulders. "Flaming arrows, you say!" He cursed bitterly. "It wasn't Indians that shot those arrows! It had to be Gunnarson or one of those other fools! Find them, Jack!"

Hargett shouted after his men, "Latham! Hoffman! Dunn! With me!" He glanced at the man who had told them about the flaming arrows. "You, too, Brinkley. Let's go."

The men whose names he had called turned back. They hurried to join Hargett and the man called Brinkley. Together, the five of them ran toward the bluff where the flaming arrows had originated.

"Kill them, Jack!" Galloway shouted after them. "Kill anybody you find up there!"

Just as Arne Winterborn had predicted, he was able to fire all six arrows while the men down below were still standing around looking confused about what was happening.

Then a small group broke away from the others and rushed toward the bluff. They were all armed, but they didn't pause to shoot.

That was a mistake on their part.

Arne would have liked to draw his sword and wait to engage with the attackers at close range, but he was a practical man as well as a warrior. He pulled a regular arrow from his quiver and nocked it on his bow. As he drew the bowstring back, he saw his companions following his example.

"Now, lads!" he called to them.

The flight of arrows whipped out of the shadows under the trees. Aiming down a slope like that was tricky. Two of the men missed completely, although they came close enough to make the attackers duck as the arrows whistled just above their heads.

One of the men stumbled and then fell when an arrow embedded itself in his left thigh.

Another staggered, dropped his rifle, and pawed with both hands at the shaft of the arrow buried deep in his chest. That was the arrow Arne had fired, and it had flown true and deadly. The man it struck lost his balance and pitched forward. When he hit the ground, that impact drove the shaft the rest of the way through his body.

One of the men yelled in alarm, and the others who were left skidded to halts and flung their rifles to their shoulders.

"Down!" Arne called to his men. They dove to the ground as shots blasted and smoke and flame spouted from the rifle muzzles. With a rattling sound, the heavy lead balls tore through the branches above Arne and the others.

Although Arne hated to leave a battle unfought, he and his companions had accomplished their goal, and he didn't want to sacrifice the lives of his friends needlessly.

"Back to the camp!" he roared at them. "Go!"

Maybe some of Galloway's men would pursue them, Arne thought. That would narrow the chances of the prisoners getting away. It seemed a worthwhile gambit. The four of them scrambled to their feet, turned, and plunged deeper into the woods.

* * *

A dozen men were running toward Preacher, Tall Dog, and Nighthawk. From the wool shirts, canvas trousers, and work boots they wore, they appeared to be men who labored in the sawmill. They had left their jobs to help fight the fire but had noticed the three raiders freeing the prisoners and turned their attention to that.

None of them were armed, which meant they were no match for Preacher's Colts. Preacher drew the revolvers as he stepped forward, but he was unwilling to gun them down mercilessly. When he opened fire, the bullets struck the ground a short distance in front of the charging men. Preacher thumbed off two rounds from each gun, the four reports so close together that they combined into one rolling roar of gun-thunder.

Galloway's men stopped so short it was comical the way they fell over themselves.

"Preacher! To the right!" Tall Dog called.

Preacher swung in that direction and saw that several other attackers were almost on top of them. These men were armed with axes, which meant they were probably members of one of Galloway's logging crews who'd happened to be in Skarkavik when the raid took place.

Preacher saw one of the long, double-bitted axes sweeping at his head. He ducked under it and then darted closer to the man wielding the axe. His right-hand Colt thudded into the man's head in a chopping blow. The axe flew from the fella's hands as he dropped senseless to the ground.

Another man with his axe held high loomed in front of Preacher. Before the blade could fall, Preacher triggered a shot that smashed the man's shoulder. He cried out in pain and fell backward.

From the corner of his eye, Preacher saw that Tall Dog had drawn his sword and was lunging back and forth as he blocked blows from two axemen. The long, heavy blade moved almost too fast for the eye to follow. Tall Dog swept it around in a swift, slashing motion that cut the legs of one man out from under him.

At the same time, Tall Dog kicked the other man in the belly and doubled him over. A hard blow to the head with the sword's hilt knocked that man out.

Meanwhile, Nighthawk was dealing with two more men in his own fashion. He charged them and got too close for them to use their axes effectively. He clamped a hand around each man's neck and lifted them off the ground. They were large, muscular men, no lightweights, but Preacher knew the giant Crow warrior was capable of feats of amazing strength. Nighthawk knocked their heads together with stunning force and then tossed their limp bodies aside like a child discarding a pair of tattered, no-longer-beloved rag dolls.

Having seen what happened to their companions, the remaining attackers turned and ran. Preacher let them go. He called to Tall Dog and Nighthawk, "Let's see if we can find Galloway."

There was something to be said for ending this today.

As his eyes swept over the village, though, Preacher didn't see any sign of Decker Galloway. The man had to be here somewhere, but he could be hiding inside one of the buildings. They would have to search everywhere for him, and if they took the time to do that, the odds might well swing against them. They had routed the first two attacks, but they were still heavily outnumbered.

And judging by the amount of smoke coming from the boat, Galloway's men were finally getting the fire on the vessel under control, which meant more of them would be free to come after the raiders.

"Let's get outta here," he said to Tall Dog and Nighthawk. "I want to make sure Axel and the others got back to the camp all right."

"Umm," Nighthawk said with a nod.

"I wish we'd gotten our hands on Galloway," Tall Dog said.

Preacher whistled for Dog, then said, "So do I, but I reckon that'll be a fight for another day. We got those gals loose, and that was the main thing we were after today."

Tall Dog couldn't argue with that. The three of them headed for the trees. Dog caught up with them and ran ahead, his muzzle flecked with blood from the damage he had done to several of Galloway's men. All four of them disappeared into the thick growth.

Galloway's hand shook from rage and caused the neck of the glass bottle to clink against the tin cups as he poured drinks for himself and Jack Hargett.

They were back in Galloway's office. The door was open, letting in the unpleasant smell of smoke and ashes that lingered in the air outside.

It was a harsh reminder, not that Galloway needed one, of what had happened.

At least half the shipment of lumber on the boat had been destroyed in the blaze. Most of the rest was damaged but salvageable. The loss was a financial blow, but not really a crippling one. In the long run, it wouldn't cause Galloway a problem.

Nor would losing the three men who had been killed in the raid. Galloway devoted even less thought to them.

Hargett was upset, though, because one of the dead men was a fellow he had recruited and brought with him to Skarkavik. Having something like that happen made him look bad, he claimed, especially when the man responsible for it had gotten away.

The loss of the prisoners was worse than the loss of the lumber, in Galloway's opinion. Not having the women around would be a blow to the men's morale. Galloway wouldn't have that to motivate them to work harder anymore.

But the absolute worst, the thing that had him so furious his hand trembled and his breath rasped in his throat, was that someone had dared to defy him . . . and gotten away with it.

Hargett picked up one of the tin cups and threw the whiskey back. He scowled at Galloway and said, "I thought you claimed you weren't having Indian trouble. According to the talk among the men, there were at least two redskins in the bunch that attacked us today."

"They may have had a couple of Indians with them, but it was that crazy bunch of would-be Vikings," Galloway insisted. "I'm certain of it."

"Shooting flaming arrows, that's something Indians do."

Galloway drank some of the whiskey, relishing the way the fiery stuff burned his throat, and then shrugged.

"Maybe so, but you don't have to have red skin to shoot an arrow. It had to be Gunnarson and his people. They staged the whole thing in order to free the women from the village. Who else would have done that?"

"What you're saying makes sense," Hargett admitted. "I suppose the Vikings could've convinced some Indians to help them." He reached for the bottle, raised an eyebrow at Galloway, and poured another drink when the red-bearded man gave him a nod. "The question is, what do we do about it now? Do you know where we can find them?"

Galloway shook his head. "That's why I sent for you. My men aren't trackers. They're loggers and sawyers, not hunters. I never even bothered to try to find their camp, because I thought they might have sense enough to give up and move on."

Hargett grunted and said, "Pretty clear now that's not gonna happen."

"No, it's not. And they've inconvenienced me too much for me to let it go. They have to be found and wiped out." Galloway gave a decisive nod. "That's going to be up to you."

"Fine. I've lost one man, but there are still enough of us to handle the job. Those two Swedes of mine, the Olafson brothers, are good trackers. I'll tell them to pick up the trail while it's still fresh. They'll find out where that bunch took the women."

"And when they do . . ."

"We'll take care of it," Hargett said. "For good."

Preacher, Tall Dog, and Nighthawk were on their way back to the camp in the canyon when they heard noise in the brush to their right. They stopped and swung their rifles in that direction. Dog snarled and bared his teeth as he crouched, ready to spring.

But it was Arne Winterborn and his three companions who broke out into the open. When he spotted them, Arne grinned and bellowed, "My friends! It was a glorious battle, was it not?"

"Well, it wasn't really much of a battle," Preacher said. "Didn't last all that long. But we sent a few of the varmints across the divide, anyway."

"Did the prisoners escape?" one of the men with Arne asked anxiously. "We didn't see what happened."

"They were freed," Tall Dog replied. "They came this way with my grandfather and the others."

Arne and his companions expressed their relief and gratitude at hearing that news, then Arne asked, "Did Galloway's men follow you?"

"Umm," Nighthawk said.

"No sign of them, eh? Well, I am glad to hear that." Arne frowned. "Galloway will not allow this to pass, though. He will have revenge."

"Let him try," Preacher said. "We'll be waitin' for him if he does." He inclined his head in the direction of the camp. "Meanwhile, we'd best get back and make sure Axel and the others made it there all right."

Together now, the group headed on to the camp. As they neared the canyon mouth, Preacher's keen eyes spotted men armed with rifles waiting behind rocks and trees. One of them stepped out and waved the newcomers on. He wore a big grin.

"I reckon that look on your face means everybody made it back here safe and sound," Preacher said to the man as they walked up.

"Yes, our women are free!" A solemn expression replaced the grin as he went on, "But they have been through a great deal and there is much anger and sadness among our people. It will get better with time, I hope, but . . ."

"But for now, folks are upset, and nobody can blame 'em for feelin' that way," Preacher said. "That's part of war, I'm afraid, and even though it's on a small scale, what we got goin' on here is a war between that varmint Galloway and the people of Skarkavik. This was just one battle."

"A battle that we won," Tall Dog put in. "But there will be more battles to come, I'm afraid."

"I reckon we can count on that."

They moved on to the camp. Axel Gunnarson was waiting for them. He grabbed Tall Dog in a rough embrace and pounded the young warrior on the back.

"You are unharmed, grandson?" he asked.

"I am fine, Grandfather. Did you encounter any trouble on the way back here?"

Gunnarson shook his head. "No, nothing." He looked around at the newcomers. "We didn't lose a man in the raid. It could not have gone better."

"The gals who were bein' held prisoner?" Preacher said. "Where are they?"

"With their families." Gunnarson frowned. "It was a difficult time for all of them. But they are strong. Like the rest of us, Viking blood flows in their veins! They will recover. And sooner or later, they will have vengeance for what they have suffered."

The group broke up then. Audie and Nighthawk were reunited, while Preacher and Tall Dog walked toward the shelter they shared.

Alfhild and Betsy were waiting there for them. Betsy wanted to know everything that had happened, so she and Tall Dog wandered off to talk, leaving Preacher there with Alfhild.

"Any trouble while we were gone?" the mountain man asked.

Alfhild shook her head. "I heard what the jarl said to you about not losing a man," she said, "but that is not exactly true."

"What do you mean by that?" Preacher asked, puzzled. As far as he knew, none of the raiders had even been injured, let alone killed.

"I have not told Jarl Gunnarson about this, but earlier I

saw Einar Lindholm slipping off toward the other end of the canyon. He never came back. I have looked all over the camp and there is no sign of him." Alfhild shook her head. "He must have found another way out of the canyon and has abandoned us. He is gone, and I believe that somehow, he means to bring us harm."

CHAPTER 25

Once again, Preacher called a council of war with Tall Dog, Audie, Nighthawk, Axel Gunnarson, and Arne Winterborn.

"I looked all over," he told them, "and Alfhild's right, Lindholm is gone. He must've taken that little trail at the far end of the canyon you told me about, Arne."

"Why would he do such a thing?" Gunnarson asked.

"Maybe he's just run out on us and don't want to have anything to do with you folks anymore, but there's a chance he's nursin' enough of a grudge that he's decided to double-cross you and throw in with Galloway."

Gunnarson shook his head and said, "It is hard to believe that any man of Skarkavik would do such a thing."

"Bah!" Arne burst out. "Lindholm has always been a weakling. The blood of our Viking ancestors runs thin in his veins, Jarl."

Gunnarson shrugged. "We must face facts. He represents a danger to us. He can tell Decker Galloway where our camp is located."

"Galloway's gonna be able to find the camp anyway," Preacher pointed out, "if he has any kind of decent trackers workin' for him. You can't take as big a bunch as those freed prisoners through the woods without leavin' plenty of sign."

"Then they may be on their way to attack us right now," Gunnarson said with a scowl.

"That's possible," Preacher allowed.

Audie said, "We'll need advance warning if they're going to launch an assault against us."

"I don't reckon they'll try it today. There ain't enough light left in the day for them to find us and figure out a plan of attack."

"Umm," Nighthawk said.

"As always, old friend, your grasp of tactics and logistics is absolutely correct," Audie said. "Given the topography of the landscape, the only way to attack the camp is straight ahead through the mouth of the canyon. Although if they were able to position riflemen on the rims, they could fire down into the camp from above and pin the defenders down long enough for another force to carry out that frontal assault successfully."

"We ain't lettin' 'em get up there," Preacher declared. An idea began to form in his head, vague at first but coming into focus.

"I can scout the area between here and the lake, beginning first thing in the morning," Tall Dog suggested. "That way I will see them coming and can bring the warning back here."

Preacher nodded. "That's a good idea. We'll be ready for 'em when they get here."

"Ready to defend the camp, you mean?" Gunnarson asked.

"Nope," Preacher said. "Ready to spring our trap."

* * *

It was after dark when Jack Hargett came to the mead hall to see Decker Galloway.

"The Olafson brothers, Nils and Arvid, picked up the trail that bunch left when they hustled the women away from here, just like I figured they would," Hargett reported. "It led inland. They followed it until the light got too bad to see the sign anymore."

"So they don't know where Gunnarson and his people are hiding, just the direction they went?"

"I didn't say that," Hargett replied with a sly smile. "They weren't able to get too close, but they saw what looked like the mouth of a good-sized canyon east of here. That would be a good place for those troublemakers to have their camp." The hired killer chuckled. "Problem is, they don't realize they've trapped themselves there."

Galloway frowned and said, "Not if there's another way out."

"My boys can find out about that tomorrow."

Galloway had been sitting in his comfortable chair, trying to distract himself by going through the ledger and seeing how his profits had risen steadily. He snapped the book closed and set it aside, then stood up and began to pace.

Through the opening between his quarters and the rest of the mead hall, he could see the main chamber where the prisoners had been kept. It was empty now, and that reminder of how the men from Skarkavik had successfully defied him put a bitter, sour taste in his mouth that no amount of whiskey would ever be able to wash away.

No, it would take blood to settle that score, Galloway told himself.

He stopped pacing, clasped his hands behind his back, and faced Hargett.

"I've called in all my logging crews," he said. "Every

man who works for me is in the village tonight. There are ninety-two of them in all. Counting the men you brought with you, that's more than a hundred. There can't be more than thirty or forty fighting men left from the village's original inhabitants. You'll have them outnumbered by more than two to one."

Hargett narrowed his eyes. "You intend on throwing everything you have at them?"

"Damned right I do," Galloway snapped. "They can't be allowed to get away with what they've done. Your scouts can make sure they're holed up in that canyon, and then we'll move against them with our full force. This has gone on long enough. I'm going to put an end to it tomorrow."

Hargett shook his head slowly and said, "Your boys can chop down trees and cut them into boards, but can they fight?"

"Of course they can! Loggers are the toughest bunch you'll ever see."

"Maybe brawling among themselves they are, but going up against a bunch of crazy fellas who fancy themselves Vikings?"

Galloway clenched a fist and shook it in front of him. "They'll follow orders, Jack, don't worry about that. A couple of them were killed today, and they're mad about that. They want to settle the score almost as much as I do."

"How are you fixed for guns?" Hargett asked.

"We have forty rifles and perhaps half that many pistols. So more than half of our force will be armed with guns. As for the others . . . well, we have plenty of axes. Get my axemen close enough and they'll make fast, bloody work of those stubborn barbarians."

"You know, I've heard that Viking women will fight, too," Hargett mused. "How are your fellas going to feel about that? Will they be able to do what it takes if some woman comes at them with a gun or a sword?"

Without hesitation, Galloway nodded. "They'll do whatever they're told."

He hoped he was right about that. He didn't feel quite as confident as he sounded. And yet he believed that while some of the men might hesitate to fight a woman, in the heat of battle, with their own lives at stake, most of them wouldn't.

Hargett shrugged and said, "All right, I'll get Nils and Arvid out on the trail again first thing in the morning—" A footstep behind him made him glance back over his shoulder. He turned and went on, "Well, speak of the devil."

One of the tall, blond, rawboned Olafson brothers had come into the mead hall. Hargett probably could tell them apart, but Galloway had no idea which one this was—not that it mattered to him.

"What is it, Arvid?" Hargett asked, confirming what Galloway had thought.

"We just caught somebody slipping around outside, Jack," Olafson reported.

"One of the men from Skarkavik?" Galloway asked sharply.

"*Ja,* he says he is one of them so-called Vikings," the big axeman replied with contempt in his voice.

"What's he doing here?" Hargett wanted to know. "Did he really think he could cause any trouble by himself?"

"He says he wants to join us."

Galloway frowned. "That's impossible. They all hate us."

"All I know is what he says, Mr. Galloway." Olafson shook his head. "You can't trust them Norskis, though. They're almost as bad as Danes."

Galloway and Hargett looked at each other. Hargett shrugged again.

"Bring him in here," Galloway ordered. "We can talk to him and find out what he's really after. And then you can kill him, Jack, if that's what needs to happen."

"You should let me and Nils do it, Mr. Galloway," Olafson growled. "That bunch killed Perry Severs earlier today, and he was one of us. We'd be happy to take our axes to him, *ja*."

Galloway shook his head. "No, not until we've had a chance to question him, anyway. Just bring him in like I told you."

Olafson scowled at the sharp tone of voice Galloway used on him, but Hargett gave him a curt nod and motioned for him to carry out Galloway's order. Olafson left the mead hall and returned a moment later, pushing a man clad in buckskin trousers and a leather shirt ahead of him. Olafson held his axe ready in case he needed to split the prisoner's skull.

Galloway faced the man and said, "Who are you, and what do you want?"

The prisoner looked nervous, but he seemed to have something driving him on that stiffened his spine. He looked Galloway in the eye and said, "My name is Lindholm. Einar Lindholm. I come from Skarkavik."

"I know where you come from," Galloway snapped. "I asked what you're doing here." His lips twisted into a sneer that the bushy mustache and beard partially concealed. "Gunnarson didn't send you to beg for peace, did he?"

"Axel Gunnarson has no idea I'm here. If he knew, he would probably try to kill me." Lindholm shook his head. "I have come to help you."

"What makes you think I need help?"

"You no longer hold our young women and girls prisoner, do you?"

Rage boiled up inside Galloway. He wanted to smash

his fist into Lindholm's face. But instead he controlled his anger and said, "Gunnarson and the rest of your people will pay for defying me."

"It's not only Gunnarson. Men arrived from the south to help us. The jarl's grandson, and a man called Preacher, along with a couple of others."

"Preacher!" Hargett repeated, sounding like he recognized the name.

Galloway looked quickly at him. "You know the man?"

"I've heard of him, that's all," Hargett replied, shaking his head. "But what I've heard isn't good. He's supposed to have clashed with some British agents a few years back and caused them all sorts of trouble. Trouble that they didn't survive."

Galloway started pacing again, the anger and anxiety so strong in him that they wouldn't allow him to stay still.

"I knew Gunnarson tried to send for help. In those days I was still pretending to be friendly, and my man Judson picked up rumors that Gunnarson was suspicious and had sent a letter to his grandson with one of the men from the village. So I sent some men south to prevent that." Galloway shook his head as he paced. "They never came back. I hoped that despite that, Gunnarson's plea for help never reached its intended recipient. Evidently it did, though."

Lindholm said, "This man Preacher is the one who came up with the plan to rescue the prisoners. He is a good fighter and a cunning man. And the others are warriors, as well." His lips drew back from his teeth as he grimaced. "I hate Preacher and would see him dead! That is why I come to you with an offer to help defeat your enemies."

Galloway stopped pacing and stared intently at Lindholm for a long moment. Then he said, "I recognize treachery and hate when I see them. I don't think you're lying to me."

"I speak the truth."

Galloway nodded. "Very well. How can you help?"

"I can tell you where the people of Skarkavik are hiding. I can even take you there."

"My men will be able to find them," Galloway said with a shrug. "We have a pretty good idea already. So your offer isn't very helpful."

"I can show you a back way into the canyon where they are camped. You can attack them from the rear, take them by surprise, and wipe them out before they know what is happening."

Galloway looked at Hargett, who cocked his head to indicate that the suggestion was intriguing, at the very least. Galloway turned back to Lindholm and said, "Tell us about this back entrance."

Lindholm shook his head. "If I tell you, what's to stop you from killing me?"

Hargett drew a pistol and aimed it at Lindholm's head. "There's nothing stopping us from doing that anyway. If that back door you're talking about is really there, my scouts can find it."

Lindholm paled slightly under his permanent tan. "Let me fight with you," he said. "I can get back in the camp. I'll find Preacher and kill him before the attack even starts. Your chances of victory will be better if he's dead."

"What do you think, Jack?" Galloway asked Hargett.

"If half the stories I've heard about Preacher are true, it would be a help not to have to worry about him," Hargett admitted.

"You think you can get back in there tonight?"

Lindholm nodded. "I'm sure I can."

"Where is this camp?"

Lindholm hesitated again but then said, "In a canyon several miles east of here."

Galloway and Hargett exchanged a glance again. Just as the Olafson brothers had speculated, the survivors from Skarkavik were holed up in that canyon.

And they would die there, Galloway vowed to himself.

"Tell us exactly how to find it," he said to Lindholm. "Then you can leave. Sneak back in there, if you can, and kill Preacher. I want him dead by dawn, because that's when we'll attack." Galloway looked at Hargett. "You can have the men in position and ready by then, can't you, Jack?"

"Sure I can," Hargett said. That wasn't much time to set up such a large operation, Galloway knew, but they stood the best chance of emerging victorious if they took their enemies by surprise.

Galloway jerked a curt nod to Lindholm and told the man, "Go on. Just don't fail me, or you'll regret it."

"I won't fail," Lindholm promised.

Galloway smiled. "And here's something you probably haven't considered, Lindholm. With Gunnarson and the rest of the ones who have been causing trouble dead, the ones who are left alive will need a new leader. How does Jarl Lindholm sound, eh?"

An ugly smile curved Lindholm's mouth. "I will not fail," he declared again. "I swear it."

Galloway waved him out of the mead hall. Lindholm left with a vicious, eager look on his face.

When the man was gone, Hargett said to Galloway, "You really think he'll be able to kill that fella Preacher?"

"I don't have any idea," Galloway answered honestly. "Either he kills Preacher or the other way around, and either way, one of them is no longer a problem for us."

Hargett nodded and said, "I'd better get busy. Dawn will come early, and we want the killing to start on time."

It was late, and the camp was quiet and dark. Preacher walked around the place with Dog padding along almost silently at his side. The mountain man wanted to make sure everything was as it should be.

Beside him, the big cur started a soft growl, but the sound trailed off almost as soon as it began, as if Dog realized that what he had seen wasn't a threat after all.

Preacher had seen the same movement that Dog had. Even in the poor light of a quarter-moon, he recognized the shape of the person up ahead.

He stopped and asked, "What are you doin' up and about? You ought to be gettin' some sleep."

The figure came closer to him. Stray beams of moonlight shone on the honey blond hair twisted into a single braid. Alfhild reached out and put a hand on his arm.

"It is difficult to sleep on a night such as this," she said, "knowing that everything may be changed tomorrow."

"That's true every night, ain't it?" Preacher asked. He enjoyed the gentle warmth of her touch and the scent of her as she stood close to him. "Folks may think they know from one day to the next what their life's gonna be like, but the truth is that damn near anything can happen in the blink of an eye, with no warnin' whatsoever."

"But to dwell on such a prospect means a person will go mad. If the world . . . if life . . . is truly so fragile and perilous, better not to think about it. We should hope that things will be good. We should believe they must be. Otherwise, what is the point of living?"

"You should have this talk with Audie. He's read all the books by them philosopher fellas, and that's the sort of thing they worry about." Preacher shrugged. "Me, I just keep my eyes open and my powder dry and deal with what comes."

Alfhild laughed softly. "Perhaps your way is truly the more profound path."

"Also," Preacher said as he slipped his arm around her waist and pulled her closer, "I try to keep my mind occupied."

A short time later, as the two of them walked around the silent camp, trailed by Dog, Preacher said quietly, "You don't have to be here, you know."

"It is better that I am. I talked about it with Betsy and the other women. We all made the choices we made for our own reasons."

"And I figured it'd be a waste of time to argue with you," Preacher said. "Told ol' Tall Dog the same thing was true about Betsy."

"She may not be descended from Vikings," Alfhild said, "but who can truly say about such possibilities? Some of their blood may run in her veins."

"Yeah, those ancestors of yours got around a whole heap, didn't they? From what Audie's told me, it'd be hard to find a place anywhere in Europe that they didn't visit at one time or another."

"They scattered their seed widely, there is no denying it." She linked her arm with his. "You may have some Viking heritage of your own."

"As fiddlefooted as I am, I don't reckon I'd doubt it."

They walked on in silence for a few minutes. The cooking fires had long since burned down to embers, but the faint smell of their smoke hung in the warm air. It was almost still tonight, barely a breeze to rustle the branches of the pine and spruce trees in the canyon and up on the rims.

Alfhild broke the hush by asking, "When this is over,

what will you do? Will you return to the mountains in the south?"

"Well, they're only south compared to here," Preacher said. "Most of the folks down in the states and the territories think of the Rockies as bein' pretty far north, especially the parts where I spend most of my time. But yeah, I suppose I'll head back down there. The country hereabouts is mighty nice, but I'm an American. It don't feel right bein' up here where there's a king or queen in charge of things."

Alfhild laughed. "Do you believe Victoria, on her throne there in London, knows or cares what's going on all the way out here in this wilderness?" She shook her head. "We do not consider ourselves to be British subjects."

"Maybe you don't, but I promise you, the Crown figures you are. About thirty years back, 'way down yonder in a place called New Orleans, I fought the bloody British, you know. Me and Andy Jackson and Jean Lafitte and a bunch of other fellas. Whipped 'em, too. Ran 'em all the way back to the Gulf of Mexico. And I've had plenty of run-ins since then with those folks. No, I don't hanker to stay permanent-like in any place that belongs to the British."

"Thirty years ago, you must have been little more than a boy."

"I was fourteen. Plenty big enough to fight."

Alfhild was quiet for a moment, then said, "I would not mind visiting London. But I wouldn't want to stay there, either. Do you think you'll ever go there?"

"I ain't plannin' to, I can tell you that. Bunch of snooty folks drinkin' tea." Preacher shrugged. "But like I was sayin' a while ago, you don't ever know what the next day might bring. One of these days, I might be paradin' down

Piccadilly . . . Ain't that the name of one of the streets? Or goin' to one of those big ol' castles, or . . . Shoot, I might even see the queen!"

The thought of that ludicrous possibility made Preacher chuckle.

His amusement didn't mean he let his guard down, though. He heard the soft scrape of a hurried footstep behind him and every instinct in his body warned him it was a threat. He whirled, pushed Alfhild aside, and barely caught a glimpse in the moonlight of the razor-sharp axe head sweeping down at him.

CHAPTER 26

Preacher threw himself the other way, away from Alfhild, and the axe went between them. It struck the ground with enough force to make the man wielding it grunt from the impact.

Before the man could lift the axe again, Preacher kicked his legs out from under him.

The attacker went down hard enough to jolt the axe out of his grip. Before he could fumble for any other weapons he might have on him, Preacher scrambled up and leaped on top of him, throwing a punch at the same time. The mountain man's fist slammed into the man's jaw, the blow guided unerringly by instinct despite the poor light.

Preacher figured that might be enough to knock the man out, but he was wrong. The man threw his right leg up, hooked it in front of Preacher's left shoulder, and levered Preacher off of him. He rolled toward the fallen axe, grabbed it again, and came up swinging.

Preacher had rolled, too, and made it back to one knee before he had to fling himself backward to avoid the slashing axe head. Even with his lightning-quick reflexes, he felt the disturbance in the air as the axe passed only an inch or two in front of his face. He landed on his back and pushed himself along the ground with his feet and elbows as more of the barely avoided blows rained around him.

The attacker came after him, chopping and slashing. He might have been lucky enough to land one of those strokes if a large, furry shape hadn't catapulted out of the night and crashed into him. Dog's weight was enough to knock the man off his feet. Once again, the axe handle slipped out of his hands.

"Dog, back!" Preacher called as he got a hand on the ground and pushed himself up. He appreciated the big cur's help but wanted to deal with this man himself. He made a shrewd guess and went on, "Decided to sneak back in like the varmint you are, eh, Lindholm?"

A voice he recognized as belonging to Einar Lindholm spewed Old Norse at him. Preacher laughed.

"If you want to cuss me out, old son, you're gonna have to do better than that. I don't speak that lingo of yours."

Lindholm charged again, reaching out with his bare hands this time. Preacher started to dart aside, then realized too late that Lindholm's move was a feint. He hadn't expected that much cunning from the enraged man.

Lindholm rammed a shoulder into Preacher's chest as he wrapped his arms around the mountain man's waist. His momentum was enough to carry both of them off their feet. They hit the ground with bone-jarring, tooth-rattling impact . . . and Preacher was on the bottom, so he got the worst of it.

That hard landing drove all the air from Preacher's lungs and left him momentarily stunned. Lindholm hammered a punch into Preacher's face that knocked him closer to slipping into unconsciousness. Lindholm was a big, tough scrapper, a more-than-worthy opponent for the mountain man.

But Preacher had never been one to give up and sure as

blazes wasn't going to start now. When Lindholm tried to ram a knee into his groin, Preacher managed to twist the lower half of his body so that he took the blow on his hip.

At the same time, he lifted his right arm and drove the heel of that hand into Lindholm's chin. That forced Lindholm's head back. Preacher arched his back and bucked his attacker to the side.

He rolled that direction, chopped with his forearm at Lindholm's throat. That might have been a crippling blow, even a fatal one, if it had landed cleanly, but Lindholm blocked some of the force with his shoulder. He caught hold of Preacher's arm and heaved. Preacher gritted his teeth against the pain. It felt like Lindholm was trying to rip that arm right out of its socket.

Preacher looped his left around and clubbed that fist against Lindholm's right ear. Lindholm yelled and loosened his grip on Preacher's other arm. Preacher hit him again in the head, and this time he was able to follow that by pulling his arm loose. It was kind of limp at the moment from all the twisting and jerking on it that Lindholm had done.

Preacher got his left hand on Lindholm's throat and clamped the fingers in place like iron bands. With his right arm not working, though, he couldn't block the punch that Lindholm threw at him, so the hold was short-lived. Lindholm's fist crashed into Preacher's jaw and knocked him to the side. Gasping for air, Lindholm rolled the other way.

The two men made it to their feet at the same time. The moonlight was enough for Preacher to see how Lindholm's chest was heaving from all the exertion of the battle. Preacher was breathing pretty hard himself. He wasn't as young as he used to be, and Lindholm was a dangerous brawler. Maybe it was time to put an end to this.

His hands dropped to the holsters on his hips . . . but the

Colts weren't there. Even though he'd had the keeper thongs looped over the hammers to hold them in place, he had been thrashing around enough during the fight that the revolvers must have worked themselves free.

Lindholm had noticed that, or more likely his hand had just happened to fall on one of the Colts while he was rolling around. The gun was clutched in his fist as he raised his arm.

"Now you die," he gloated. "Just like I promised Gal—"

A heavy *thunk!* interrupted him. His eyes widened until the whites of them were visible even in the dim light. He took a clumsy step forward. The hand holding the gun sagged. The Colt slipped from nerveless fingers and thudded unfired to the ground at his feet.

Einar Lindholm pitched forward and landed on his face. He didn't move again. Preacher saw the handle sticking up from where the axe head was buried in the back of Lindholm's skull.

Alfhild stood behind where he had fallen, looking at the motionless body. She wasn't breathing hard and didn't even seem to be particularly upset by the fact that she'd just cleaved Lindholm's skull.

Yeah, plenty of Viking blood flowing in those veins, Preacher thought.

"I'm sorry if you didn't want him killed," Alfhild began.

"No, don't worry about that," Preacher assured her. "Seein' as how the skunk was about to shoot me, I'm just as happy you stepped in."

"I heard what he said about how he promised Galloway he'd kill you. He really did turn on us. I didn't think he would."

"Neither did Axel," Preacher said. "But sometimes a fella gets so twisted up inside his head that you can't tell what he's liable to do. I reckon that's what happened to Lindholm."

"I should have known when he abandoned his wife and children that there were no depths to which he would sink." Alfhild looked up from the body. "If he has been to see Galloway, he might have been able to tell us what Galloway is planning. I should not have killed him!"

"We know what Galloway's plannin'," Preacher told her. "He's gonna attack this camp, sooner or later. I'm bettin' on sooner. And when he does, we'll be ready for him. That's really all that matters."

Alfhild looked around the dark, silent encampment and said, "I suppose you are right. How long do you think we will have to wait?"

"No way of knowin' for sure," Preacher said, "but I've got a hunch he'll be here first thing in the mornin'."

In the village of Skarkavik, nobody got much sleep that night. Galloway had assembled all the men and explained the plan to them. Before daybreak, Jack Hargett and his men would enter the camp of their enemies by using that steep, narrow trail out of the canyon that Einar Lindholm had told them about. They would launch a surprise attack at dawn.

Meanwhile, the rest of Galloway's men, except for a small group that would be left here at Skarkavik with Galloway himself, would move into position for a frontal attack that would sweep right through the canyon mouth. Caught between the two forces that way, the defenders would be wiped out.

"Don't take any of the men prisoners," Galloway ordered bluntly. "They're no use to us. Spare as many of the women as you can, but I warn you, some of them will fight. You may not have any choice except to kill some of them. I don't like that any more than you do, but it's a simple fact: A woman can kill you just as dead as any man. Do what you have to."

As far as he was concerned, he didn't care what happened to the children, either. But other than Hargett's men, who would kill anybody if the price was right, he knew he couldn't ask the others to slaughter children. They would fight to the death against men they knew were trying to kill them, or even women, but they would draw the line at disposing of the little brats.

"When this is over, there'll be bonuses for all of you," Galloway promised. "Once we no longer have to worry about those troublemakers, more lumber will flow out of here than ever before . . . and that means more money flowing in."

Nobody was going to complain about that. In fact, a few scattered cheers went up.

When the time came, these men would do what was necessary, Decker Galloway told himself.

Hargett took charge of passing out rifles, pistols, and ammunition. Galloway had made it clear to the men that Hargett was in command of the assault and they were to follow his orders just as they would have Galloway's own. Galloway went back to the mead hall, figuring he would try to get some sleep.

Slumber proved elusive, though. He was too eager to have this mess over and done with. Everything had seemed so clear-cut at first. Taking over, getting what he wanted, should have been so simple. If only those would-be Vikings hadn't been so stubborn about wanting to hang on to the village of Skarkavik . . .

He hated that name, Galloway realized as he paced in his quarters, long after midnight. Skarkavik . . . It was so alien, so harsh on the tongue. There was no reason he had to keep it, he told himself, no reason at all. He would change the name of the place . . . Deckerville . . . No, Galloway City, that was better. And from the humble beginnings, it would grow and grow and become more and more prosperous until it was a real city, a shining light in the vast, endless forest . . .

He didn't know what time it was, probably a couple of hours before dawn, when Hargett came into the mead hall with a frown on his wolfish face and said, "We're going to have to change the plan."

Annoyed that Hargett had broken into his reverie, Galloway demanded, "What are you talking about?"

"We can't slip into that canyon through the back door," Hargett said. "It's blocked by some boulders. We could clear them away, but it would take a couple of days and make a lot of racket. They'd know what we were doing."

"But Lindholm got out that way!"

Hargett shrugged. "Then there's been a rockslide since Lindholm left. Either that, or they know we're coming and decided to block it themselves."

Galloway stared at him and asked, "Why would they do that? If they cut off the only possible escape route, that means they've trapped themselves in that canyon!" A canny look came over Galloway's face. "Unless they've already fled."

Hargett shook his head. "I thought of that right away, but they're still there, all right. My scouts and I watched the place for a while. Some of the women are already up and have got the cooking fires going for breakfast."

"A ruse," Galloway suggested.

"No, the children are still there, too. I saw one of them helping his ma by carrying some water. If they were trying to slip away, they would have taken the kids with them."

That was undeniably true, Galloway thought. If the children were still in the canyon, then the grown-ups had to be, too. But why had they stayed? Why hadn't they sought out some new hiding place? They had to know that he would strike back at them for raiding the village.

"This makes no sense," Galloway muttered.

"It does if they intend to hold that canyon. They must figure that they've got a good place to defend, and they're going to just hunker down there."

"We can starve them out."

"Maybe," Hargett said, "but there's water in there, and if they've taken all their supplies with them, they might be able to hold out for quite a while. Especially since they'll figure out you can't afford to keep all your men tied up by laying siege to the place."

"That's true," Galloway admitted with a scowl. "Besides, the men are worked up and ready to attack now. We can't let that go to waste."

"So we go ahead with the plan, only without the surprise attack from the rear?"

"I don't see any other choice," Galloway said. "With our superior numbers, we'll still wipe them out."

"May pay a little higher price to do it," Hargett said.

"I can always hire more men."

Hargett thought about it and nodded. "I'll send some of my boys up on the rim. They can pick off the defenders at the canyon mouth. That'll let us get in there among the shelters quicker. It'll be a damn slaughter, Decker."

"I've known from the first that this day was coming, sooner or later," Galloway said. "I'm ready to get it over with, no matter how much blood is spilled!"

* * *

The Olafson brothers preferred to do their fighting at close quarters with the axes they were so skilled at using. With the two of them close behind him, Jack Hargett knelt in the brush where he could see the mouth of the canyon about a hundred yards away. The eastern sky was turning gray with the approach of dawn, and in that weak light, the canyon was a dark, gaping slash in the rearing bluffs.

Like stars in the night sky, though, scattered cooking fires in the encampment burned here and there. Figures passed in front of them, telling Hargett that the group's women were busy preparing the morning meal. A small figure scampered past one of the fires, carrying a bucket. The women were keeping that youngster busy fetching water.

Nils Olafson touched Hargett's shoulder and then pointed up. "The signal," he said.

For a brief moment only, Hargett saw the light on the rim above the camp. It moved back and forth once, twice, three times, just as it was supposed to. Then the candle was snuffed out.

"They're ready up there," Hargett breathed. "All we have to do now is wait for the sun to come up." He glanced over his shoulder. More than eighty men were assembled behind him, poised to charge into the camp and wreak bloody havoc on the people of Skarkavik.

In addition to firearms and ammunition, Galloway had broken out jugs of rum and whiskey and had them passed around among the men. They hadn't been allowed to guzzle enough to make them drunk; a drunk man couldn't fight as well. But the liquor had warmed their bellies and put a fire in their blood, creating enough of a haze in their brains to allow their natural savagery free rein.

Hargett believed that every man, at heart, possessed

that savagery. Civilization was just a thin veneer, and it didn't take much to rip away that veneer and reveal the bloody-handed killer behind it.

Under the right circumstances, any man was capable of . . . anything. And Hargett had made a damn good living exploiting that buried savage.

He smiled. In a short time, the wolves would be loosed again . . . as soon as the sun began to peek above the horizon.

CHAPTER 27

Preacher struck without warning in the gray light, looping his arm around the man's neck, jerking him backward, and sliding the knife expertly through the ribs so the point penetrated the man's heart. The man died instantly, in silence, his passing so quick he probably never had any idea what had happened.

Preacher withdrew his knife and lowered the dead man to the ground, still without making any noise.

He knew that at the other end of the line of hidden riflemen, Tall Dog had disposed of another of Decker Galloway's men in similar fashion. The two of them had watched from hiding as six men climbed the bluff and then made their way to the canyon rim overlooking the encampment below. They had seen one of the men pause and kindle a tiny fire with flint, steel, and tinder, then light a candle from the flame and signal with it.

That was even more confirmation that Galloway was about to launch an attack on the camp, probably at dawn. Galloway would figure that was the best time to take the people of Skarkavik by surprise.

Instead, Galloway's men were going to be the ones who were surprised when they didn't get the help from above they were expecting.

Nor were the people in the camp asleep, ready to be slaughtered.

Two of the bushwhackers on the rim were taken care of. Preacher moved on to the next one, knowing that Tall Dog would be working his way toward the center of the line as well. Even though the hidden killer lurked in the shadows behind a rock, the mountain man's keen senses pinpointed his location. Preacher could smell the whiskey on him.

The way the man was crouched, Preacher wouldn't be able to grab him from behind and stick a knife in his heart, as he had done with the first of the bunch.

Instead he moved in until he could reach around, cup his hand under the man's chin, and yank his head up and back, exposing his throat and drawing it tight. The razor-sharp blade whispered through flesh.

Preacher saw the dark fountain of blood that spurted out against the rock where his victim had taken cover. With Preacher's hand under his chin that way, he couldn't open his mouth enough to make any noise as he died, not even a gurgling gasp.

Two down, Preacher thought as he lowered this corpse like the first one.

Ghost Killer still prowled the shadows, silent and deadly.

Preacher catfooted along the rim, searching for the third man he needed to kill. He glanced toward the eastern sky and saw rosy streaks beginning to run through the gray. The gray itself began to take on a golden hue. The sun wasn't far below the horizon now. He realized it was light enough for him to make out the trees and bushes and boulders along the rim.

He saw the third man at the same moment the would-be killer spotted him.

Twenty feet separated them as the man whirled away

from the tree where he had taken cover. He started to bring his rifle up. Preacher's arm flashed back and then forward in less than the blink of an eye. The knife flashed across that distance and buried itself in the man's throat before he could pull the trigger.

He staggered back against the tree and pawed at the knife's handle with his left hand. It was purely an instinctive gesture. He couldn't do anything to save his life now. Even if he managed to pull the knife out, that would just speed up the rate at which blood spilled from the wound.

Leaning against the tree, he slid slowly down the rough-barked trunk. When he finally reached the ground, he sat there with his legs stretched out in front of him and the rifle lying on the ground at his side. His head drooped forward in death.

Tall Dog trotted up, barely glanced at the dead man, and looked at Preacher. The mountain man nodded to indicate that the chore was finished. Tall Dog returned the nod. No words needed to be said.

Tall Dog turned and waved toward a thick stand of trees. Half a dozen of Axel Gunnarson's men emerged from the concealment and ran forward. Each man carried a rifle. Moving quickly because they were just about out of time, Preacher and Tall Dog positioned them along the rim, putting a man near each spot where one of Galloway's men had been hidden.

They knew the plan. As soon as the sun came up, they would fire a volley of shots to make the men outside the canyon believe the attack was underway. Galloway's men, thinking they had help from above and that they were attacking a drowsy, unsuspecting camp, would charge forward into the canyon mouth.

They would find a much different reception waiting for them than they expected.

Preacher pointed to the east and told one of the men, "Watch for the sun. You'll start the ball as soon as it pokes its head up, got that?"

The man nodded his understanding. Preacher clapped a hand on his shoulder for a second, then joined Tall Dog in hurrying to a pile of brush they had placed near the rim earlier. They threw the loose branches aside, revealing two coiled ropes that were tied securely around the bases of nearby trees. They tossed the other ends of the ropes over the edge and let them fall into the canyon, where the shadows were still thick enough to conceal them as they descended.

Preacher grinned at his young friend. "See you at the bottom," he said.

Hargett leaped to his feet as a ragged volley of shots sounded from the canyon rim a few minutes later.

"Let's go!" he called to the men with him. He charged forward, hearing the pounding of their feet behind him.

Those shots would alert the people in the camp that they were under attack, but Hargett knew his force could cover the distance to the canyon mouth quickly. And the sentinels who'd been posted there ought to be dead, since he had sent only good marksmen up there to the rim.

No one put up a fight as Hargett and his men ran into the canyon. Hargett spotted some unmoving shapes sprawled here and there and knew those were the guards who had been cut down by the bushwhackers.

It was darker here in the canyon, since it would take a while before the sun was high enough to spill its light over the walls, but he could see well enough to know where he was going. Up ahead, figures scurried around the shelters and the cooking fires. Panic was probably setting in right about now . . .

He never noticed the so-called dead men scrambling to their feet behind him, and neither did any of the men with him.

But he saw the dozens of men who suddenly leaped into the open from behind tents and trees and rocks, rifles in their hands already loaded and ready to fire. Hargett saw the wave of smoke and flame that erupted from those rifles, heard the roar of gun-thunder that filled the canyon . . .

And then something smashed into his chest with terrible force and he felt himself going backward, his charge abruptly ended.

He didn't feel it when he hit the ground, or anything else.

Preacher had drawn a bead on the fella who seemed to be leading the charge. He didn't know who the man was, only that he wasn't Decker Galloway. But that wasn't surprising. Preacher hadn't figured Galloway for the sort of man who would get in the thick of the fighting himself when he could pay other fellas to do it for him.

Even though he didn't know the man in charge of the attack, Preacher felt a surge of satisfaction when his rifle ball punched into the varmint's chest and threw him backward. Preacher could tell from the limp way the man landed that he was drilled through the heart, dead and gone.

At least half of the remaining force went down, too, scythed off their feet with wounds either fatal or serious enough to put them out of the fight.

That might not have evened the odds exactly, but it made them pretty damned close. Close enough, Preacher thought as he tossed the empty rifle aside and charged forward to take on the enemy close up. Dog leaped out ahead of him. Tall Dog, Audie, and Nighthawk were to his right, Axel Gunnarson and Arne Winterborn to his left. The six men and the big cur formed the tip of the spear that ripped into the ranks of attackers.

A lot of the men still on their feet were armed with rifles or pistols. Preacher filled both hands with his Colts and began thumbing off shots, alternating between the guns. Each time one of the revolvers roared, one of the attackers fell. It was a devastating display of deadly accuracy.

While Preacher was doing that, Tall Dog waded into the enemy with sword in hand. The blade flickered in the dawn light as it danced back and forth in the young warrior's skilled hands. The tip darted in to skewer a man's throat, then a slash of the blade chopped another man off his feet. Tall Dog was so fast it was impossible to follow his actions or know how many men he killed or wounded.

Nighthawk grabbed men by the throat and slammed their heads together with bone-splintering force. Audie emptied a Paterson Colt he had bought in St. Louis after seeing the weapons gifted to Preacher by the Texas Rangers. Arne Winterborn and Axel Gunnarson fought with sword and shield, battling in the old ways that would have done their ancestors proud.

The group of attackers broke apart, unable to retain any cohesion in the face of the shocking resistance they had never expected. The battle spread out through the canyon and became a wild melee, a bloody rampage that saw Galloway's men fall one by one . . . but not without the defenders paying a grim price of their own. Some of the survivors from Skarkavik went down with mortal wounds, too.

A handful of women led by Alfhild and including Betsy

Kingsley took part in the fighting, as well. They had stayed in the camp to fool Galloway's men into believing that the entire group was still there, but once the fighting started, they pulled off the dresses they had worn over leather breeches and vests, grabbed the swords and shields they had ready, and charged into the fray. From what Preacher heard about it later, they accounted themselves with honor, too.

With his Colts empty, Preacher didn't take the time to switch out cylinders in the weapons. Instead, he pouched the irons, drew his knife and tomahawk, and began fighting hand to hand. He plowed through a knot of the enemy, hacking and slashing, and suddenly found himself face to face with the two axe-wielding brothers.

They charged at him, swinging those axes, and for a long moment, it was all Preacher could do to avoid the sweeping blows. If any of them had connected, they would have lopped off an arm or even his head.

As he twisted past one of the men, he lashed out with his knife and carved a long, deep wound in the man's upper right arm. The axe started to fall, but the man reached across his body with speed and determination and caught the handle in his left hand. The head flicked up toward Preacher's throat. The mountain man jerked back to avoid it.

That put him within reach of the second brother. The man whipped his axe up and struck at Preacher's head, but before the blow finished falling, Dog slammed into the man from the side and knocked him off his feet. The axe missed wildly.

The man hung on to the deadly implement, though, and slammed the flat of it against Dog's head. The big cur went rolling from the impact and didn't move after he came to a stop.

While that was going on, Preacher blocked a blow from the other brother with his tomahawk, although the force with which the axe handle hit the tomahawk made Preacher's right arm go numb.

That didn't matter, because the mountain man had his knife in his left hand and brought it around in a looping strike that sunk the blade in the side of the man's neck. The man's eyes widened in shock and pain as the keen blade severed his spinal cord. Muscles that no longer worked dropped him to the ground. Preacher ripped the knife free in a spray of blood, ensuring that the man wouldn't have to worry about being paralyzed. He was dead in seconds.

Preacher turned around in time to see Dog lying motionless on the ground. The other axe-wielding brother was getting back to his feet. Preacher dropped his knife and tomahawk and snatched up the first brother's fallen axe. With an enraged yell, he charged the man who'd hurt the big cur.

The axes crashed and clanged and spun and leaped and slashed and chopped. It wasn't Preacher's weapon of choice, but he had fought with axes before and brought all his speed, reflexes, and instincts to the battle. Neither man realized that the fighting had come to an end around them, and their clash was now the centerpiece on the bloody, corpse-littered field.

The blur of action continued for what seemed like long minutes but was probably only a few moments. Then Preacher slipped for a second and lost his balance. His opponent sprang forward, the axe swinging with blinding speed as he tried to take advantage of that split-second opening.

Preacher went to a knee as he felt the enemy's axe head brush his hair. One-handed, he brought his axe up and over and buried the head in the middle of the man's face. It was a hideous wound. The man was able to take a couple of steps back before he collapsed.

Preacher was still on one knee, breathing hard, when he felt something nudge his side. He looked down and grinned as he saw Dog standing there. The big cur had been knocked senseless for a few moments but was all right again.

Preacher looped his arm around Dog's hairy, muscular neck and pulled his old friend against him. "You big old varmint," he said, laughing. "I thought you was done for. I should've knowed better, shouldn't I?"

That was when he became aware that the sounds of battle had died away in the canyon. Nighthawk stepped up in front of him and extended a hand. Preacher clasped the giant Crow's wrist and Nighthawk hauled him effortlessly to his feet. Preacher looked around and assured himself that Tall Dog, Audie, Alfhild, Betsy, Gunnarson, and Arne Winterborn were all still alive, although they were spattered with blood from the battle. Some of it might have been their own, but none appeared to be hurt badly.

"What a glorious battle!" Arne shouted, causing cheers to go up from the other survivors of Skarkavik. "They are singing songs about us in Valhalla, my friends!"

"Maybe so," Preacher said, "but this ain't over yet."

"Galloway isn't here," Axel Gunnarson said. "That is what you mean, is it not, Preacher?"

"That's right," the mountain man said. "We've still got some settlin' up to do."

The silence got on Decker Galloway's nerves. He was accustomed to hearing the rumble of the engines in the sawmill, the high-pitched whine of the saws, the ripping sound as the blades cut through the logs, and the shouts of the men as they worked.

A hushed quiet like the one that hung over the village today meant that he wasn't making any money.

But that inactivity was in the service of a good cause, he told himself. Those who opposed him would be wiped out once and for all. They wouldn't plague him any longer, wouldn't chip away at his profits. And with that opposition gone, he could really begin building his empire here in the wilderness. Someday, all of this vast land would be his domain . . .

Cecil Judson, who had been left behind in the village, ran into the mead hall and reported in an excited voice, "Boss, somebody's coming!"

"That'll be Jack Hargett and the others," Galloway said confidently as he walked toward the entrance. "I didn't really expect them back this soon—"

"It's not Hargett." The fact that Judson interrupted him was a sign of just how upset the man was. "It looks like those . . . those damned Vikings!"

Galloway took a step back, almost as if he had been punched. He started to reel to one side, but he caught himself and imposed a steely grip on his nerves.

"Impossible," he muttered.

"Maybe so, but the fella walking in front of the bunch sure looked like that Axel Gunnarson. The jarl, or whatever crazy name those folks call him."

Anger welled up inside Galloway as he strode forward. He shoved Judson aside.

"Out of my way, damn it," Galloway said as he stalked out of the mead hall.

The other men who'd been left behind were standing there gawping at the woods. Galloway looked in the same direction and saw the large group approaching the village.

Even though it seemed beyond belief, he saw that Judson was right: Axel Gunnarson was leading the heavily armed contingent, flanked by two men Galloway had never seen before.

Both of those men wore buckskins like the outfits fur trappers sported. One was older and had a broad-brimmed brown hat on his head. The other was bareheaded. His fair hair was cut like that of an Indian, and his clothes were decorated with beads and feathers like a redskin's.

The young man might be Gunnarson's grandson, Galloway thought. Which likely made the older man . . .

Preacher.

Not everyone in the group was male, Galloway noted despite his shock. Several women were among them, but those women carried swords and short-handled axes and shields. Many of the men were armed with such primitive weapons, too, but quite a few of them carried rifles. Galloway's men were outnumbered at least two to one, and he could tell by looking at them that none of them wanted to fight these savage-looking barbarians. They were ready to throw down their arms and surrender.

Gunnarson and his two companions came on ahead while the others stopped at the edge of the village. "Galloway!" Gunnarson shouted.

Galloway drew in a deep breath, clenched his hands into fists at his sides, and bellowed back, "What do you want, Gunnarson?"

"For you to get out of our home!"

Galloway shook his head. "Skarkavik is mine now. Or should I say . . . Galloway City?"

A dark red flush came over Gunnarson's face. "You thief! You liar!" He stepped forward. "Are you armed?"

Galloway spread his hands and held his arms out at his sides in response.

Gunnarson unbuckled the belt that held a scabbarded sword at his waist. He handed it and his short-handled battle axe to the tall, blond young man with him. Then he swung back toward Galloway and said, "We will settle this with our bare hands, you and I."

Galloway took off his coat and tossed it aside, followed by his cravat. He rolled up the sleeves of his shirt, revealing brawny forearms covered with coarse red hair. They were still heavily muscled, as they had been when he worked in the sawmills.

"It was always going to come down to this," he said, then with a roar of rage he charged straight at Axel Gunnarson.

CHAPTER 28

After Tall Dog took the weapons from his grandfather, he barely had time to glance at Preacher and ask, "Is this a good idea?"

Then Gunnarson and Galloway came together with a crash, grappling like two titans vying for control of the world. Which, Preacher supposed, in a way they were.

"This is the best way to settle it," the mountain man said. "Galloway was never gonna give up. If he left, he'd just go and hire more men, then come back and try again to kill your grandpa and all the other folks from Skarkavik."

"That means my grandfather will have to kill him."

"What it comes down to," Preacher said with a nod.

The battle went back and forth. Gunnarson and Galloway slugged, kicked, gouged, wrestled, and choked each other. The faces of both men were swollen and bloody. Their clothes were ripped. Barrel chests heaved and breath rasped in throats. And the spectators on both sides watched in awed silence. The two battlers might not be giants, but they seemed to tower over everything.

Then Galloway got the upper hand. He forced Gunnarson backward and tripped him. Gunnarson went down hard, but his arms shot around Galloway's neck and pulled him down, too. They rolled and flipped, and even though

Gunnarson was on the bottom, he had twisted Galloway around so that the red-bearded man faced away from him. His right forearm was around Galloway's throat, under the beard, pressing on Galloway's windpipe like an iron bar. Gunnarson's left hand clamped on his right wrist, locking the grip in place.

Galloway kicked and thrashed, tried to reach back and claw his fingers at Gunnarson's eyes, but Gunnarson jerked his head out of reach. He kept up the pressure. Galloway's legs flailed. His arms began to beat the ground on both sides of him. Spasms rolled all through his body until finally one last jerk of his muscles stiffened him for a second before he went limp.

Gunnarson held his grip for a good minute to make sure Galloway was dead before he shoved the corpse off him and rolled onto his side. Gunnarson gasped for air, and his drawn, haggard face showed how much the fight had taken out of him.

But it was over, and Decker Galloway was vanquished.

For once, Arne Winterborn didn't cheer. He looked as grim as the rest of the group. This victory had been necessary, but it had been ugly and brutal, too. The cheers and the celebrations would come later.

Preacher faced Galloway's remaining men and said, "You fellas put your weapons in the mead hall. Behave yourselves, and you'll live to see the next boat arrive. You can leave on it. Otherwise . . ."

One of the men said hurriedly, "You don't have to finish that, mister. It's over as far as we're concerned." He looked around and got emphatic nods from the others. "We just appreciate you letting us live."

"Considerin' the way some of the folks from Skarkavik got treated, it's probably more'n you deserve," Preacher said. "Get rid of those guns and make yourselves scarce."

Tall Dog helped his grandfather to his feet. Gunnarson cast a contemptuous glance at Galloway's body, then looked at the sawmill and said, "We should burn that abomination to the ground."

Audie said, "You might want to think twice about that. I'm sure your men could learn to operate it, and then you could reap the profits from these forests just as Galloway intended to."

Gunnarson frowned and shook his head. "That is not what our ancestors would have wanted. Would you have our names bandied about with dishonor in Valhalla?"

"I'm just saying that the world changes whether we wish it to or not," Audie said. "And sometimes all we can do is make the best of it."

"You fellas can wrangle about that some other time," Preacher told them. "For now, let's bring everybody home."

The mead hall was full of feasting and drinking that night. The somber mood earlier in the day had dissipated as the people began to understand that their long ordeal was finally over. They could return to their homes, heal from their wounds, and resume their lives.

As he sat at the end of one of the long tables with Preacher and Nighthawk, Audie said, "You know, strictly speaking in terms of legalities, Galloway had as much right to be here as Axel and his people do. None of them were here with the approval of the Crown. We might be regarded as lawbreakers every bit as much as Galloway and his men."

"We never enslaved no women and gals and molested 'em," Preacher said.

"Umm," Nighthawk added.

"Indeed, morally speaking, there's no doubt Galloway

was reprehensible and deserved everything that happened to him. And speaking from a strictly practical standpoint, there's no legal representative of the British government within several hundred miles, so I think it's highly doubtful any of us will ever have cause to worry about being prosecuted for what we've done here."

"All I know is, I ain't gonna lose any sleep over it," Preacher said. He changed the subject by saying, "Question now is, what's Tall Dog gonna do? He said he wanted to go back home, but I reckon Betsy wants to stay here. I heard her say she's got nothin' in St. Louis to go back to, and she likes these folks and they seem to like her. So that leaves Tall Dog sort of hangin'."

"Umm."

"I won't be surprised if he stays, too, old friend," Audie said. "At least for a while." He nodded across the room and added, "What about you, Preacher?"

The mountain man looked where Audie had indicated and saw Alfhild there, sitting with Arne Winterborn and laughing. He smiled with genuine pleasure and said, "I reckon I'll be movin' on." He reached down and scratched the ears of the big cur lying at his feet. "When have I ever done anything else?"

The bear seems harmless—at first. Just a lost and confused grizzly poking around Big Rock. Then the killings begin. A horse wrangler is mangled. A rancher mauled. Then a bartender in the heart of town is found clawed to a bloody pulp. Now every man in Big Rock is taking up arms to hunt down the beast before it strikes again—which worries the local sheriff. He's afraid this amateur hunting party could turn into a mass funeral real fast. So he asks Smoke Jensen to help keep everyone calm and contain the panic. Unfortunately, it's too late. The panic is out of control. And the hunt is on . . .

While the gun-toting locals head for the hills in search of the bear, a ruthless gang of bank robbers ride into the half-empty town—armed to the teeth. Then a professional wild game hunter shows up offering to kill the grizzly— for a price. If that wasn't enough, a traveling medicine man claims the bear is part of his act—and wouldn't hurt a soul. Smoke Jensen isn't sure what to believe or who to trust. But one thing is certain: Where there are jaws, claws, and outlaws, there will be blood . . .

**National Bestselling Authors
William W. Johnstone and J.A. Johnstone**

DARK NIGHT OF THE MOUNTAIN MAN

On sale wherever Pinnacle Books are sold.

Live Free. Read Hard.
www.williamjohnstone.net

Visit us at www.kensingtonbooks.com

CHAPTER 1

It was safe to say that Nelse Andersen had been drinking when he encountered the bear. Every time Nelse drove his ranch wagon into Big Rock to pick up supplies, he always stopped at the Brown Dirt Cowboy Saloon to have a snort or two—or three—before heading back to his greasy sack outfit northwest of town.

Smoke Jensen happened to be in the settlement that same day, having come in to send some telegrams related to business concerning his ranch, the Sugarloaf.

A ruggedly handsome man of average height, with unusually broad shoulders and ash blond hair, Smoke stood on the porch of Sheriff Monte Carson's office, propping one of those shoulders against a post holding up the awning over the porch.

The lawman was sitting in a chair, leaning back with his booted feet resting on the railing along the front of the porch. His fingers were laced together on his stomach, which was starting to thicken a little with age.

At first glance, neither man looked like what he really was.

Smoke was, quite probably, the fastest and deadliest shot of any man who had ever packed iron west of the Mississippi. Or east of there, for that matter.

As a young man, he'd had a reputation as a gunfighter and outlaw, although all the criminal charges ever levied against him were bogus. Scurrilous lies spread by his enemies.

These days, he was happily married and the owner of the largest, most successful ranch in the valley. In fact, the Sugarloaf was one of the finest ranches in all of Colorado. Smoke was more than content to spend his days running the spread and loving Sally, his beautiful wife.

Despite that intention, trouble still had a habit of seeking him out more often than he liked.

At one time, Monte Carson had been a hired gun, a member of a wolf pack of Coltmen brought in by one of Smoke's mortal enemies to wipe out him and his friends.

It hadn't taken Monte long to figure out who was really in the right and switch sides. He had been a staunch friend to Smoke ever since, even before Big Rock had been founded and he'd been asked to pin on the sheriff's star.

Pearlie Fontaine, another member of that gang of gun-wolves, had also changed his ways and was now the fore-man of the Sugarloaf. Smoke couldn't have hoped for two finer, more loyal friends than Monte and Pearlie.

Or a finer day than this, with its blue sky, puffy white clouds, and warm breeze. Evidently Monte felt the same way, because he said, "Sure is a pretty day. Almost too pretty to work. What do you reckon the chances are that all the troublemakers in these parts will feel the same way, Smoke?"

"They just might," Smoke began with a smile, but then he straightened from his casual pose and muttered, "or not."

Monte saw Smoke's reaction and brought his feet down from the railing. As he sat up, he said, "What is it?"

"Hoofbeats. Sounds like a team coming in a hurry."

Monte stood up. He heard the horses now, too, although Smoke's keen ears had picked up the swift rataplan a couple of seconds earlier.

"Somebody moving fast like that nearly always means trouble."

"Yeah." Smoke pointed. "And here it comes."

A wagon pulled by four galloping horses careened around a corner up the street. The vehicle turned so sharply as the driver hauled on the team's reins that the wheels on the left side came off the ground for a second. Smoke thought the wagon was going to tip over.

But then the wheels came back down with a hard bounce and the wagon righted itself. The driver was yelling something as he whipped the horses.

Monte had joined Smoke at the edge of the porch. "What in blazes is he saying?"

"It sounds like . . . bear," Smoke said. "Is that Nelse Andersen?"

The wagon flashed past them. Monte said, "Yeah, I saw him drive by a little while ago, not long before you showed up. Looked like he was on his way back to his ranch."

They watched as the wagon swerved down the street and then came to a sliding, jarring stop in front of the Brown Dirt Cowboy Saloon. Nelse Andersen practically dived off the seat and ran inside, leaving the slapped-aside batwings swinging to and fro behind him.

"Well, I have to find out what this is about," Monte said. "He can't be driving so fast and reckless in town. He's lucky he didn't run over anybody."

"I'll come with you. I'm a mite curious myself."

By the time they reached the saloon and pushed through the batwings, Andersen was standing at the bar with a group of men gathered around him. A rangy, fair-haired man, he had a drink in his hand, which was shaking so badly that a little of the whiskey sloshed out as he lifted it to his mouth.

The liquor seemed to steady him. He thumped the empty glass on the bar and said, "It was ten feet tall, I tell you! Maybe even taller!"

One of the bystanders said, "I never saw a grizzly bear that tall. Close to it, maybe, but not that big."

"This wasn't a regular bear," Andersen insisted. "It was a monster! I never saw anything like it. It had to weigh twelve hundred pounds if it was an ounce!"

He shoved the empty glass across the hardwood toward the bartender and raised expectant eyebrows. The apron looked at Emmett Brown, the owner of the place, who stood nearby with his thumbs hooked in his vest pockets. Brown frowned.

A man tossed a coin on the bar and said, "Shoot, I'll buy him another drink. I want to hear the rest of this story."

Brown nodded, and the bartender poured more whiskey in the glass, filling it almost to the top. Andersen picked it up and took a healthy swallow.

"Start from the first," the man who had bought the drink urged.

"Well, I was on my way back to my ranch," Andersen said. "I was out there goin' past Hogback Hill, where the brush grows up close to the road, and all of a sudden this . . . this *thing* rears up outta the bushes and waves its paws in the air and roars so loud it was like thunder crashin' all around me! Scared the bejabbers out of my horses."

"I think it scared you, too," a man said.

Andersen ignored that and went on, "I thought the team was gonna bolt. It was all I could do to hold 'em in. The bear kept bellerin' at me and actin' like it was gonna charge. I knew I needed to get outta there, so I turned the team around and lit a shuck for town."

Emmett Brown had come closer along the bar. "You had a gun, didn't you? Why didn't you shoot it?"

Andersen tossed back the rest of the drink and once again set the empty firmly on the bar.

"I didn't figure that rifle of mine has enough stopping power to put him down. I could'a emptied the blamed thing in him and it might've killed him eventually, but not in time to keep him from gettin' those paws on me and tearin' me apart." Andersen shuddered. "I wouldn't'a been nothin' but a snack for a beast that big!"

"I still say you're exaggeratin'," claimed the man who had said he'd never seen a grizzly bear ten feet tall. "You just got scared and panicked. Maybe it seemed that big to you, but it really wasn't. It couldn't have been."

Andersen glared at him and said, "Then why don't you go out there to Hogback Hill and see for yourself? I hope that grizzly gets you and knocks your head off with one swipe o' his paw!"

"I don't cotton to bein' talked to like that—" the man began as he clenched his fists.

"That's enough," Monte Carson said, his voice sharp and commanding. "You're not going to bust up this saloon because of some brawl over how big a bear is."

Enthralled by Andersen's story, the men hadn't realized that Smoke and Monte were standing at the back of the crowd, listening.

Now they split apart so that the sheriff and Smoke could step forward. Nelse Andersen turned from the bar to greet them.

"Sheriff, you better put together a posse and ride out there as fast as you can."

"Why would I do that?" Monte asked. "I can't arrest a bear. Assuming there really is one, and that he's still there."

"You don't believe me, Sheriff?" Andersen pressed a hand to his chest and looked mortally offended.

"Those do sound like some pretty wild claims you're making."

Smoke said, "I've seen some pretty big grizzlies, but never one that was more than ten feet tall and weighed twelve hundred pounds. I think you'd have to go up to Alaska or Canada to find bears that big."

"Well, Smoke, no offense to you or the sheriff, but I'll tell you the same thing I told Hodges there. Why don't you ride out there and have a look for yourself? A critter as big as the one I saw is bound to have left some tracks!"

Smoke exchanged a glance with Monte and then said, "You know, I think I just might do that. Especially if you come along and show me where you saw him, Nelse."

Andersen swallowed hard, opened and closed his mouth a couple of times, but then he nodded and said, "I'll do it. I got to go home sometime, and I'll admit, I'll feel a mite better about travelin' on that stretch of road if you're with me."

"I'm ready to go if you are." Smoke looked at Monte again. "Are you coming?"

"No, I'd better stay here in town," the sheriff said, adding dryly, "since I don't really have any jurisdiction over bears. But you'll tell me what you find, won't you, Smoke?"

"Sure," Smoke replied with a chuckle.

One of the bystanders said, "How about the rest of us comin' along, too?"

"Might be better not to," Smoke said. "A big bunch might spook that bear and make him attack, if he's still out there."

The real reason Smoke didn't want them coming along was because he knew how easy it was for a group of men to work themselves up into a nervous state where they might start shooting at anything that moved. That could lead to trouble.

A few men muttered at the decision, but Smoke was so well respected in Big Rock that no one wanted to argue with him. He and Andersen left the Brown Dirt Cowboy, but not until Andersen cast one more longing glance at the empty glass on the bar and sighed in resignation.

Smoke's horse was tied at the hitch rail in front of the sheriff's office. Smoke swung into the saddle and fell in alongside the wagon as Andersen drove out of Big Rock. The Sugarloaf was located off the main trail that ran due west out of the settlement, but Andersen followed a smaller trail that angled off northwest toward the small spreads located in the foothills on that side of the valley.

As they moved along the trail, Smoke chatted amiably with the rancher, who was a bachelor, well-liked but not particularly close to anybody in these parts. Andersen asked after Sally, as well as Pearlie and Cal Woods, another of Smoke's ranch hands. He didn't seem to be affected much by the whiskey he had consumed. Smoke had heard that Andersen had a hollow leg when it came to booze, and now he was seeing evidence of that.

They covered several miles before Andersen pointed to a rugged ridge up ahead on the right and said, "That's Hogback Hill."

"I know," Smoke said. "Good name for it. It looks like a hog's back, sort of rough and spiny."

Andersen was starting to look apprehensive now. "That brush on the right is where I saw the bear. He must've been down on all fours in it. When I came along, he just reared up bigger'n life. I really thought he was gonna eat me."

Smoke's sharp eyes scanned the thick vegetation they

were approaching. "I don't see anything moving around in there," he said. "Or hear any rustling in the brush, either."

"I didn't see or hear anything out of the ordinary until suddenly he was right there, no more than twenty feet from me. He's a sneaky one, that bear is. He was layin' up, waitin' to ambush me."

Smoke tried not to grin as Andersen said that with a straight face. The rancher appeared to believe it. Smoke supposed he ought to give the man the benefit of the doubt. As far as he could recall, Andersen didn't have a reputation for going around spreading big windies.

"We'll be ready, just in case," Smoke said as he pulled his Winchester from its saddle scabbard under his right leg. He laid the rifle across the saddle in front of him.

A moment later, Andersen pulled back on the reins and brought his team to a stop. "This is it," he said. "This is the place." He pointed into the brush. "Right there. I'll never forget it."

Smoke studied the bushes and listened intently. There was no sign of a bear or any other wildlife, other than a few birds singing in some trees about fifty yards away.

"I'm going to take a closer look," he said.

"Are you sure that's a good idea?"

"I don't think there's anything in there." Smoke swung a leg over the saddle and dropped to the ground, still holding the Winchester ready in case he needed it. He had spotted something that interested him, and as he moved into the brush, using the rifle barrel to push branches aside, he got a better look at what he had noticed.

Quite a few of the branches were snapped around the spot where Andersen said the bear had been, as if they'd been broken when something large and heavy pushed through the brush. A frown creased Smoke's forehead as he spotted something else. He reached forward and plucked a tuft of grayish brown hair from a branch's sharply broken end.

That sure looked like it could have come from a bear's coat.

Smoke moved closer, pushed more of the brush aside, and looked down at the ground. Some rain had fallen about a week earlier, so the soil was still fairly soft, not dried out yet.

After a long moment, he turned his head and called, "Come here, Nelse."

"I ain't sure I want to," the man replied. "What did you find?"

"Better you come take a look for yourself. There's nothing around here that's going to hurt you."

With obvious reluctance, Andersen set the brake on the wagon, wrapped the reins around it, and climbed down from the seat. He edged into the brush and followed the path Smoke had made.

When Andersen reached Smoke's side, Smoke pointed at the ground and said, "Take a look."

Andersen's eyes widened. He breathed a curse as he peered at what he saw etched in the dirt.

It was the unmistakable pawprint of a gigantic bear.

CHAPTER 2

"So he was telling the truth? There really is a monster bear roaming around out there?"

Monte Carson sounded as if he were having trouble believing what he had just said.

Smoke, straddling a turned-around chair in the sheriff's office, said, "We only found three tracks, and they were scattered some. I couldn't tell from them exactly how tall the varmint is, but they were deep enough that I can say he's pretty heavy. Might go a thousand pounds."

"So not as big as what Nelse claimed, but still a mighty big bear."

"Yeah," Smoke agreed. "I don't recall ever seeing one that big around here."

"What did you do with Nelse?"

"Rode with him back to his ranch." Smoke smiled. "He didn't much want to travel alone. He kept looking back over his shoulder like he was afraid that bear had climbed into the wagon with him."

"Then you came back here instead of heading home?"

Smoke nodded. "Sally's not expecting me back at any particular time. I thought it would be a good idea to let you know there was some truth to what Nelse said. There was a good-sized bear within a few miles of town earlier today. The tracks prove that."

The broad shoulders rose and fell in a shrug as Smoke continued, "Of course, that doesn't mean it's still anywhere around these parts. When you watch bears moving around, they look like they're just lumbering along, but they can move pretty quickly when they want to."

"Yeah. Kind of like runaway freight trains."

"Anyway, this one has had enough time to cover some ground. He could be a long way off by now."

"Or he could be wandering around the edge of town." Monte sighed. "I'm going to have to warn folks, Smoke. They need to be on the lookout, and especially keep an eye on their kids."

"I agree, but I wish there was some way to avoid a panic."

"It was too late for that once Nelse Andersen started guzzling down whiskey and spewing his tale," Monte said. "You know some of the fellas who were in the Brown Dirt Cowboy have already started spreading the story by now."

"More than likely." Smoke rested his hands on the chair's back and pushed himself to his feet. "Let folks know that first thing tomorrow morning, Pearlie and I are going to try to pick up that bear's trail and find out where it went from Hogback Hill. If it left this part of the country, then people can stop worrying about it."

"And if it's still around here somewhere?"

"Pearlie and I will find it and drive it on out of the valley if we can."

"What if it won't leave?"

"Then we'll deal with it," Smoke said with a note of finality in his voice.

* * *

For such an apparently huge creature, the bear proved to be surprisingly elusive. Smoke and Pearlie found its tracks leading north from Hogback Hill the next morning and followed them for a while, but the trail disappeared when it entered the rocky, mostly barren foothills at the base of the mountains in that direction.

When they finally reined in and admitted defeat after casting back and forth among the hills for several hours, Pearlie shook his head disgustedly and said, "We need Preacher with us. That old boy can follow a trail better'n anybody who ever drew breath."

"I can't argue with that," Smoke said. The old mountain man had been his mentor and like a second father to him for many years. It was said he could track a single snowflake through a blizzard. "There's no telling where Preacher is, though. He could be anywhere from Canada to old Mexico."

Pearlie rubbed his beard-stubbled chin and said, "We're liable to have folks from town roamin' around out here on the range lookin' for the critter, figurin' they'll shoot it and be acclaimed as heroes. But more than likely they'll accidentally shoot each other."

"I know," Smoke said, nodding. "But I'm hoping the bear actually has moved on and that as time goes by without it being spotted again, people will forget about it. It may take a while, but things ought to go back to normal eventually."

"Maybe." Pearlie didn't sound convinced. "Problem is, when folks get worked up about somethin', all their common sense goes right out the window."

Smoke couldn't argue with that statement.

* * *

Three days later, a middle-aged cowboy named Dean McKinley was following one of his boss's steers that had strayed up a draw. Water ran through here when it rained very much, but that dried up quickly, sucked down by the sand underneath the rocky stream bed.

The iron shoes on the hooves of McKinley's horse clinked on those rocks as he rode slowly, swinging his gaze back and forth between the draw's brushy banks.

McKinley had heard about the bear. Another cowboy who rode for the same spread had been in the Brown Dirt Cowboy that day and brought back the tale of Nelse Andersen's run-in with the giant beast.

As far as McKinley was concerned, Andersen was a loco Scandihoovian who drank too much, but the story had had the ring of truth to it.

And the last thing McKinley wanted to do was run into a grizzly bear while he was out here alone on the range.

Maybe the smart thing to do would be to turn around and hope the steer found its way back home, he told himself.

But then the blasted critter had to go and bawl piteously, somewhere up ahead of him. To McKinley's experienced ears, it sounded like the steer was scared of something.

He hesitated for a couple of heartbeats, then muttered a curse under his breath and dug his boot heels into his horse's flanks, sending it loping forward.

He had just rounded a bend in the draw when something loomed in front of him, moving fast toward him. McKinley couldn't hold back a startled yell as he tugged hard on the reins and brought his horse to an abrupt stop. His other hand dropped to the butt of the revolver holstered on his hip.

Then he realized it was the steer charging toward him,

wild-eyed with fear. McKinley jerked his mount to the side to get out of the way. The steer's run was an ungainly thing, but it was moving pretty fast anyway as it charged past him.

"What the devil?" McKinley muttered as he twisted in the saddle to look behind him. The frantic steer disappeared around the bend, heading back the way McKinley had come from.

The cowboy was still looking back when his horse let out a shrill, sudden, terrified whinny and tried to rear up. McKinley hauled hard on the reins to keep the horse under control as he looked in front of him again.

Twenty yards away, from around another bend, came the bear.

The creature was enormous, even on all fours. To McKinley's eyes, it seemed like the bear was as big as the horse he was on, maybe even bigger.

And it was coming fast toward him, panting and growling.

"Yowww!" McKinley cried as he realized what was happening. The steer had fled in blind panic from the bear. Now it was his turn. The massive beast had already covered half the distance between them by the time McKinley got his mount wheeled around and kicked it into a run.

The horse took off like a jackrabbit, so fast that McKinley had to reach up and grab his hat to keep it from flying off. He didn't really care about the hat. Grabbing it was just instinct.

The bear was so close McKinley could hear its breath rasping. He thought he could feel the heat of it on the back of his neck, but that was probably just his imagination. The cow pony, once it got its hooves under it, was running fast and smooth now.

Unfortunately, a bear could run just about as fast as a horse. That was what McKinley had heard. It appeared to be true, because he wasn't gaining any, he saw as he glanced back over his shoulder.

It might come down to which animal tired first, or whether the horse tripped.

If they went down, McKinley knew, it would be all over.

He suddenly remembered that he had a gun on his hip. He knew better than to think a Colt would stop a huge grizzly bear, but he clawed the iron out of leather anyway and triggered it behind him without looking. Maybe the racket would make the bear stop, if nothing else. He pulled the trigger until the hammer clicked on an empty chamber.

A bellowing roar sounded. McKinley looked back and saw that his desperate ploy might have worked. The bear had stopped and reared up on its hind legs. It swatted at the air with its massive paws and continued to roar.

But at the same time, the racing horse was putting more distance between it and the bear. McKinley clung to the saddle. They swept around another bend, and he could no longer see the bear.

Of course, it could resume the chase, if it wanted to, but with each stride, the horse put the huge, hairy menace that much farther behind.

Even so, McKinley didn't heave a relieved sigh until the draw petered out and he emerged onto open range again. He reined in, turned his mount, and looked back.

No sign of the bear.

The monster had gone back to wherever it had come from, McKinley thought.

The steer he had followed up the draw stood about fifty yards away, cropping calmly on grass as if nothing had happened. McKinley glared at the steer for a moment and then shook a fist at it as he called, "Next time you go wanderin' off and find yourself on the menu for a bear,

I'm gonna let the dang thing have you, you blasted cow critter!"

The next day, Smoke and Pearlie were leaning on one of the corral fences, watching as Calvin Woods cautiously approached a big gray horse.

"He's givin' you the skunk eye, Cal," Pearlie called to his young friend. "Don't trust him."

"I wasn't planning on it," Cal replied. "But I'm not gonna let some jugheaded horse think he's gettin' the best of me."

"Now, I don't know why he'd think that," Pearlie drawled, "just 'cause he's already throwed you half a dozen times today."

Cal scowled over his shoulder, then turned his attention back to the gray. He spoke softly to the horse as he reached out with one hand. The gray blew a breath out, making his nostrils flare, but he didn't shy away as the young cowboy stroked his neck.

"All right now," Cal said. "You and me are gonna be friends, horse. You just take it easy." He lifted his left foot, fitted it in the stirrup. "No need to get spooked. I'm not gonna hurt you."

He grasped the reins and the horn and lifted himself into the saddle. His eyes were wide with anticipation as he settled down in the leather.

The gray didn't budge, just stood there calmly.

"Well, son of a gun," Pearlie breathed. "Maybe the boy's done it."

Equally quietly, Smoke said, "Look at the way that horse's tail is flicking."

From atop the gray, Cal said, "See, I told you I'd—"

The horse exploded underneath him.

The gray was a sunfishing, crow-hopping, end-swapping dynamo as Cal yelled in alarm and clung to the saddle for dear life. It was an effort that was doomed to fail. Only a handful of seconds elapsed before Cal sailed into the air and came crashing down on the ground inside the corral.

The horse bucked a few more times as it danced across the corral, seemingly celebrating its triumph.

"Are you all right, Cal?" Pearlie called.

Cal groaned, sat up, and shook his head groggily. He had lost his hat when he flew out of the saddle. He looked around for it, spotted it, and started to crawl toward it on hands and knees.

"You'll get him next time," Pearlie said, then added under his breath to Smoke, "or not."

Smoke smiled. He was glad that Cal wasn't hurt and admired the young cowboy's determination, but something else had caught his attention.

"Rider coming," he said with a nod toward the trail that led to the Sugarloaf from the road.

Pearlie squinted in that direction and then said, "That's Monte, ain't it?"

"Yep," Smoke replied. He turned away from the corral and started toward the ranch house, intent on finding out what had brought the lawman out here.

Sally must have sensed somehow that company was coming, because she came out the front door onto the porch as Smoke walked toward the house. She wore an apron over a blue dress, and her thick dark hair was pulled back and tied behind her head. She'd been cooking and dusted flour off her hands as Smoke approached.

She was the prettiest woman he'd ever seen. The smartest, bravest woman he'd ever known. The former Sally Reynolds had been a schoolteacher when he first met her up in Idaho. It was her students' loss and his gain when she'd agreed to become his wife.

"Did you know Monte was coming out here today?" she asked.

"Nope," Smoke replied. "He must have news of some sort."

And it probably wasn't good news, he mused. Otherwise he would have waited until the next time Smoke came into Big Rock to talk to him.

Monte loped up and reined in. Sally smiled and said, "I hope you're in the mood for some nice cool lemonade."

"That sounds like the next best thing to heaven," he replied. "I'm much obliged to you."

Pearlie had followed Smoke from the corral. He took the horse's reins from Monte when the sheriff had dismounted.

"I'll take care of this ol' boy for you, Monte."

"Thanks, Pearlie."

Smoke said, "Come on up onto the porch and sit down."

Sally had gone back into the house. She returned a few moments later carrying a tray with a pitcher and three glasses on it. She poured lemonade for all of them, then joined Smoke and Monte in the wicker-bottomed rocking chairs on the porch.

"What brings you out here, Monte?" Smoke asked after taking a sip of the cool, sweet beverage.

"That bear again," Monte said.

"The giant bear Nelse Andersen saw?" Sally said. "Smoke told me about it."

"It's been spotted again?" Smoke asked.

"More than spotted. It chased Dean McKinley and nearly got him."

"McKinley . . ." Smoke repeated as he tried to put a

face with the name. "Puncher who rides for Bart Oliver's Boxed O brand?"

"That's right," Monte said. "He followed a steer up a draw, and that bear nearly got both of them."

The Boxed O was a small outfit bordering the foothills to the northwest, five or six miles from the Sugarloaf. Bart Oliver, who owned the spread, worked it with his two teenaged sons and a couple of hired hands, one of whom was Dean McKinley.

"McKinley wasn't hurt?"

Monte shook his head. "No, he was able to get away on horseback."

"He was lucky, then. Bears are mighty fast when they want to be."

"Yeah. McKinley said he emptied his six-gun at the beast. He probably missed with all his shots, and even if he didn't, a .45 slug wouldn't do more than annoy a grizzly unless you hit it just perfectly."

"Not likely from the hurricane deck of a running horse, especially when the fella pulling the trigger was probably scared to death."

"No probably about it," Monte said. "McKinley still looked pretty shook up when he came into town and talked about it this morning."

"So now folks are all worked up about the bear again," Smoke said. "I sure was hoping it had moved on."

A week had passed since Nelse Andersen's encounter with the bear. Phil Clinton, editor/publisher of the *Big Rock Journal*, had printed a story about it on the paper's front page that was picked up and reprinted by one of the Denver newspapers, so it was doubtful that anybody in this whole part of Colorado hadn't heard about the giant bruin.

But after a few days of hunting parties going out to

search for the creature, with no success, most of the interest had died down.

This latest development would change all that.

"I'm hoping you'll agree to try to track it again," Monte said. "I'm going to issue an order for everybody in the valley to stick close to home and stay out of the way so you can find the bear and deal with it."

"Kill it, you mean?" Sally said with a slight frown of disapproval.

Monte shrugged. "I'd be fine if the varmint just wasn't around these parts anymore, but I don't know how you'd guarantee that. Even if you drove it off a long way, it could come back. They can range for hundreds of miles."

"First thing is to find it," Smoke said. "I'm certainly willing to try again. I'm not sure you'll be able to get people to stay home, though."

"It'll be easier if I can tell them that you're on the trail. They'll want to give you a chance to succeed. I appreciate you taking on the chore, Smoke."

"I'll do my best."

Monte drank some of his lemonade and then sighed. "I hope you can get him. Andersen and McKinley were lucky. That luck probably won't hold up. Sooner or later . . ."

"Sooner or later, somebody who runs into that bear is going to wind up dead," Smoke said.

Visit our website at
KensingtonBooks.com
to sign up for our newsletters, read
more from your favorite authors, see
books by series, view reading group
guides, and more!

Become a Part of Our
Between the Chapters Book Club
Community and Join the Conversation

Submit your book review for a chance to win exclusive
Between the Chapters swag you can't get anywhere else!
https://www.kensingtonbooks.com/pages/review/